D1252113

Zermatt

Zermatt

"Frank" Schaeffer

CARROLL & GRAF PUBLISHERS
NEW YORK

ZERMATT

Carroll & Graf Publishers
An Imprint of Avalon Publishing Group Inc.
161 William St., 16th Floor
New York, NY 10038

First Carroll & Graf edition 2003

Library of Congress Cataloging-in-Publication Data is available.

ISBN: 0-7867-1259-7

Book design by Paul Paddock
Printed in the United States of America
Distributed by Publishers Group West

Zermatt is for my beautiful wife, Genie.

Author's Note:
Portofino, Zermatt, and *Saving Grandma* are all about the Becker family and their adventures, as narrated by Calvin Dort Becker. Each novel is a stand-alone work, though taken together they form a trilogy.

Frank Schaeffer, May 30, 2003

Chapter 1

"NOW WE WILL ALL DIE because of the filthy Roman Catholics," said Janet. "This would never happen in Vaud."

"Valais is a dark place," Mom said, and sighed.

"Typhoid in Switzerland, unbelievable," murmured Rachael gloomily.

"*Catholic* Switzerland," said Dad, as he turned another page of his big old Bible with a swish-slap that made Mom wince. "Where there's superstition there's corruption. And where there's corruption there's dirty water. In Vaud they may all be liberal Protestants, but at least there is enough of a memory of the Reformation so that they wouldn't hide a broken sewer pipe so as not to scare away the tourists!"

"I'm just thankful we're going straight up to Riffelberg this year and not spending the night down in the town," said Mom. "That was very clever of you, Ralph; I mean the way you figured out all these train schedules so we could make it up to Riffelberg in one day. And you were so perceptive to ask about the water supply! How marvelous that the hotel has its own spring, so we don't have to worry!"

"Don't try and butter me up, Elsa!" Dad snapped.

"All those people want to be down there because they play jazz at the Hotel Zermatterhof. Now look, they're dying!" said Janet with grim satisfaction.

"They're not *all* dying," whimpered Rachael with a quiver, in a voice as gentle as the cooing of a slightly depressed wood pigeon. "The conductor says most of them are just sick. All the cases are in one hotel where the water got contaminated he said."

"And dying!" snorted Janet.

"Anyway, I'm just thankful that we're going to be staying above all that," Mom added primly.

"I still would have liked to have our usual night at the Hotel Zermatterhof," I mumbled. "No one is sick there, are they?"

"Calvin Dort Becker, you only want to be down there because of the jazz!" said Janet. "I saw you dancing last year!"

"I was not. I just tapped my foot," I muttered.

"You stood right next to the orchestra and moved your legs. I saw you!"

"Well, no one is dancing now," said Mom. "I only hope that the typhoid has made some of them turn to the Lord."

"Maybe we should go down there to witness to them," said Rachael. "I mean after we're settled."

"Are you crazy?!" exclaimed Janet, "We'll catch it!"

"We're supposed to be missionaries," said Rachael.

"We're on vacation," snapped Dad.

"Poor, poor people, they're so lost, so confused," said Mom.

"But most of them are Church of England—the skiers, I mean," whispered Rachael, "not Catholics. Dad said most of the skiers are English, so maybe they're not all lost."

"Yes," said Mom, "but C of E is just as bad. They call communion 'Eucharist' and believe in the 'real presence,' just like the Catholics. I don't believe there's a Real Christian anywhere in England these days, unless you count a handful of small Reformed Presbyterian churches in Scotland, and I'm not even sure about them."

"They're all in the same boat," said Janet. "All dying."

"Or just very ill," whimpered Rachael.

"Filthy water, bad theology. I can't think of a Roman Catholic country where you *can* safely drink the water," said Dad.

He glared at us, then looked back down at the enormous Bible on his lap, turned a page hard, and started reading again and marking passages with his fountain pen. It was clear that Dad did not want to talk anymore. So the rest of us kept quiet.

Usually we spent the first night in Zermatt, then the next morning took the cog railway up the mountain to where the Hotel Riffelberg—the alpine lodge we always stayed in on our annual ski vacation—was perched high above the town. When Dad learned there was an outbreak of typhoid in Zermatt, he told Mom to cancel our vacation. But once it was established that the typhoid was only in the main town and that due to a new train schedule we would not need to spend the night there but could just change trains and go straight up to Riffelberg, Dad had relented.

To the south, the Hotel Riffelberg overlooked the cliff, the Matterhorn, the Zermatt Valley, and a range of peaks ringing the town. To the north, the hotel faced a steep snowfield perfect for skiing, which swept up for a mile or more to the top of the Riffelhorn and, beyond that, kept going for another few miles to the summit of the Gornergrat Mountain.

We stayed at Hotel Riffelberg because it was less expensive than the hotels in town and also because we would not be corrupted by the lures and wiles of the après ski nightlife. As Mom said, "There will be no smoke-filled taverns for *this* family! We have come here to *ski* and enjoy the wonders of God's creation!"

Even the old farmhouses, naked fields, and leafless orchards were barely visible through the swirling gossamer mist of snow stirred up by the rushing train. The familiar mountains that I knew were towering above me were hidden in the clouds. Only the dark pine forests on the lower slopes remained visible. I glanced at Mom sitting next to me and at Dad and my two sisters, Janet and Rachael, across from me. Janet was staring accusingly. I had not done anything in particular to annoy her. That was the way she usually looked at me. Rachael smiled sweetly and reached out to give my hand a friendly squeeze.

In the winter of 1966 Janet was eighteen years old, stocky and dreadfully strong. Rachael was sixteen, slender, with wrists almost as thin as bread sticks. I was fourteen and, at last, taller than both of my sisters.

Janet had Dad's olive complexion. Her brown eyes were dark and peered suspiciously out on the world. She wore her plain brown hair pulled back in a ponytail tied with a rubber band.

Even when Rachael shouted she was quieter than Janet talking in her normal voice. Rachael's hair frizzed out around her head in a little halo above soft gray-green eyes and skim-milk-pale skin.

Mom was a very pretty woman with high cheekbones and what she called a "trim figure." She had bright, sparkly blue eyes. Although she was forty-six, Rachael said Mom looked more as if she were a "young thirty," and she was right. Mom's teeth were white and straight, and she smiled most of the time to "show forth Christ's love."

Dad had not had "the privilege of good dental care," Mom said, when I asked her why Dad did not smile as much as she did. His teeth were somewhat crooked and stained by the tea he drank all day. He had a square jaw and dark eyes, which Janet said were "a little closer together than is comfortable to look at." This was especially so when he was glaring at you. Those deep-set eyes, under a big fore-head made even bigger looking by his receding hairline, gave him an angry look even when he was not in a Mood. Dad had heavy pow-erful shoulders and hands with short fingers sprouting from wide palms that made getting a spanking from him a serious business. He was six feet tall, but walked as if he were carrying a weight that some-times stooped him right over. He looked a lot older than Mom, even though they were the same age. Mostly he just seemed tired.

I was sort of in between the rest of my family. I had Dad's build in the strong legs department and could hike in the mountains above our village for hours without resting. Rachael said that with my shirt off I looked very manly. But Janet's forearms were thicker than mine, and when she hit me I stayed hit! I had Mom's straight nose and her eyes, which according to Janet made me the "fortunate one in the looks department."

On my most recent birthday—September 3, 1966—Dad measured

me and marked my height on the inside of his cupboard door, where he kept all of our heights. I was five foot ten.

Jennifer Bazlinton had said, "Calvin Becker, you've become rather handsome." Jennifer was my beautiful friend from England, whom I met every year in Portofino. She was my age and always stayed, along with her parents, at the same *pensione* we stayed at. Jennifer and I had played together on the beach every year since we were both little. She let me kiss her during our last summer vacation. That was during the same vacation she called me handsome. So I guess she meant it. I liked that kiss a lot.

I had never kissed a girl before (not counting my mom and sisters, but it was not that sort of a kiss). Jennifer kissed me only once. I had been thinking about it ever since.

No matter what I was doing, even while singing hymns in the Monday morning Bible study, I was thinking about the girls around me. I liked the smell of their skin, warm and sweet, something like melting butter and my pet cat's tummy back when she was a kitten. Girls loomed up in my mind a lot, or at least certain parts of them did. But the girls at the mission were not the sort who let you kiss them. They had come to learn about Jesus and were all much older than I was, mostly in their twenties, and mostly dressed in a godly way that hid everything I longed to get a better look at. . . .

I caught Janet's smirk. She always seemed to know what I was thinking about. I hastily turned to the large plate-glass train window and stared at the white blur of flying snow.

I sighed. Dad shot me an angry look. I saw his grimace reflected in the window. I tried to smile at him in a way that would let him know that mine was a genuine, unplanned sigh, not like one of Mom's. But it did no good. He looked down again too quickly to catch my friendly nod and went right back to staring at his open Bible.

As we shot around a bend in the track I heard a rattle. I glanced at our five pairs of skis swaying in the rack at the back of the train car, including the new ones I had gotten for Christmas. I cheered right up. However strange my family was, I had ten days to be normal!

I loved our vacations. The summer vacation was a twelve-hour train trip away, in Portofino, Italy. We took our winter vacation in Zermatt. We had been going to both places since I was five.

This meant that every September and February I was able to slip away from my parents and sisters for a few glorious days. I would walk to Portofino by myself and visit the Italians I had gotten to know over the years. In Zermatt I might meet on a ski lift. I would tell these strangers—I thought of them as the normal people—that my dad was a teacher and that we lived in America and were just regular tourists. They might ask what programs I liked on TV "back home" or what movies I had seen or where I went to school. I tried to play along by making things up and hoping they did not guess that I had never been to a movie, that my family did not have a TV, and that I was home-schooled and had not even lived in my own country since I was three years old, when my parents were called by God to save European youths from papacy, secularism, liberal theology, and Roman Catholic superstition.

If the normal people figured out that I was part of a family of missionaries—or, worse yet, if Mom and my sisters got to them first and explained about how we Beckers were trying to keep ourselves "apart from the world," and how we were "serving the Lord" and did not want to "defile ourselves with worldly entertainments" or by listening to Catholic teachers who might try and turn us into papists (that is why I got home-schooled)—then the normal people got horrified looks on their faces. When I saw that look, I knew that soon the normal people would drift away as fast as they could without actually running.

I pored over scraps of Swiss newspapers to find out about movies so I would have something to talk about with normal people. I looked at maps of the USA to see where I was from in case they asked. My most treasured possessions were five old copies of *Mad* magazine. I received these from the son of a visiting pastor from Muskegon, Michigan, and kept them stashed up in the attic. I studied the yellowing pages to learn about things American kids my age were interested in, such as barbecues, high school proms, cheerleaders, two-car garages, band practice, football, "hot rods," "nerds," "jocks," and chest-expanders you sent six cereal box tops in for—at least you could send them in if you lived in America—as well as jokes about braces getting locked when teenagers kissed after "dates."

Gathering worldly information was particularly difficult. My home schooling had not worked out. I still did not read well, even though I was on "the threshold of manhood," as Mom put it. Sometimes I asked Andy Keegan (the son of one of Mom and Dad's coworkers) to read difficult words to me. Sometimes I risked asking Rachael to read something. Rachael would laugh at some of the jokes in *Mad,* and then she would blush because she had laughed. Rachael once told me that it was hard to be a Real Christian, and she had to admit that she, too, was "tempted by worldly interests." If Rachael deemed the newspaper or magazine was "too worldly," then she would begin a lecture that always started with: "Calvin Dort Becker! *Where* did you get this unseemly trash?" But she never told on me.

My middle name, Dort, was for a town in Holland where theologians got together during the Reformation to decide on the Five Points of Calvinism, upon which our Reformed Presbyterian denomination was founded. I was also named for the French Reformer John Calvin, who had lived in Geneva, Switzerland. I hated my stupid names but I guess that I was fortunate that I did not get called Guillaume Farel after another of Mom and Dad's favorite local Reformers.

Chapter 2

IN SWITZERLAND THE VALLEYS and mountains might have been conquered by cog railroads, daring tunnels, and high bridges, but it still took a long time to get from one alpine town to another on public transportation. Zermatt was a seven- to ten-hour journey (depending on train and bus connections) from our village of Trois-Torrents.

Trois-Torrents was a smaller and much less famous village, which also nestled in the southern Swiss Alps. Zermatt and Trois-Torrents each sat in their own valleys beneath towering mountains. Both were in the canton (state) of Valais near the French and Italian borders. Zermatt had many ski lifts. Trois-Torrents had none.

In some flat place, say Kansas, where, as a young pastor, my dad had his first church, the trip from Trois-Torrents to Zermatt would have taken less than two hours by car. We Beckers did not have a car. The Lord "provided bounteously" for the needs of our missionary work, but not *that* bounteously. In fact, no one could get to Zermatt by car. Even the rich, even the "Very Wealthy"—as Mom called just about everyone who came to ski in Zermatt besides us—parked their cars in the medieval towns of Sion or Visp and took the narrow gauge railroad from Visp (where we changed from the main line) up to Zermatt. There were no cars allowed in the town. In winter, horse-drawn sleigh taxis were provided. In summer, there were carriages. When we stayed down in Zermatt for the first night, the best part—besides the music at the Grand Hotel Zermatterhof—was the sleigh ride up the main street, with the jingling harness bells echoing merrily off the wide overhanging eaves that lined the street while the sweet steam from the horse billowed around us in the icy air.

The trip from Trois-Torrents to Zermatt began at the low, wide front door of Chalet Tulip (our chalet's name), with my mother running down the stairs while Rachael and Janet acted as a kind of relay team whose duty it was to both relate information about Mom's progress to my father and to hurry Mom along out of the chalet. They bundled her down the icy steps, along the path cut through the snow, through the gates, then, at last, down the steep stairs to the road. Mom's descent was watched by my exasperated father, the furious driver of the yellow postal bus, and the angry passengers who—mostly heavyset and malodorous peasant women on errands to Monthey, our "big town" in the valley—were by now ready to make good their threat to drive off and leave Mom and the rest of us *"Américaines"* to find another way to get to the station.

"Tell Elsa," Dad yelled, "that if she's not here in ten seconds everyone in this bus will miss their connections in Monthey and Aigle! Tell her we've probably already missed the ten-forty to Visp and the connection to Zermatt! Tell her that if we miss the twelve-ten to Zermatt there isn't another one until five-eighteen and we'll miss the Gornergrat train and won't get to Riffelberg tonight!"

"Yes, Dad," I said.

"And tell that woman that if we miss the Gornergrat connection she can just forget the whole thing because we are *not* spending the night in Zermatt! Not this year! I forbid you to even leave the station or wash your hands or go to the toilet in that place! On the way over to the Gornergrat train we will have to let other people open doors. Don't even touch the handles! Do you understand?!"

"Yes, Dad!" I said.

"Well, tell her!"

The driver added a sour comment: *"Non, mais! C'est pas possible! Je pars en trente secondes! Nom de Dieu! Non, mais! Merde!"*

The Swiss peasants muttered and shook their heads. Some wagged thick red fingers at Dad in a cautionary gesture, as if scolding a child. One called out that this was Switzerland, not America, and that if this was how our family behaved it was no wonder that America was full of gangsters.

Janet relayed this scene and all the information to Rachael, who, in turn, dashed inside to tell Mom, who was still packing last minute necessities. Rachael repeated it all word for word except the part where the bus driver took the Lord's name in vain.

"He swore, Mom," was the way Rachael conveyed the profanity. I wondered, but of course never said aloud, if Mom was not responsible for causing the bus driver to stumble and blaspheme, since it was she who made him late. But this never seemed to occur to my sisters or mother. All Mom said was, "It is so unfortunate, darling, that he and his kind use words like that in front of children, and the fact he does it in French is no excuse!"

At last we made the bus. By that time Dad was in a Mood. He almost always was when we traveled. Janet was grimly satisfied that her prediction had come true. She had said that Dad "looks to be in a Mood for the whole day." He was.

On the cog rail line (during the last leg of our journey up to Riffelberg), I was sitting hunched over and staring at the snow-covered pine trees. Their branches were weighed down so heavily that the snow formed an almost straight white sheath, making the trees look strangely narrow. Through the trees the high peaks could be glimpsed: dazzling white and towering above everything as the view unfolded. It had stopped snowing and the sky was clearing.

Some years there was hardly enough snow to ski. This was not one of them. My heart raced at the thought of what the slopes were going to be like, judging by the amount of deep powder piled in sparkling drifts along the track. I knew I would soon be gliding from the top of Gornergrat all the way to Zermatt without even having to slow down, even on the lower slopes just above the town where, during some bad snow years, the *piste* got rocky and icy where it ran past the little barns, the ones that sat up on stilt feet topped off with huge round flagstones so that the rats could not get in and spoil the grain.

We were sitting huddled over the heater that ran along the baseboard under the row of wooden seats. Our feet were almost warm but I could still see my breath. This was the last train of the day. Through the trees I glimpsed a few straggling skiers on their way down the *piste* to the town.

The little brown two-car cog railway was empty of everyone but the driver and us. I breathed in deeply. I loved the familiar smell of that old railway car: slightly rancid axle grease; the damp wood floor; the hot electric-ozone odor from the motor under the train; stale cigarette smoke; the onion-carrot-cabbage smell of raw vegetables coming from the stacked crates full of supplies being hauled up the mountain to our hotel; and the fresh, dank, glorious stench of cigar.

There was no separate engine on the cog railway, just the two cars. The first, in tramlike fashion, was both the engine and a passenger car. Since the train was empty, it was the only car where the driver had bothered to turn on the heat, so that is where we rode. Mom coughed politely several times and stared at the unshaven driver with her most meaningful look, but he paid no attention. He stood, slouched over the eerily luminous green dials, chewing on "that foul thing" till his saliva soaked the cigar so completely that it went out and smelled even worse.

Riffelberg was only a few miles above Zermatt, but the cog railway slowly meandered for twenty minutes through dense forest and over several high bridges, as well as through various glistening icicle-crusted tunnels before it ground its way slowly out into the open above the tree line. The pine forest suddenly ended and the splendid twilit view of the town of Zermatt far below and the pale mountains above exploded around us. The first stars were visible in the arch of sky. Rachael cupped her hands around her face and leaned forward.

"Isn't it magical?" she whispered.

Rachel turned and put her arm around me and hugged me excitedly. Janet shot her a pitying look.

"Well, it is!" said Rachael.

Janet shrugged.

"Rachael's right," I said.

"Then you're a sentimental sop too," said Janet.

The driver turned on the train car lights, and the view through the big windows was replaced by our reflections. Janet gave Rachael and me a satisfied nod, as if somehow it served us right.

"Don't mind her," whispered Rachael. "She has a heart of stone."

"I heard that!" snapped Janet.

The low drone of the grinding cog deepened as we pulled into the Riffelberg station. The eight-foot-high bank of snow opened to reveal a small concrete one-room station. Two hundred yards down the steep snowy slope was the Hotel Riffelberg. It was the only building at our stop—besides the station and the tiny sheds at the base at and the top of the hotel's small ski lift. The hotel was a large oblong six-story stone building, which sat less than fifty feet from the top of a stomach-churning precipice that fell thousands of feet down to the Zermatt Valley. Painted a drab yellow-beige, it had been built in the late 1800s and had a heavy sheet-metal roof that could withstand howling alpine gales and hold up under the weight of ten feet of snow.

The warm light from the dining room spilled out through fifteen-foot-high picture windows onto the sculpted snowdrifts. The hotel, Dad once told me, was built to accommodate "serious skiers" and mountain climbers who wanted to stay up in the high mountains rather than down in the town, but "who also wanted three hot meals a day, a parquet dance floor, hot water, and a bath."

Night was falling quickly. I was hungry and could smell French fries and some sort of roasting meat wafting from a kitchen vent that was sending up clouds of fragrant steam into the frigid air. One of the stocky Italian maids was waiting with a large sled to take our bags. Even Dad looked a little more cheerful when he smelled the food.

At dinner the first night Mom barely had sat down before she looked up and choked back a startled little cry.

"What's wrong, Mom?" Janet asked. Mom was staring across the hotel dining room. We followed her gaze. Janet and Rachael gasped.

"Good night, shirt! I can't believe it!" barked Dad.

"Ralph, dear, be careful of your blood pressure," said Mom.

We all stared. There, tucked away at the side of the room behind the bar, was a drum set, three music stands, stools, an electric guitar, and an upright piano. The drum set was made of some kind of gray plastic that sparkled. The guitar was bright red.

There had never been music at our hotel before. Mom had always said that it was a blessing that the dance floor was "mercifully unused." My heart leaped for joy as I shook my head sadly along with the rest of the family.

Dad called Eva, the hotel's waitress, over to our table. Dad had been a missionary in Switzerland for over ten years, but still could not speak either French or German because so many of our young people spoke good English. Dad had not bothered to take lessons the way Mom had and always said he was "no good at languages." So when Dad addressed Eva, he spoke in English.

Eva spoke English quite well, though she mixed in French and German words. Eva's voice would go up into a fluty trill at the end of each sentence. In her soft, rather high little voice, everything she said almost sounded as if she were singing it.

"Eva, what is that?" said Dad, pointing across the dance floor.

"*Herr* Becker, *wounderbar!* Thees year we have *la music!*" said Eva. She smiled with her most friendly smile and waved her plump hands as if leading an imaginary orchestra. "*Tr-la, la, la!* Elvis, *non?*"

Eva giggled. We all looked at her in horror, or in my case, with the best pretend horror I could muster. Eva smiled back and stood waiting to see what else we wanted. Then she stopped smiling and glanced behind her to see what we were all looking at in such horror. She did not see anything very awful as she looked at the bar, dance floor, and the other diners quietly eating their food. She turned back to us and her brow furrowed.

Eva was nice to look at. She was not as old as Mom, but older than Janet—a lot older, about thirty or thirty-five. Eva was round all over, but all in proportion, and not very tall. Eva's figure was "very Swiss," Rachael once said. From the front she looked like an hourglass and from the side a curvy *S*. She had been several inches shorter than me for the last two or three vacations. By this vacation I was a good six inches taller than Eva, and when we had walked in a moment before, she had exclaimed, *"Mais, Calvin, comme tu as grandi!"*

Eva's face was round, her mouth small—kind of like a little pink rosebud that has just started to open. She had a little bit of a double chin and big blue eyes that opened wide when she was surprised. Her hair was strawberry blond and so thick that it stood out from her head in two wavy wedges. She parted it down the middle and sometimes pinned a flower to one side under a little silver beret shaped like a skier. We all liked Eva.

"Een a moment, even before zee *Baba au Rum*! Zen it you may dance! *C'est bien, non?*"

"But it's low season," said Mom. "I was given to understand that the hotel only provided music and after-dinner dancing during high season."

"Mais oui, Madame Becker, mais thees year zee hotel ees fulling zan usual *et puis c'est très bien, non?* Zee manager, he keep *la music* when *les réservations c'est mieux que normal.*"

Eva turned away to serve the English General his émincé de veaux and spëtzli. Dad glared after her as she made her way across the shiny oak parquet floor with little mincing steps that made her wide hips swing and the ribbons of her small white apron swish back and forth like a cat's tail. Then Dad glared at us.

Mom was sitting even more bolt upright than usual. Two vivid spots of crimson appeared on her cheeks. We children fidgeted with the edges of the stiff white tablecloth. Not only had we been invaded by the World, or soon would be when the musicians arrived, but the dessert choice that night was our least favorite. The rum-soaked Baba au Rum was out of the question.

"Oh dear," sighed Mom.

"Elsa, why didn't you call ahead and make sure that there was going to be no music?"

"Why, Ralph—"

"Don't you 'why, Ralph' me!" snapped Dad.

The vein was pulsing in the right temple of Dad's forehead. My heart was racing with excitement at the thought that here, unexpectedly, was a wondrous thing: worldly music had followed us up the mountain!

The thought of the music was compensation for the disappointment I suffered moments before when I looked around the dining room. There were no other young people my age. Of course, what I was really looking for were girls. The year before, there had been one. She was a pretty German of fifteen, called Ingrid. Rachael tried to witness to her the very first day, and Ingrid avoided all of us for the rest of the vacation. I even saw her timing her ski runs so that no matter how long I waited at the bottom of the lift she was never there to ride the T-bar with.

This year, as usual, almost everybody seemed even older than Mom and Dad. By the time we took our "low season" vacation, all the normal kids were back at school. We were able to take our holiday during low season because Janet had finished her schooling, and was waiting for the Lord's leading on the next step for her life, whether to go to a Bible school in the States or to stay on at the mission and help teach the young people. Rachael was, like me, being home-schooled. That was why we could vacation in February when Mom got the best low-season prices.

"Where will we be able to sit now in the evenings?" asked Rachael. There was a slight quiver in her voice.

"In the lobby?" I asked.

"You know perfectly well we'll hear the music from the lobby," said Janet. "I know what you're up to!"

"We'll sit here until our meal is done. Then we'll go upstairs and read," said Mom cheerfully. "We have *Wind in the Willows* and the *Voyage of the Dawntreader* with us."

"But, it'll be so early," I said.

"We're not going to stay here and listen to worldly music!" said Janet in a triumphant tone.

"You stay out of this, Janet," said Dad.

"Maybe they'll play classical music," said Rachael, ever hopeful.

"With a drum set and electric guitar?!" snapped Janet scornfully. "There's only one kind of music that's good for!"

"I'm afraid Janet is right," said Mom. "Oh dear, what shall we do now, Ralph?"

We all looked at Dad.

"The Spirit of the World is like a poison gas," muttered Dad. "It creeps in everywhere. We can only hope it's frivolous dinner music and not hard-core rock and roll."

Rachael shivered. Janet glared around with her I-told-you-so look. I hoped it was hard core.

Judging by the three small middle-aged men in seedy gold jackets and threadbare white pants who walked into the dining room at that moment, we were about to find out exactly what kind of music was going to attack our family that evening. They detoured on the way to their instruments via the bar. Mom and Janet exchanged a very meaningful look as the three men not only ordered drinks from Eva but lit cigarettes as they waited for her to mix their cocktails. Rachael smiled at the men until Janet hissed at her to stop.

Eva bustled behind the shining polished mahogany bar, taking various glasses from the gleaming copper-covered shelves suspended in front of a large mirror, in front of which all the bottles were arranged in a glittering, brightly colored row. The bar itself was quite small. There were only six matching red-leather-covered bar stools set off to one side of the dance floor. Next to the bar was a small platform. That is where the instruments sat.

Around the dance floor, the tables and comfortable dining chairs upholstered in red-and-white checked fabric sat in a semicircle. All the tables but one were filled with guests. Dinner was served precisely at seven-thirty, and you were expected to be on time. Each guest used the same table; his napkin from the meal before was waiting at his place, in a wooden ring that had his or her name written on a piece of tape stuck to it, as well as whatever wine was left from the last meal, the bottle marked with the guest's room number.

Behind the tables was a space that ran around the edge of the room. It was covered with a thin red carpet that tended to bunch up under the dessert trolley. Behind everything else were the huge plate-glass windows.

The tables seemed to shine. They were draped with heavy white cloths that felt smooth to the touch and were set with heavy old silver-plate flatware. Each huge soup spoon, fork, and knife was stamped on the handle with the words *Grand Hotel Zermatterhof,* which meant—as Dad once explained—that at some point the Hotel Riffelberg had bought up the old silverware from the Zermatterhof. Wine and water glasses glittered.

It was always a moment of sorrow and humiliation when Eva arrived at our table and swept it bare of two of the three long-stemmed glasses at each place, and left only the smallest glass, the one on a short thick stem. For whatever reason, Eva never told the Italian assistant maids to leave the wineglasses off our table, so each evening I felt as if we were being demoted to a lower rank of guest in front of all the normal people. Most guests had a glass of white wine with their first course and some red with the second, all except for the English General, who always brought his glass of whisky with him from the bar. He would then send Eva back to the bar three times during his evening meal—and once at lunch—to, as he barked loudly, "fetch me another spot of the life-giving, pet!"

The first night back we just had time to change and come down for dinner. All the guests dressed for dinner: men and boys in jacket and tie; women in evening gowns of one sort or another, some long and flowery (the English ladies), some short and black (the Swiss, Germans, Swedes, and French); but everyone was nicely attired. Mom always dressed up even more than most of the other women. She said she wanted them to see that "Real Christians are as stylish as anyone else." Janet brought one bright-blue knee-length dress, and Rachael wore the same black-and-green checked plaid skirt and white blouse with long lacy sleeves almost every night. Dad was in his preaching suit—it was his only suit—and one of his three striped ties. I wore a white shirt, yellow tie, my good gray flannel pants, and my good jacket, a blue blazer.

"Maybe they ordered tomato juice," said Rachael, nodding toward the musicians.

"Look at those glasses she's using!" hissed Janet. "Those aren't 'tomato juice' glasses! Those are *cocktail glasses*, aren't they, Mom?"

"I'm afraid so, dear."

"The World is clever," said Dad. "Have you ever noticed how all the fancy, glamorous glasses are used for alcoholic drinks? Water and soda are served in plain glasses. What's the unspoken message? I'll tell you what it is. It's that fun and sophistication come in fancy glasses!"

"That's so true, Ralph," said Mom.

"Those are martini glasses," I said.

"How do you know that?" asked Janet accusingly.

"Eva told me."

"When?" asked Janet.

"One time last year."

"Where were you?"

"I just happened to ask her."

"Were you hanging around her at the bar?" asked Janet.

"Janet, he has a right to just ask," said Rachael.

"No, he does not!" said Janet. "He's fascinated by all those sorts of things. That's dangerous, isn't it, Mom?"

"Well, dear, it can be. It's a small step from being overly interested in what kind of glass is used to serve a cocktail to wanting to take that first sip. We have to be very careful where such curiosity leads."

The three men, each with a lit cigarette in one hand, drink in the other, made their way to the stainless-steel adjustable stools, music stands, and their instruments. They moved deliberately and slowly, set their drinks down and slid their ashtrays into easy reach. Then they began to tune the instruments. One plugged his guitar into the small amp and speaker. It let out a momentary crackle and low buzzing noise. Then he tuned up from the piano. At each strum my heart raced.

"Real musicians would never drink, smoke, and try to play at the same time," said Mom. "If you ever see a choir singing the Messiah, they won't be drinking at the same time! You see, children, sin is always self-defeating."

"And look, he's put his drink on the piano!" said Janet. "A real musician wouldn't do that, would he?"

"Never, dear," said Mom. "He would have too much respect for his instrument and for the talent the Lord gave him."

"Bach was a Real Christian, wasn't he, Dad?" asked Rachael.

Dad said nothing. He was scowling at his plate.

"Yes, he was a Real Christian, dear," answered Mom.

Dad was glaring at his spëtzli. He did not like the little Swiss noodles. And with no dessert in sight, one look at his face let us all know that his Mood was deepening into a dark brooding storm that could burst at any moment.

Mom shot us one of her let's-work-to-get-Ralph-out-of-his-Mood looks. Then she smiled her brightest being-cheerful-in-the-face-of-adversity smile.

"Bach was very Reformed, wasn't he, dear?" asked Mom, while nodding encouragingly at Dad. "Tell us all about the Dutch and German Reformation and the wonderful culture it produced. There is no finer music than Bach, is there, dear?"

"I don't like this stuff. You like this stuff, right?" said Dad, pushing his plate of spëtzli across the table.

Eva marched over from the bar and reached for Dad's plate.

"*On a bien mangé?* Excuse, have you eat well?" she asked.

"I'm not done yet, Eva," said Dad, and he waved her away with a scowl.

Mom smiled her special smile so that Eva would understand that she, Mom, would never push a plate of food across a restaurant table, but that Ralph, poor thing, came from a working-class background, "very earthy," as Mom sometimes put it. Dad did not practice the great truth of etiquette that her mother had taught her: "Always behave at table as if you are dining with the King and Queen of England at Windsor Castle!"

Dad knew *exactly* what the tilt of Mom's head meant, combined with her rueful sweet-sad smile, the little shrug, the eye contact with Eva, the sorrowful patient laugh. Dad's neck was red. It was a bad sign. And on top of everything, the band was tuning up quite loudly and trying a few opening bars of what sounded a lot more like hard-core rock and roll than jazz, let alone dinner music.

"Eva?"

"Oui, Herr Becker?"

"That music will be too loud. Listen to the volume of that electric guitar!" said Dad.

"I theenk eet ees only for during zee preparations, but I weell asking," said Eva.

"We're eating. Do the other guests want to be disturbed while they eat?" asked Mom.

"Madame Becker, zee music ees so very nice, *non?*"

"Dinner music, my dear, is a violin or harp, *not* an electric guitar! When my dear father took us to the Palm Court in New York City, they played violins."

"I shall speak to zem to play *doucement*," said Eva.

"Don't bother," snapped Dad. "I don't give a damn!"

Janet, Rachael, and I exchange horrified glances. Mom had made Dad furious, mad enough to swear! With her smile, capped off by her mention of her father taking her to the Palm Court in New York City, she had driven Dad right over that edge.

Dad hated Mom's references to her privileged background and her stories about her father, how he cut his meat so daintily. "It was like watching a ballet when that fine old gentleman picked up a knife and fork," Mom often said. Dad knew that his hands were "working-man's hands," as Mom put it. He knew that when she looked at me when I was eating and said, "Think of the Queen of England," what she was really doing was commenting on the way Dad slurped his soup or chewed with his mouth open. She did not even need to look in his direction.

"Eva?" barked Dad.

"Oui, Herr Becker?"

"Don't you dare bother those men! You let them do their damned jobs and play any way they want to! We look forward to being entertained."

Eva gave us all a polite but mystified stare, nodded, and hastily retreated and began to clear the English General's second-course dishes.

"But dear, I thought—" said Mom.

"Just be quiet, Elsa!" barked Dad.

We heard a loud smack. The English General was sitting alone at his small table, as he did every night. His tall frame and narrow sloped shoulders barely filled out his heather-colored tweed jacket. His bald head and long, usually pale horsy face was now an angry red. The General's small white mustache was bristling. He had just slapped Eva's hands with a resounding smack as she tried to take his empty dishes.

"Blasted girl! I'm *not* bloody well finished this dreadful meal! *Bloody girl!*"

"He's always so difficult," whispered Mom.

I laughed. Janet glared at me.

"Mental illness isn't funny, Calvin!" Janet hissed.

"Do you think he really *is* crazy?" Rachael asked, and giggled.

"Of course he's crazy," hissed Janet. "Isn't he, Mom?"

"The General is a little bit unbalanced, yes. But he's a fine old English gentleman, when he's feeling well, at least."

"Nutty as a fruitcake," Dad said with a chuckle. "The English are all nuts. They all hold their forks backward!"

Chapter 3

THAT NIGHT, WHEN I STEPPED OUT of the hotel door, the snow squeaked under my boots. Even without a moon the starlight illuminated the Matterhorn, Ober Gabelhorn, Zinalrothorn, Weisshorn, Brunegghorn, and all the other peaks that ran in a line of sharklike teeth down the Zermatt Valley. The field of snow shimmered in a long smooth sweep of sparkling white above our ski lift.

I wanted to walk along the side of the hotel where there was a narrow path cut in the snowbank, so I could peer through the dining-room windows and get a look at the band in full demonic rock-and-roll swing. It was the best I could do to participate in the night's festivities, seeing as the hotel had only one entrance to the dining room and that ran smack through the lobby. To go that way meant I would risk being seen by the manager's wife who, next morning, in good polite Swiss fashion, might ask—probably in front of my parents—how I had enjoyed the music.

When I tiptoed down the hall past my parents' room, Dad was still yelling at Mom in fits and starts, as he had been off and on for an hour since dinner. I could hear Mom's murmured replies. I figured Janet and Rachael were in their room.

By going down the back service stairs, along the dingy staff-quarters hall, past the kitchen, out the kitchen entrance to the ski room (where all we guests kept our skis), and along the path, at last I came to the picture windows.

I could hear the pounding beat the moment I stepped out of the ski shed and began to make my way down the path between the two high banks of snow. It was a very cold night, but not bitter. The light from the dining room cascaded across the snow so brightly that the little shed a hundred yards away at the bottom of the ski lift cast a stark shadow up the smooth slope. The band was playing "Itsy Bitsy Teenie Weenie Yellow Polka Dot Bikini." I knew the tune. It had been played over and over on the jukebox by the snack bar on the Paraggi beach the summer before.

The General was dancing with one of the Swedish ladies. The Swedish sisters—pale, tall, identical twins in their mid-fifties—had been coming to Riffelberg for the last six or seven years. The General was old, and the Swedish twins were older than Mom, a lot older, but that didn't stop them from dancing. Close, too. I laughed when I saw the General reach down and place his hand on one Swedish twin's bottom and she reached back and slapped it away. I wondered if this was what he had meant last year, when he asked me while riding the T-bar, if I had had any "luck with the damn fillies. You know, old boy, in the gee-gee department?" Was a women's bottom the "gee-gee department"? I wondered.

As I peered around the thick vertical divider between one window and the next I saw something that made me feel as if the mountain were swaying under my feet. *Janet was dancing!*

Several years before, Mom had announced that Janet had "entered the difficult years between childhood and womanhood, when it's so hard to be a young person in today's awful world." Mom said that Rachael was now in the "same phase" and that for young women today "the temptations are greater than ever." Well, Janet seemed to have given in to them! She was dancing with the cook. He was an Italian named Sergio.

Sergio was in his late twenties and short but strong. He had olive skin, a big nose, wide friendly lips, and wiry black hair that started low on his forehead and swept upward. Although he spoke no English or

French, I liked Sergio and sat in the kitchen some afternoons (if it was snowing too hard to ski) while he ran the huge potato-peeling machine that spit dirty water and peel directly into the floor drain. He would let me sit there until the manager's wife came in and shooed me out. Rachael called him "dreamy." Janet made fun of her for saying that. Mom told Rachael she should not talk like that, because we did not know "where thoughts like that could lead."

Judging by the way Janet was letting Sergio hold her around her waist, hold and bump up against her, her thoughts had led to a very bad thing! I was stunned.

The Hotel Riffelberg had forty-seven rooms on five floors, and about thirty guests there at that time. There was a staff of twelve or so, not including the band. They all lived up at the hotel throughout the winter. During low season, life at Hotel Riffelberg was casual. The year before, Sergio had often come into the dining room after dessert was served and sat at the bar having a drink. Sometimes one of the guests would have a drink with him. Sometimes he turned around and winked at Janet, and she would flush a deep red and mutter, "Really! What does that disgusting little man want?!"

Sergio had changed out of the gray-and-white checkered pants he wore in the kitchen. He was wearing a shiny black suit and red tie. Janet had on her blue dinner dress. It was longer and a lot more shapeless than what the other women were wearing but tight enough on top to show the "developed" part.

My first thought was, how does Janet dare? How could she be certain, short of murdering all the rest of us in our beds, that Mom or Dad might not decide to look in on the dining room? Why would she risk such a thing?

My feet were going numb. Sergio held Janet close. I stayed rooted to the icy path as the last feeling drained from my frozen feet. He was pressing himself against her more and more! The band was playing something else now; I didn't know what, a slow sort of song. The drummer had put away the drumsticks and was using wire brushes. The piano player switched to a saxophone. Janet smiled at Sergio. She seemed to be breathing hard. Her smile wasn't happy, but kind of excited: the way she looked that time when she came with me to the village and watched Farmer Ruchet kill a pig. I had thought she would say it was disgusting, the way Rachel did when I killed the chickens after they stopped laying eggs. Rachel had run away, but Janet didn't.

Mom once said the saxophone had been invented for only "one reason," that there was "no real music for a saxophone," that a saxophone was "a thoroughly modern and worldly instrument," that the only reason it existed was to "rouse an animal desire for all the wrong things."

Besides Eva (who was behind the bar), Janet was the only woman in the room under fifty. A Swedish twin was letting the English General hold her close. The bald, rotund, and sweating hotel manager was holding his thin, severe wife.

When the piece of music was done Janet glanced over her shoulder and said something to the cook, who held on to her hand as she pulled away. Janet giggled and kept pulling away and the cook finally let her go. Then Janet walked toward the door to the hall. The cook asked Eva to dance—she shook her head no and he walked out of the dining room—and the band started another number, a fast kind with a real pounding demonic beat of the kind "that only serves to inflame." By that time I knew I was risking frostbite.

I raced up the back staff stairs as fast as I could on numb feet. I wanted to see if Janet went back to her room. I wondered if the dancing had led to the ultimate temptation and if Janet was in the kitchen ruining her life for a "few moments of fleeting pleasure." By the way Sergio had held on to Janet, I had no doubt that he would gladly "take advantage of her innocence," thereby proving the sad fact, as Mom put it, "that young people don't want to wait these days."

Janet was made of stronger stuff than Mom credited. About thirty seconds after I opened the door at the top of the staff stairs and lay down on the cold floor in the dark to peer out unseen, Janet stepped into the light of the single dim bulb that hung on the landing and tiptoed to her and Rachael's room down the center of the red jute runner that stretched the length of the hall. She was carrying her shoes.

I stayed where I was until I heard Janet's door click and the key turn. Then I crept past Janet and Rachael's room, past Mom and Dad's room, opened my door softly, and stepped in. When I passed their room Dad and Mom were talking in low voices.

I did not turn the light on until I had locked the door behind me with the big old key, which had a heavy, solid orange rubber ball the size of an apple hanging from it. (The ball made it impossible to forgetfully slip a room key into your pocket and walk off with it instead of handing the key in at the desk each morning, where the manager could hang it on the hook in front of your letter-and-message box, where it belonged.)

Once my door was locked and the light was on I sat down on the edge of my bed to think. The room was cold and I was chilled to the bone. I pulled what I called my "puff" (the large, shapeless white eiderdown comforter) up around me. I was so preoccupied, it was several minutes before I remembered to bury my nose in the crisp white cover and sniff the delicious smell of hot irons, starch, laundry soap, and fresh air (from the daily airing when, even in winter, all the bedding was hung out our hotel windows for a few hours in the morning before the beds were made up). That night I hardly thought about the delicious Swiss-clean smell. I was wondering if the world was ending.

I sat on the bed and studied the knots in the old pumpkin-colored pine paneling and thought deeply. There was plenty to think about! Janet was worse than Mom and Dad combined when it came to telling on me, suggesting punishments, and making snide comments about The World and its evil ways. Yet here *she* was, *Janet Becker,* who wanted to make sure I had my eyes closed when I prayed and told if I didn't; Janet, who gave me Indian wrist-burns to help "prepare" me for the martyrdom that she said awaited each of us when the Russians invaded in order to torture all American missionaries in Europe for Christ's sake; here was Janet, the future missionary nurse, *sneaking down to dance to the very worst kind of worldly music!*

Janet the Bible teacher had been in the arms of the Italian cook! That Janet the terrible and holy one should dance, which was even worse than smoking because smoking could not lead to the "fleeting pleasures of the flesh" but only to ill health; that *Janet* should have *danced* to hard-core rock and roll of the "very worst, most debased sort" with some young oily Roman Catholic, one who wore a cross around his olive neck and worshiped Mary and the Saints—a Real Christian did not need these "external symbols" because we had Christ in our hearts and no need for "the traditions of men"—that *Janet* could dance with such an unsaved man, who was not only *exactly* the kind of person Jesus had died for but that we, the Becker family, were called to Switzerland to bear witness unto; that *Janet* should *dance,* when the most that she should have done was to share Christ with that cook and share Christ at a *safe distance* no less; that *Janet* let herself be *rubbed* and *touched,* be *pressed* in her Temple with her "womanly gifts" shaking and bobbing to demonic rhythms while rubbing her body on someone not of God's choosing for her; that *Janet* did this all *before marriage* and did not wait until after marriage to be with that *one other person only; THAT JANET SHOULD HAVE DONE ALL THIS,* kept me sitting on my bed pondering for a long, long time.

Janet's dancing seemed so momentous, so strangely apocalyptic, that all I could think of was that it was time to check the sink, maybe even the toilet, to make sure Jesus was not on his way back or, worse, had already come back and caught Rachael up to meet him in the clouds while leaving the rest of us. Maybe Rachael was gone! Maybe *this* was why Janet dared to dance!

Janet would have been so angry when she figured out that it was she of whom Christ had spoken when he said there would be those on Judgment Day to whom he would say, "I never knew you. Depart from me into everlasting punishment," even when they thought they were saved. So I went down the hall and flushed the toilet. (There was no bathroom, only a sink, in each bedroom. The baths and toilets were at the end of the hall and we guests took turns.)

It says in the Bible that several amazing things will happen when Jesus zooms back to earth to snatch his elect up into the clouds at the Rapture. The moon will turn to blood. The water will turn to blood too. So I flushed the toilet to see if Janet was dancing because it was the End Times and we had all been left, rather Janet and I had been left and Mom and Dad too, maybe because they had been fighting.

There is nothing that will cause more despair than getting left behind. So I thought, maybe Janet had been in her room getting undressed and Rachael was already in bed asleep or quietly reading her bedtime scripture portion, and just like it says in the Bible, two will be on the rooftop and one will be taken and the other left, and two will be in a field and one will be taken and the other left; well, there was Janet just about to take off her stockings and all of a sudden this ray of light hit Rachael's bed and Rachael started to float up to the ceiling and went right through it and disappeared. Then Janet rushed over to the light beam and jumped into it and reached up, because of course she would have known *exactly* what was happening, and got set to go too, while maybe wondering why Rachael was taken up to be with the Lord first, since Janet was the oldest, but still happy that Jesus had arrived at last and that we were about to be proved right about everything. And then the light just went out and then *nothing!*

So Janet waited while staring up at the pine boards of the ceiling and expecting her own beam. What would Janet think? First of all, it was not as if Jesus might come back later for her, because the Bible is very specific: it says it is all going to happen in the "twinkling of an eye." No matter how you interpret "twinkling," it has to be faster than spread out over five minutes. The seconds were ticking by, way past any kind of twinkling. We were Calvinist, Reformed, Presbyterian fundamentalists, so there would be no comfort for Janet in any sort of liberal interpretation of what twinkling meant! Twinkling meant *twinkling!*

Six or seven minutes had passed and Janet knew by this time that the elect were long gone. There would be no second thoughts in the Second Coming, no second chances. You were in or out!

So there Janet was with the full realization sinking in that she was the one left while Rachael was the one taken, like the ones on the rooftop and in the field Jesus talked about. So what was the point of just standing there worrying? If you were left, that was it—you were left. And the reason we did not dance was that we did not want to displease Jesus, because dancing grieves the Lord. But if you were not going to be taken up with the Lord, then what was the point? You were way past worrying about grieving the Lord. Grieving the Lord? Ha! He had just left you standing there with your mouth open watching Rachael slide through the knotty pine ceiling of room 27 without even mussing her flannel nightgown! Who cared about what Mom and Dad thought now? Let them see you dance!

So Janet might have slipped on her shoes and dress and marched right back down in a mood of defiance and despair of the same sort New York atheists and the Antichrist will feel when they find out that they have lost the fight against God. Then Janet, having decided to taste the carnal pleasures before the end, and in a very wayward and rebellious mood sure to lead to all sorts of things, in this case the cuddling of Italian chefs, headed down to the dining room, drawn forward by the pounding demonic beat. Then Janet tapped the Italian cook on the shoulder and said, "*Sí,* I *will* dance with you, Sergio!"

So that is why I flushed the toilet, twice, to make sure the water had not turned to blood. And it had not.

The fact that, after what I did to Andy Keegan, I still flushed the toilet in the Hotel Riffelberg to see if Jesus had come back showed how Janet's dancing really scared me.

I once put Mom's red food dye in the toilet tank at Andy's chalet. I did it when I knew Mom, Dad, and Andy's parents, Dick and Jane Keegan, and all the young people had gone for a hike to have an outdoor Bible study. Mom had said, "You wait until Andy gets off the bus and tell him where we all are up on the path to Champéry, then you two come on up the mountain and meet us."

I had waited around, and as I waited I thought about how quiet the chalets were with all the young people gone. That made me think about how this was about how the unsaved Swiss Roman Catholics in our village would find our chalets after the Lord came back. Madame Ruchet might walk in to deliver eggs and she would call out, *"Madame Becker!"* high and low, but no one would answer. Finely she would figure out that we had all been taken up in the clouds, and now she would know we were right and that Mary and the pope could not save you, that only the finished work of Christ could. But it would be too late and Madame Ruchet would wish she had accepted Jesus when she had the chance, because now she was left behind.

Thinking about that—I was sorry because I liked Madame Ruchet and her husband, Farmer Ruchet; he let me help make sausage every year when he killed his pig before Christmas—made me think that if Andy got off the bus from Monthey, where he had gone to the doctor for another one of his ear infections, and I ran out and said, "Andy! They're all gone! I think Jesus came back and we've been left! We'd better check the toilet!" Andy would run inside, which he did, and be all wide-eyed and attentive and maybe even cry when I flushed.

Sure enough the food dye, from Mom's little bottle of cake-frosting dye somebody sent her from America, made the water run dark pink, almost red, red enough to make Andy yell out, "Oh no! We got left! But I really *do* believe in Jesus!"

When Andy started to cry—he had an excuse, this was back when he was only nine years old—I felt bad and showed him the red dye bottle floating in the tank and how I had done it. Then I told him I thought he was really one of the elect after all and not to worry so much. Then Andy hit me, but not too hard, and we made up and I promised not to tell anyone he had cried and I gave him a bar of chocolate.

So I felt kind of hypocritical when I was relieved the water was still just water when I flushed the toilet. I still could not figure out why Janet had dared to dance. It was a long while before I got to sleep.

Chapter 4

I WOKE UP and lay still for a moment, wondering why I had a strange sinking feeling in my chest. Then I remembered Janet and the dancing. I reached out in the pitch dark and turned on my bedside lamp. I looked at my watch. It was five minutes to seven. I picked up the little bell-shaped ivory electric switch that sat on the bedside table and had the word "*SERVICE*" printed on the side. I pushed the button so Eva would know I wanted my breakfast.

The shutters of the Hotel Riffelberg were different from the ones on our chalet. Ours had a life-size shape of a tulip cut out of each center and were made of thick unpainted pine, silvered by the weather. At the hotel the shutters were made of even thicker pine planks painted a dark maroon. Back home the shutters kept my room pitch dark and warm all night, but in the morning the tulip let in the sun so I could see a bright splash on my thin cotton curtains. In the hotel the shutters had no shape cut out of them and closed so tightly that I had no idea when it was morning.

At home when I opened my curtains, if the sun was shining at a certain angle, a brilliant shaft of light shot through the tulip and across my bedroom, lighting up glittering dust particles. When I smacked my pillow and stirred up a dazzling explosion of dust, it seemed as if a whole universe had suddenly sprung to life, complete with galaxies, suns, and worlds swirling and twinkling in the light beam that cut through the thick dark. Then I would wedge myself between my bed and the wood-paneled wall—my bedroom was very small, only about six feet by ten—on a narrow patch of faded blue linoleum. And I would stare up at the dust-mote-filled shaft of light. Maybe, I thought, our own Planet Earth is nothing more than a dust mote floating in some huge bedroom.

What if on one of my dust planets there was a boy lying on his back watching dust glitter in *his* sunbeam? What if his mother was downstairs preparing to lead the Monday morning Bible study and telling her young people—assuming they had lost Roman Catholic youths in other universes too—that God was watching over them and had a wonderful plan for their lives? Maybe the microscopic boy was thinking the *exact same thing* and was blowing the dust in *his* room at the *exact same moment* and making it dance and twinkle above him and was also whispering, "In the beginning God created the heavens and the earth. The earth was without form, and void; and darkness was on the face of the deep."

I would get dizzy. No matter how hard I concentrated on one particular mote, sooner or later I lost track of it as it swirled up over the bookshelf above my bed to be lost in the darkness.

Had God had lost track of our world too? Then it would not matter what I thought. If God could not see me, maybe I was safe when I imagined Jennifer and how her bathing suit straps slipped and the force of the water peeled her suit down when she pushed off the bottom of the sea and shot to the surface so that for one glorious instant I glimpsed her small new breasts.

I would forget all about my dust planets and concentrate on Jennifer and all the women on the beach, from the big Italian mothers with their rolling bellies to the slender tall girls in sunglasses who stepped off the teak speedboats, then sauntered across the beach with everyone watching. Those tall girls would swing their hips and act as if it was the most natural thing in the world to be just about naked in their tiny bikinis, no more than four little triangles of bright cloth, three in front and one behind. . . .

A few minutes later I would open my bedroom shutters and make sure I got what Mom called the "Precious Seeds" cleaned up. That way Mom would not find any stains and give me a lecture about not defiling my body—the Temple of the Holy Spirit—with "animal desires."

In the Hotel Riffelberg there were no dust-beam universes. The rooms were dust free and the shutters solid and thick. The unsmiling elderly Swiss-German maid—she wore her hair in the tightest bun I had ever seen, something like a compressed tennis ball made of steel wool—and her two round and friendly middle-aged Italian assistants were a lot more thorough in their cleaning than my mother was. In my hotel bedroom the honey-colored oak floor shone with a polished waxy sheen so smooth that, when wearing socks, if I put my foot down wrong I was sent flying. The eiderdown and huge fluffy pillows were bright white and crisp. There was a thick felt mat by the door to put my ski boots on, so that if they had any snow on them it would not puddle up and mark the floor. There was a cloth pen-wipe on the nightstand sewn into a little embroidered cloth booklet. That way, if I happened to be using a fountain pen, I would not be tempted to wipe the nib on my sheet or on one of the two thin little hand towels that hung stiff with starch from the thick chrome bar next to the small old-fashioned bedroom sink. Everything had its place and was covered or glass-topped, varnished or waxed, or had a lace doily under it to stop whatever, say the bedside lamp, from marking what it sat on. Even the wood-paneled knotty-pine walls were smooth and varnished.

To see whether it was morning, I had to pull back the faded burgundy brocade drapes, then draw the gauzy white lace curtains aside and open the large double-paned window, fastened in the middle by a big brass handle that worked a latch at the top and bottom. After that I unfastened the iron bar that hooked into the middle of each shutter. Then I folded the shutters back and fastened them to the outer masonry wall.

The first morning back, the trip to the window was worth it in spite of how cold the floor felt to my bare feet as the blast of frigid air drained the room of heat the instant I opened the window. The iron bar that hooked the shutters was so cold that my hands stuck to it, not painfully the way my tongue once froze to the metal laundry-line pole back home when I was young enough to try that trick—Rachael saw me and ran for hot water so I did not lose too much skin—but just enough to let me know that the temperature was way below zero.

I flung the shutters wide and the view appeared suddenly out of the stuffy darkness. Even at dawn the snow and sky were bright and made me blink and rub my eyes. Before I got the second shutter open my fingers were so cold that I could not feel them as I pinned it against the wall while fumbling with the six-inch, cast-iron hinged fastener shaped like a soldier, which I clicked neatly into place.

I stood rooted to the floor for so long that I could not even feel my hands when I shut the window. No postcard or painting came close to telling the truth about the peaks, just how huge the jagged teeth were and, at the same time, how delicate they seemed, like something made of sugar in a fancy bakery window.

I gazed lovingly at the Matterhorn. She was always bigger and more dangerous looking than my memory of her. She perched above everything, her famous craggy pyramid presiding over the world, the essence of mountain, and the very heart of Switzerland. The Matterhorn seemed so close that it was disorienting to look down and measure the distance between the hotel and her foot—about three or four miles—by letting my eyes wander down the cliff, across the narrow top of the Zermatt Valley, then up the forested lower slopes to where the trees stopped and bare rock was covered by thick snow from which the granite peak, too steep for the snow to cling to, shot skyward to her squared-off summit.

My eyes ran from the Matterhorn's top down the line of the ridge to the hump at her foot, where the spidery cables ran in a long arc from steel pylon to pylon and carried the Zermatt-Furi-Schwarzsee *téléphérique* up to the high ski pistes on the glacier. I rode the Zermatt-Furi-Schwarzsee téléphérique once per vacation with Dad on our father-son day out. I wondered if this year we would take our usual trip or if Dad would not want us to get that close to the town because of the typhoid.

Usually, about the second or third day we would skip breakfast and leave at first light, heavily muffled against the cold. We had to be extra careful. The blue shadowless predawn light flattened out all the contours of the piste. What looked smooth could actually be a series of bumps that would unexpectedly send me spinning out of control, legs thumping up and down like pistons as I flew over ridges.

We skied in silence. The only sound was made by the metal edges slicing into the icy slope. By the time we arrived in the valley the wool mufflers in front of our mouths were crusted white with moisture from our frozen breaths. Dad and I would be waiting at the cable car station, and munching on the chocolate bar Dad always brought, long before the other skiers arrived.

Once Dad and I were on the second leg of the journey—we changed cars halfway at Furi—the ascending téléphérique would leave the Zermatt Valley and rise up until we burst into the brilliant white sunshine that had turned the tips of the peaks gold. The interior of the big boxy car would turn from the monochrome of twilight to vivid color in one dazzling instant.

The car would sway gently a thousand feet above the snowy ground that was swiftly gliding past. The only sound would be the far-distant hum of the electric motor steadily pulling us up and up, its deep hum carrying down the miles of thick cable that looped around huge wheels at the top and bottom and over the banks of pulleys under each towering pylon. If I then looked straight back down, there was a tightening in my stomach that made me feel as if someone had just grabbed my "little seed sack" with an icy hand. . . .

I leaned far out of the hotel window and listened. The total silence was so powerful that I held my breath until I began to feel faint. I wanted to get the full benefit, soak up the solitude and listen to the thud of my heart.

Eva knocked on my door. I closed the window and hopped back into bed as she bustled in and put the huge wooden tray, with a big old battered silver pot of hot chocolate, two fresh croissants and two *ballon* (crusty rolls), a saucer filled with butter curls, and four miniature pots of different kinds of Héro jam, on the top of the dresser. She had stubby hands—usually red from washing glasses at the bar—with dimpled knuckles. She picked up the second of my two pillows off the floor and stacked it behind me so I could sit up and lean back comfortably and eat. She poured me a cup of steaming hot chocolate, then turned and picked up the tray and placed it on my lap on top of the puff.

"Merci," I said as I watched her.

Eva kept her short nails polished a bright red.

"C'est rien," said Eva. "Eet ees a beautiful day! *Très beau mais froid!"* Eva paused and smiled. "Calvin?"

"Yes, Eva?"

"Do you have a leetle friend?"

"What little friend?"

"Chez toi, at home, a leetle friend?"

"There's Andy."

"Ees she *très belle?* "

"Andy's not pretty!"

"C'est un garçon?"

"Of course he's a boy."

"Mais tu as une petite amie, not a boy?"

"Girl? Girlfriend?"

"Oui."

"I don't have a girlfriend," I said, and I could feel my cheeks getting hot.

"*Pauvre petit,*" laughed Eva.

She gazed at me. Her blue eyes were sparkling. She shook her head and smiled.

"*Dit moi, Calvin. Ne mentais pas.* You must telling zee truse!" Eva laughed, put her hands on her hips, and cocked her head at me.

"Of course there's Jennifer," I mumbled.

"*Oui?*"

"In Italy. In the summer we go to Portofino on vacation."

"You have *le petit ami en Italie?* " asked Eva and smiled brightly. "You have kees her?" asked Eva.

I shook my head NO.

"*Non? Pourquoi pas?*"

Eva laughed. I did not want her to think I was just a child, or worse, some kind of missionary who never got kissed while all the normal kids in the world got kissed all the time. So I added, "Once I did kiss her."

"*Une fois? Pourquoi?* Why not many kees?"

"Because she's English I guess. Jennifer is, I mean."

"Ah! *Les Anglais ils sont très difficiles!* But, Calvin, you are so handsome, so *carrée.* Me, I would kees you many times! *Les Anglais ils sont fous, non?* So handsome, so *carrée!* "

"What?"

"*Carrée!* Ees a compliment, to say you are so handsome and like zee box weeth zee strong shoulder, zee shape ees square. How old you are thees year?"

"Fourteen."

"*Oo, la, la! Très beaux!*"

"Square?"

"*Oui!* Wide, weeth les *muscles.*"

"Oh."

"Me, I kees *mon petit ami* many times!" Eva laughed. "I have a friend he ees een Montreux."

"Is that where you're from?"

"*Oui.*"

"But I thought you're Swiss-German," I said, feeling a little bit relieved that we were talking about something more everyday than kissing.

"*Mais oui,* from Zurich. Not after my fasser work as zee concierge of zee Hotel Excelsior. Then we live to Montreux. You like Montreux?"

"Yes. We go there for a day off sometimes and walk by the lake."

"But eet ees long weenter here een Zermatt!"

"Do you ever get a chance to ski, Eva?"

"*Mais non!*" Eva laughed. "I am worker, not on oleeday. Work, work, work! You are zee only one who get up so early but een one hour I work, work, take *le petit déjeuner* to everyone. No time *pour le ski!* "

"Don't you like it here?"

"*Mais oui.* But I do not have *le petit ami.* My friend ees too far, and sometimes when I bring *le petit déjeuner* to the gentleman Englais *oo, la, la!* "

"The General?"

"*Oui!*"

"Our English General?"

"*Oui!* He try to kees me each morning. What is 'poppet'?"

"It's an English word. I've heard it in the books Mom reads sometimes, but I don't know exactly what it means, something like sweetheart or something."

"He say, 'come here, my poppet!' He open hees bed, *comme ça,* and he pat *le duvet ici.*"

Eva demonstrated. She took a step over to my bed, sat down next to my knees, and patted the bed.

"He wants you to get into his bed?!"

"*Comme ça,* "said Eva as she patted the bed. "Last morning he have no pajama!"

"What?!"

"He have on hees pajama here"—Eva pointed to her chest—"but down"—she pointed to my lap—"*en bas,* down he have no pajama. He open *le duvet! Voilà! Je le vois tu est nu, tout prêt!* I see him. And he was *tout prêt,* you understand?"

"Ready? Ready for what?"

"His, how you say, was *grande.* Stand ready for of the loved."

Eva slowly lifted her arm to demonstrate, her arm was sticking straight out from her shoulder. As she raised it to a right angle, she laughed.

"The General had his pajamas off and his, his . . ."

"Bien sûr! Comme ça!" Eva laughed, stuck her arm straight up, then slowly dropped it to her side.

All I had been expecting was breakfast, and now this day had started with one of the greatest things that I could remember ever happening to me. No one in my life, I mean no grown-up, let alone any grown-up woman, had ever talked this way, let alone used her arm to demonstrate what she was talking about. To see a woman almost as old as my mother stick up her arm to show how the General's Little Thing had been standing up and to have this be said to me by her while she laughed and her bosom heaved up and down no more than a couple of feet away was so wonderful I could hardly stand it.

"Did you t-tell?" I stammered, trying hard to keep my voice steady.

"But of course not! *C'est normal.* Zee gentleman are like thees."

"But it's not allowed, is it?"

"For zee gentleman to ask for the *petit service c'est normal, non?*"

"What?"

Eva laughed and placed one of her plump warm hands on my arm.

"You are never looking at me and are thinking of *l'amour, mon petit?*"

"No," I muttered. "No, of course not."

"*Pourquoi?* I am not preety?"

"Oh, of course, but I just meant . . . "

Eva threw her head back and laughed. Her white blouse heaved up and down over her really huge bosom in such a way as I could see the pattern of her lace bra for a moment when the thin white cotton of her blouse stretched over it. My cheeks felt as if they were on fire. Her blouse stretched tighter than ever. Right there in front of me was that lacy bra showing under the cloth of her blouse!

"But, Calvin, you are a *très gentil garçon, non? I am une belle femme, non?*"

"Yes, but. . ."

"Would you like a leetle kees before your *petit déjeuner?*"

When she bent forward over the tray to kiss me I did not pull away even though I felt as if the room were tipping over. I heard the dishes on the tray rattle and a couple of the jam pots hit the floor and roll. And still Eva kissed me. At last she pulled back, smiled, and took a deep breath.

"*Voilà!*"

Eva straightened the dishes on the tray. Then she retrieved a stray butter curl off the puff cover and returned it to the dish. She smiled, stood up, smoothed down her apron, and walked out. I sat and stared at the skin forming on my untouched hot chocolate. My lips tingled.

The kiss was exactly the kind of thing I was supposed to tell Mom about so she could decide if she should tell Dad. But I gave up telling Mom anything years before, after she started asking me if I was touching my Little Thing. After that I never mentioned anything private again if I could help it.

Mom said that all "physical intimacy between boys and girls" should be reserved for marriage and that the Europeans, Catholics, and the like were "tragically secular" and "sadly free with the precious gift the Lord means only for husbands and wives." She also said if anything of "that kind" troubled me I was to talk to her about it.

Eva had kissed me! That was certainly "that kind" of thing! But it sure was not troubling me! Besides, it was not my fault. All I had ordered was breakfast. I had not done anything to make her kiss me, but still I knew Mom would not like it. In fact, I think she had tried to prepare me for just such an eventuality by relating the story of Joseph. In the Bible story, Joseph ran away from Potophor's wife. She wanted to kiss him and do even worse things. Mom would have wanted me to respond as Joseph did. He ran out of that room so fast, he left his cloak in the clutches of his worldly seducer. But I liked Eva's kiss. Besides, I had a heavy breakfast tray on my lap.

Chapter 5

I WAS ALWAYS THE FIRST PERSON in our family, usually the first from the hotel, to clip on my skis and make the short trek over to our ski lift. After it had snowed and yet another layer was added on top of the deep snow pack, as had happened during the night, I cut a fresh track. I used my poles as little as possible. That way, when I got to the lift and looked back, my path made a clean cut in the fresh powder.

I was waiting at the lift before the men who ran it came to work on the early train, the one that carried the railroad workers, the lift attendants, and the first skiers up the mountain. I watched the two lift attendants ski the short distance down from the station. The first took off his skis, jammed them into the snowbank, and started the lift's electric motor humming. Then he lit a fire in the little wood stove in his hut. The second attendant, the one who minded the top of the lift, then rode a T-bar up the mountain.

The trains kept coming all day, about every half hour. They were packed with skiers on their way to Rotenboden and Gornergrat, the two stops above our hotel. Rachael and I categorized skiers' skills by whether or not they were "Gornergrat skiers" or just "Rotenboden skiers." Intermediate skiers got out at Rotenboden to avoid the start of the piste at Gornergrat and the incredibly steep slope that Janet called "the wall of death." Mom never took the train all the way to Gornergrat and always got out at Rotenboden. Janet, Rachael, and Dad continued on to Gornergrat, and so did I. Mom mostly used the little hotel lift a few times in the morning, then sat on the bright sunny terrace outside the hotel and wrote letters.

About twenty minutes after a train full of skiers passed our station, the first of them would be back, having made the run down. They might stay, skiing for a while on our piste, but usually they sailed past on their way back down to Zermatt to take the train again, or perhaps the téléphérique to Schwarzsee or the big chair lift to Sunnegga.

I envied the other skiers their freedom, the money that allowed them to afford the big lifts and the train, to ski at will over all the slopes that fanned out from Zermatt. Because we were guests in the hotel we could buy a book of tickets for our T-bar lift from the manager at a reasonable price. To take the train all the way to the top of Gornergrat, let alone ski down to town and take the big cable cars or chairlifts, was a big treat.

I spent the morning of the kissing skiing up and down the Riffelberg slope. The day was perfect; "splendid," as the English General said while we rode the T-bar together. When I tilted my head back and looked through the cables, the sky was such a dark blue it seemed almost purple.

There was not a shred of ice anywhere. The sun was hot on my face but the air cold enough so that my mitten, wet from brushing myself off after a fall, froze to the metal clip that reinforced the T part of the T-bar.

On the first morning of any other vacation I would have begged Mom for money for a ticket to ride the train from Riffelberg up to Gornergrat, so I could get at least one long run in besides the short up-and-down runs our little lift provided. But that day I was not thinking about skiing. I was in a daze. All I thought about was Eva. When I rode up with the General I thought about how he had dared to pull the covers back with his pajama bottoms off, to see what Eva would do about it. When the General said it was a splendid day, it was all I could do not to stare at him with my mouth open. I was wondering if other men did the kind of thing he had done to Eva, whether he was crazy or if this was an English thing, the way Mom said body odor was a "French thing" and cleanliness a "German thing."

Just before noon I rode the T-bar with Rachael.

"Rachael?" I said.

"Yes?" Rachael answered with a cheery smile.

"If I tell you something really interesting, will you promise not to tell?"

Rachael gave me a wide-eyed, searching look.

"What have you done now?"

"Nothing. I didn't do it. Eva did."

"Did what?" said Rachael, staring at me so hard she forgot to watch her skis and they jumped the groove and she veered wildly and almost fell off the lift.

"Be careful!" I shouted.

We steadied ourselves.

"Okay, what?" asked Rachael breathlessly.

"Eva kissed me."

"What?!"

"At breakfast."

"You mean she kissed you on the cheek, kind of a good morning kiss?"

"No. On the mouth, like a boyfriend or girlfriend, even a wife or something."

"WHAT?! Why?"

"I don't know. She just did."

"How could you let something like this happen?!"

"It happened fast."

"We must tell Mom. She'll know what to do."

"But you promised!"

"I did not! I only nodded."

"If you tell, you know they might take us home."

Rachael thought about this for a moment. She pensively sucked some ice off her mitten.

"Well, you may be right, and it would be a pity to . . . to spoil our vaca—Oh, Calvin, if I keep silent, will you promise to not let anything like this ever happen again?!"

"Yes. Absolutely."

We arrived at the top. After we skied away from the oncoming path of the lift we stopped and adjusted our ski poles, then stood silently side by side. Rachael let out a long shuddering sigh.

"What was it like?" whispered Rachael at last.

"Sort of nice," I said, without looking at her.

Rachael sighed again.

"I wish somebody kissed me! I mean, of course I'll wait for the man of God's choosing, I just mean *if* somebody did do that, then I'd know without it being my fault."

"Maybe the manager will kiss you. Sometimes he brings up trays when Eva is too busy on the other floors."

Rachael looked horrified.

"How disgusting! He's an old, old man, fifty at least! No, I meant maybe, uh, somebody like, uh . . . "

"Sergio?" I asked, and laughed.

"Well, maybe," said Rachael with a shudder. She blushed a deep red. "But, Calvin, don't let it happen again. You need to wait for—"

"The girl of God's choosing. I know, I know."

Rachael gave me a hug and we skied off together. Rachael called over her shoulder, "If Jesus was watching, what would you do? Mom says this should be our first thought upon encountering any dubious situation!"

"She says lots of things!" I yelled back.

"And you know He *is* watching!" Rachael yelled.

I sighed. I did not like that idea at all. No corner was so dark, no blanket thick enough, no hotel room so well hidden that Jesus could not see what, *exactly what,* I was doing, and worse yet, imagining, not only doing but planning to do, thinking about, wishing for! He could even hear half thoughts, ones I stopped thinking before I finished them. He even knew what I was *thinking* of thinking and what my real intentions were!

Intentions were "half the battle," as Mom put it. There were only a very few things in life that did not lead to something else even worse.

And there were very few "Real Christians." We, the Becker family, were Real Christians. At least Mom and Dad were, and Rachael. (Janet was so tough it was hard to believe she was.) I knew I was not.

A real Real Christian would never long to hear the jazz band in the Hotel Zermatterhof, or pretend to be adjusting his ski bindings to give some girl at the ski lift time to catch up so he could ride the T-bar with her, his heart full of joy because of her extratight ski pants!

Real Christians were mainly found in our denomination. Not even all other Presbyterians were Real Christians. Most were not. In fact, even in our mission Mom and Dad were clearly closer to the Lord than their coworkers, some of whom had been to the wrong seminary—our denomination's "other seminary," the one with "unsound views" about infant baptism and the Second Coming of Christ, just to mention a few of their many errors.

Real Christians were "Kindred Spirits," as opposed to "just nominal Christians." So many people who seemed at first like Real Christians turned out not to be. In fact, who was and was not a Real Christian was something that had to be closely watched. Anything could get a person demoted from the A list to the B list, from being Kindred to being "merely saved," from being merely saved to "not even a Christian at all." A drink of alcohol, a mention of jazz or rock and roll in some casual way that betrayed an "overfamiliarity with the

World," a "dubious theological opinion," even an "inappropriate joke" about the Things of the Lord, even what someone wore, what their wife wore, any kind of opinion that deviated from what the Lord had laid on Mom's heart concerning the "direction of the Lord's Work" and the "Lord's leading," all this and more could lead to a "break in fellowship."

Few were called and even less chosen. Other than our family, God, in his wonderful plan for mankind, had apparently decided to save very few people.

I thought about Janet dancing, too. But even that seemed unimportant compared to our waitress-barmaid kissing me. It was not that I had never thought about Eva before. I liked her, but not the way I liked Jennifer. I liked Jennifer in a way that made me blush when Janet teased me about it.

Eva was not beautiful the way Jennifer was with her tall, thin figure, high cheekbones, and long blond hair. But then Jennifer was not a woman, not yet. She was only a girl who, just a few vacations ago, had started "blossoming." We kissed that one time, then after that she acted as if nothing had happened. When I tried to kiss Jennifer a second time, the next day, while we were climbing out on the rocks under the huge villa that sat out at the point of the Paraggi cove, she just laughed and told me not to be daft, called me "a silly twit" and shoved me away in the friendly teasing way she always did everything.

Eva was fully blossomed! If she blossomed any more she would split out of her dress! She was as full and round everywhere as any woman could be. When she bent down to kiss me, her bosom had sort of poured toward me. She had not laughed at the kiss or pulled away in a hurry. She was glued to my mouth so long that I could feel her breath blowing sweet and warm into my mouth and nose as we breathed in and out a couple of times. At the same time I picked up a little of what Mom called "that unfortunate European aroma."

Eva was one of those kinds of Swiss women Mom said it was a mystery to figure out. The mystery was, Mom said, "Why these local women keep their houses so clean and yet have that unfortunate European aroma." It was the same kind of mystery as why Swiss women did not shave their legs or under their arms. Mom said, "Our habits of personal hygiene are part of our American evangelical inheritance." That was the closest I came to getting these things explained.

Eva was a Protestant. I knew this because of the type of gold cross she wore around her neck. It had a little dove above it attached by a little gold link. It was the Huguenot Cross. The Huguenots were the French Protestants that the Roman Catholics burned at the stake and massacred, which was why, Dad said, "France is the way it is." The French, Dad explained, missed their chance because the Protestants preached the truth but were martyred for it. As a result, the French had the worst case of unfortunate European aroma and also had guillotined their own peasants in their bloody revolution and later handed over the Jews to the Nazis way before they were even forced to, Dad said.

So Eva was a bit of a contradiction. She wore a Protestant cross, yet she had a strong case of that unfortunate European aroma, almost like a Frenchwoman, though of course not that bad. However, the right kind of cross or not, Eva had kissed me on the lips! No born-again woman would ever do that!

So, as I skied, what I was thinking about was not how splendid the day was; the typhoid in Zermatt; Janet dancing; or even whether Dad was still in a Mood; but about what might happen at breakfast the next day! Whatever I had promised Rachael, I resolved to make sure that, as usual, I would ring for my breakfast before anyone else in the hotel was up. The very second Eva walked into the big kitchen, turned on the lights, started the coffee urn boiling, and then tramped up to the train station to get the fresh rolls and croissants (they arrived with the milk and newspapers in the dark), I would be ready.

Chapter 6

AT DINNER I WATCHED EVA closely. She served the English General his drink. Then she served the Germans their dinner. Then she brought us our first course of half a grapefruit with a maraschino cherry in the middle.

"Do you not liking?" asked Eva, when she came to clear the first course dishes and saw we had all left the cherries. I smiled at her and tried to catch her eye, but she looked away. She did not pay any special attention to me all during dinner. In fact, it seemed as if she was avoiding my looks. My heart sank.

"Too sweet," said Dad.

"Like a candy wrapper," I said.

"That's very descriptive, dear," said Mom.

"Calvin is clever, isn't he?" said Rachael.

"He's not so clever," said Janet.

"Why must you always be so unpleasant, dear?" Mom asked.

"He's bad enough without getting puffed up," said Janet. She glared at Rachael. "Don't encourage him."

I shot Eva a look and hoped she had not heard Janet's cutting remark. Eva did not seem to have heard anything.

"There's nothing wrong with giving a compliment or being nice, is there, Dad?" asked Rachael.

"They cheat you with a first course like this," said Dad. "Can you imagine in the States what would happen if you served half of a grapefruit about the size of a baseball to some trucker in a diner and told him that this was his 'first course'?"

"A 'trucker in a diner'?!" exclaimed Mom. "But, my dear, this is *Switzerland* and what we are paying for is the view and this lovely place, *and* the culture!"

"With that fool band and grapefruit for a first course, what's next? A slice of Spam for dinner?"

"Really, dear!" said Mom. "We need to appreciate what the Lord has given us. Think of all the missionaries at the other PCCCUSA missions around the world tonight! Think of Stan and Betty in the Congo!"

"I'm thinking," said Dad.

"Well?" asked Mom.

"Well, what?" said Dad.

"Oh, look!" exclaimed Rachael. "Roast pork, my favorite!"

"There you are, dear," said Mom.

"Two paper-thin slices, great!" said Dad bitterly.

"I'll share mine with you, dear."

Mom reached over the table and laid a slice of pork on Dad's plate.

"Did I ask you to do that?" asked Dad angrily.

"No, dear, but if you're so hungry, I don't want you to be unhappy. Isn't this lovely? Look, a sprig of rosemary!"

"They don't get vacations in the Congo, do they, Dad?" asked Rachael brightly.

Dad gave Rachael a grim look. He did not like it when Rachael sounded like Mom, cheerful and saying things in a voice that sounded as if she was talking to a little child. Mom waited to see if Dad would answer Rachael.

"Well, Rachael," said Mom, "they get a furlough the same as everyone else every four years, but if they take a summer vacation they certainly don't go to a place like Portofino, and they could never dream of skiing in Zermatt. The Lord has been *so* good to us. Hasn't He, Ralph?"

"Why?" asked Janet.

"Well, dear, that's hard to say," answered Mom brightly. "He knows what we each need in our lives and gently leads us into still waters and green pastures."

"So the other missionaries don't need nice vacations?" asked Rachael.

"Well, dear, it's not for us to say. The mission board prays so hard for the Lord's guidance on where to post each missionary couple, and we got sent to Switzerland, not Africa or Indonesia."

"Luck of the draw," muttered Dad.

Mom gave Dad a sad, shocked look.

"Ralph, tell the children you don't mean that," said Mom with a nervous laugh. "We don't believe in 'luck,' do we, dear?"

Dad looked up from his plate, chewed, swallowed, and grinned.

"The mission board meets and throws dice once a year," said Dad. He shot Mom a teasing smile.

"Oh, Ralph!"

Dad laughed. Mom shook her head ruefully and gave us her he's-only-joking-pay-no-attention-whatsoever-children look.

"You throw a six and go to Switzerland, five for the Congo, four for India. Now, why four is for India nobody knows, but that's how we Presbyterians of the Presbyterian Church of Christ and Covenant United States of America do it, right, Elsa?!"

"Oh, children, your father is joking, aren't you, dear?" Mom said and glared at Dad.

Dad paid no attention to Mom and kept right on talking.

"But see, in the old PCUSA—that's the Presbyterian Church of America, in case you've forgotten who we were before the last church split, children—they read tea leaves to decide who goes where in the mission field, and that's why we split from that denomination!" Dad laughed. "We didn't agree with their method of 'discerning the Lord's leading,' right?"

Mom's cheeks flamed up red and her eyes sparkled angrily. She took a fast deep breath that sucked her nostrils flat till her nose looked pinched.

"No, dear, the reason we left was over the errors in the doctrine concerning Christ's millennial reign, that and the people they let teach at the seminary," Mom said quietly, and glared.

She waited for him to agree with her. Dad said nothing.

"Our mission board seeks the Lord's will for months before they come to a prayerful decision," said Mom primly.

"But it doesn't hurt to have Elsa's uncle on the mission board, does it, Elsa?"

Dad grinned, then burst into laughter.

"Ralph! How can you say that?"

"Why pretend, Elsa? I'm not saying I'd rather be in India, just that seeing as your grandfather founded the mission . . . well, children, it's like marrying into royalty. Talk about the Queen of England! That's why we're sitting here eating pork served by Eva, and Stan and Betty McDonald are trying to keep some kind of lice down they just scraped out of the inside of a log with a wooden stick! We're sitting here looking at the English General while they're sharing a grub with some guy that has a bone through the end of his nose!"

The men in the gold jackets were walking over to their instruments, drinks and cigarettes in hand. Dad glanced at them and kept on laughing heartily. Janet, Rachael, and I exchanged glances.

"Ralph! How can you?!" exclaimed Mom.

She jumped up and ran from the dining table. Janet and Rachael and I looked at our plates hoping Dad would not say more, that his Mood would stop and the "dark spirit," which overcame him when Satan attacked him at his weakest point—in other words, his "working-class crudeness and temper"—would be conquered by the prayers we knew Mom would be offering as she sat fuming in the lobby or up in her bedroom or wherever she ran to.

"Children?" said Dad quietly.

"Yes, Dad?" we answered nervously.

"Elsa is a wonderful woman of God, but she's a little *too* sensitive."

None of us spoke. Dad ate for a while and the rest of us pretended to. After Dad cleaned his plate and had carefully sopped up all the pork juices with a hunk of crusty bread, he looked up and smiled, not an angry or sarcastic smile but a nice friendly grin.

"See, Elsa likes to pretend that everything is just so great, so special! But there's a real world out there and I get sick of all her pretending."

We all held our breaths, tried to do nothing wrong that would push Dad over the edge.

"It boils down to this question of predestination," said Dad.

We all nodded.

"God has ordained all things before creation."

We nodded. Eva cleared the plates. Dad said nothing more for a while. He was staring out the dark windows at the ghostly mountains. We did not dare move. Eva's bosom brushed my shoulder as she reached for Janet's plate. I tried to catch her eye but she looked away again. We sat waiting for Dad to show us what to do next, if he was in a vacation-wrecking Mood or just angry about the usual things. The band started to play. People came and went. Dessert was served. After a very long and fidgety ten minutes or so, Dad shrugged, sighed, and spoke.

"But God also uses human agents to do his will," said Dad. "Not that we have any choice in the matter, because it's all foreordained."

We nodded.

"Now, I have no trouble admitting that it's a good thing to have connections on the mission board, because the way I see it, that is all part of the Lord's will too. But your mother is embarrassed by the fact, and would rather pretend God 'led us' to Switzerland without using any family connections. But let's be honest. Janet, would you rather be in Switzerland reaching out to Catholic youth or in India looking for toilet paper?"

Janet gulped. Dad rarely went this far. And he was being so calm and reasonable that it only made it worse.

"I, I . . . " stammered Janet.

I felt sorry for Janet.

"Speak up," said Dad.

"I like Switzerland," said Janet.

"And do you like toilet paper?" asked Dad.

"Yes," Janet whispered.

"So we're lucky that from before creation God chose Elsa's uncle to be the missionary board president, at least to be president back when they sent us out to Switzerland, and picked Stan and Betty to go to the Congo, where now they're eating worms and bugs while we have toilet paper."

"The Lord is good," murmured Rachael miserably.

"Rachael?"

"Yes, Dad?" said Rachael in a quivering voice.

She did not dare meet Dad's look. Rachael kept her eyes glued to the tablecloth.

"Do you like toilet paper?"

"Yes, Dad," Rachael murmured.

"Calvin?"

"Yes, Dad. I like it too."

"Good! So we *all* like toilet paper!" said Dad and stood. "Good night, children!"

Dad strode from the room.

"Poor Mom," sighed Rachael.

"Poor us!" snapped Janet.

"What a Mood," I said.

"I wonder what set him off," said Rachael.

"He's like Richard the Third," muttered Janet darkly.

"Everything seems to set him off these days," said Rachael.

"He's just pure evil," said Janet.

"Janet! Oh, how can you?" wailed Rachael.

"You sound exactly like Mom," said Janet. "I'll tell you how. I don't mind telling you at all. You better get used to the idea of being orphans, that's what!"

"*Whyyy?*" wailed Rachael.

"Because I bet he gets locked up someday or worse."

"Worse?" I asked.

"Arrested! Executed!"

"For what?" I asked.

"Murder!"

"Janet!" Rachael shrieked so loudly that heads turned and even the drummer glanced over to our table.

"He's just the kind to grab an ax some night and kill Mom and all of us in our beds!" said Janet.

"That's a terrible, terrible thing to say!" said Rachael.

"You wait," said Janet with grim satisfaction.

Mom walked back in past the bar.

"Shhh!" I whispered.

Mom smiled and sat down. Her eyes were a little red and puffy. Anyway, I thought to myself, we're getting to be down here while the band plays, so that's something even if Eva won't look at me and Dad seems to have gone over the edge. . . .

Mom was saying something that interrupted my thoughts. When she spoke, it was in her extracheerful what-the-Lord-has-done-for-me-lately Monday morning Bible study voice.

"Your father is like the apostle Paul, a great man of God but one who is tortured by a thorn in the flesh. Oh, how I wish the Lord would deliver Ralph from these times of grievous testing!"

"And deliver us, too," muttered Janet.

"Poor Dad," said Rachael.

"Yes, we must pray for him," said Mom.

"While you were out of the room that terrible man asked if we like toilet paper," said Janet.

"He did?" asked Mom.

Mom looked aghast. I laughed. I tried not to, but I did. Mom shot me an aggrieved frown. Janet kicked me under the table.

"Calvin!"

"It's *not* funny!" said Rachael, while trying not to laugh.

Mom bowed her head.

"Dear heavenly Father," Mom prayed loudly over the music, "we just come before Thee and cast ourselves on our faces before Thy mighty throne and beg for deliverance from the spirit of anger and ungodly despair that in Thy infinite wisdom Thou hast allowed Ralph to be tested by. Lift poor Ralph up, Lord, we ask in the name of Thy precious son Jesus, for his deliverance from his working-class brooding, and his bitterness that he has not yet brought to the foot of the cross to be washed in the blood, which he gets from his very, very unpleasant and difficult, unregenerate, and uneducated mother that Thou hast chosen to not call to Thyself in order that we might be tested in our faith. We just ask you that Ralph's last vestiges of the crude and godless background that he suffers from be removed from him. Lord, help each one of us gathered at this table to, like David, playing his harp before King Saul when an evil spirit filled *him,* help Ralph in his troubled spirit. In Jesus' name we pray, Amen!"

Mom looked up and smiled her most forgiving and loving smile. People were beginning to dance. Sergio was making his way across the dance floor, smiling at Janet. The English General was with a Swedish twin and dancing while looking in our direction and laughing. He must have been watching Mom pray. Janet caught sight of Sergio, turned pale, jumped up, and said, "Mom, I really don't think we should be in this place now that the dancing has started! . . . Think of Calvin seeing all—all this!"

Janet bolted from the room just as Sergio reached our table.

"She's quite right, my dears. I am forgetting myself. Come!"

Mom stood up and ignored Sergio. We all marched out, following Janet. Sergio gave us a disappointed look and shrugged, holding out his hands palms-up in a gesture of resignation.

Janet was waiting at the foot of the stairs. As we slowly walked up the three flights we could hear the band down below striking up a very fast and demonic beat.

"King Saul threw a spear at David," said Janet bitterly, just as we rounded the top landing and were stepping off the granite steps onto the wood floor of our hallway. "I think Dad is a sick evil man, like Saul."

Mom stopped dead in her tracks.

"Janet Becker! You can just go to your room if you are going to talk that way," said Mom.

"Or dance," I muttered under my breath.

Mom and Rachael did not hear my remark. But Janet did. She gave me a piercing look.

"Go to your rooms. There will be no reading out loud tonight, but I'll be in to pray with you in a few minutes once I get him settled down," said Mom.

When I got to my room I put on my pajamas and waited for Mom to come in and pray with me. While I waited, I worried. No one in their right mind goaded Janet unless they had a pretty good reason. That remark about dancing just slipped out. I was very sorry it had.

If Mom or Dad ever discovered Janet had danced, we would probably get taken home. At the very least Janet would be sent to her room for a whole day, maybe even strapped. I was not sure about the strapping part; maybe she was too old. I still got strapped, of course. Rachael never was because she never did anything. A stern word of admonition was enough to make Rachael cry, repent, and beg forgiveness through puffy red eyes. No one had ever needed to hit Rachael, not officially, though Janet slapped her from time to time just to keep things orderly.

Mom never did come in to pray. I fell asleep to the distant murmur of Dad yelling. I knew the fight was not too bad or Mom would have come to my room. Sometimes she even woke us children up. After a really bad fight Mom would come to my room or to the girls' rooms to sit on the edge of our beds and pray for Dad. And then she would say all the things she never dared tell Dad. Mom would tell us about how he was "such a trial" and how we should be "very careful to marry people who are truly Kindred Spirits." And she would tell us to find out if the person we were going to marry was as refined as her dear, dear father had been and to "find this out before it's too late."

Chapter 7

BREAKFAST THE SECOND DAY surpassed my wildest hopes. Eva put the tray down on my dresser, then sat right down next to me on the bed and kissed me before she even opened the curtains. She kissed me for so long, I had trouble breathing. She kissed me so hard that later my lips felt bruised. She kissed me in a way that Andy Keegan once told me about but that I had not actually believed people really did: Eva put her tongue in my mouth!

After a good long time Eva pulled away and we both took a couple of deep breaths.

"*Voilà,*" said Eva. "*Tu aimes ça?*"

"*Oui,*" I answered. "*J'aime ça beaucoup!*"

"*Bien,*" said Eva.

Then she leaned over to kiss me some more, only this time she pressed against me closer. Before I thought about what I was doing I reached out and put my arm around Eva's waist.

Eva did not stop me or stand up and rush out or sock me in the stomach or anything like that. She just kissed me more. Then I got emboldened and, with my other arm, touched the side of one of her huge breasts. Of course it was through layers of blouse and whatever other female undergarments were hidden beneath that. So I actually did not feel very much more than something like a big pillow with a blanket over it. I hoped she would not notice I was touching her.

Suddenly Eva grabbed my wrist. I was expecting that she might do that if she discovered what I was doing. What I was *not* expecting is where she moved my hand to!

Eva moved my hand from the bottom part of her breast to the middle of it! My hand was now on the round centermost pointy part. To be allowed to touch this spot was beyond my wildest dreams. Girls clutched towels to their breasts, folded arms over them, and if you walked into the bathroom, when Janet was in her bath her hands would fly up and cover this spot. I had seen a nipple twice (not counting statues): once on the beach when an Italian mother fed her baby and briefly that time Jennifer's top slipped as she shot up from the sandy floor of the sea. So I knew what the center of a breast looked like, knew what lay under my trembling fingers!

I had never touched a breast, not on purpose, not on a full-grown woman. (Once while roughhousing with Jennifer I put my hand in the wrong place and pulled it away fast, but that hardly even counted compared to this.) Eva had just pressed my hand against her breast, *on purpose!* She did not call my mother, slap me, or jump up and run out! And the way she asked me about it was more as if she were discussing my breakfast and how I liked the hot chocolate, as if things like this happened every day!

"*Tu aimes ça?*" asked Eva, very matter-of-fact.

"*Oui,*" I whispered.

"*Tu veux toucher l'autre?*" she asked, and smiled.

"*Oui,*" I whispered.

Then Eva moved my hand from one breast to the other and let me feel that one too! The breasts were softer than I imagined they would be. I had always thought breasts must be like balloons, bouncy. But Eva's breasts felt more like my mother's bread dough after it had been sitting in the big bowl rising for an hour on the windowsill in our chalet. This surprised me very much.

Also the breasts were heavier than I expected. I jiggled one a little with the palm of my hand and could tell it weighed as much as a small bag of oranges, though less than a bag of sugar, but a lot more than any balloon I had ever held.

It turned out that breasts were soft but quite heavy. There was more to them than I had thought. I wanted to touch Eva's breasts for a long time. I would have liked to learn more about them, to study them from every angle, measure them and take the rest of the morning learning all I could about them. I wished Eva did not have on so many clothes.

Eva got up, lifted the tray onto my lap, and marched out as if nothing unusual had happened, besides the fact that because it was Sunday instead of fresh rolls all we got was zwieback toast to dip in the hot chocolate. They did not deliver fresh bread on Sundays.

Eva had let me touch her breasts! It was the greatest moment of my life. Breasts had always been hidden: secrets that ran away screaming down the hall if I happened to catch Janet stepping out of the bathroom when her towel slipped. Breasts were created to feed babies and for marriage when they were part of a "beautiful picture of Christ and his church." Breasts were not to be squandered before the right time. Marriage would solve everything and every mystery would be explained at that far-off right time referred to as "the wedding night." Meanwhile, breasts were never displayed through immodest or worldly clothes, never shown off.

Breasts were to be covered and wrapped, to be seen only by husbands and doctors and always behind closed doors. Breasts required special clothes. These garments were not to be hung out to dry in public with boys' underwear. Bras were hung between the sheets, on the line in the middle of the six clotheslines stretched between metal posts behind our kitchen. They were hidden away so that I could not get a good look unless I ducked under the sheets.

I always liked the journey to the feminine heart of the laundry maze. I liked to smell the fresh wet cloth and lemony soap. I liked the feeling of the wet sheets and towels clinging to my face as I slid between them until I found the girls' underwear where it hung, mysterious, in a soft cluster in the laundry inner sanctum.

Once I got to the huddle of bras and panties, they were so much more complicated than anything boys wore that, stare as I would, I could not always understand what everything was for. The big question was why? Why the lace? Why all the fluttery little bows and different colors? I could not figure out why the bras were this way or why women wanted to wear things that were so fancy yet so hidden. What did girls want?

On a glorious afternoon during the autumn before the "typhoid vacation," Mom found me looking at the bras.

"Calvin, what are you doing in there?" Mom called from beyond the edge of the laundry.

I said nothing.

"I can see your feet. Now you just come right out."

"I was playing between the sheets, playing army," I answered, as I made my way slowly from the cool damp netherworld into the bright sun. The larch trees were turning gold. The summer growth on the tall pines was a deep green that framed the mountains and made the dusting of snow on the high peaks stand out against the deep blue. The sun felt warm on my face. There was a gentle drone coming from some wasps buzzing over the laundry. It was a perfect autumn day, except for the fact that Mom was standing there holding on to me.

"Darling, I was looking out the bathroom window and I saw you touching a brassiere. Why?"

I glanced longingly up the forested slope of the mountain behind our house. I knew I could pull away from Mom and run for it. I also knew this was out of the question. When Mom wanted to have an "honest talk" with me, there was nothing to be done.

"I was just looking, for a second," I mumbled. "It was in my way. I was trying to get by."

"But, darling, how silly! A brassiere is just an undergarment like your underpants. Only it's a little differently made but nothing to look at, my dear. You leave them alone."

"I was just looking," I muttered.

"Well, dear, it's natural enough that a young boy might want to know about how he is different from a young woman. You see, once a young woman begins to develop, she needs to attend to her modesty, to see it does not become a stumbling block to males and give them thoughts they should only think about the girl God has chosen for them from before creation to be their helpmeet for a lifetime. And they should only have those thoughts *after* their wedding night, just as we wait to open the presents under the Christmas tree until Christmas morning. Otherwise it spoils it all for everyone."

"Yes, Mom. I understand now. Can I go now?"

Mom did not even bother to answer that last question, as I knew she would not. She was just getting started. I sighed and looked up to the seven peaks of the Dents du Midi. The first snow had come early and made the mountain that towered over our village seem even bigger. I was hopeful that this would be a good snowy winter, one where the skiing on our vacation would be perfect. . . .

"A bra is something just like anything else. And you should ignore it like you ignore this pillowcase because, in its way, it serves a similar purpose, to cover up and hold, keep modest and healthy and clean. You see a young woman . . ."

"Who, Janet?" I asked and sighed.

"Yes. Janet, and others, all of the young women."

"In Africa?"

"In Christian countries."

"Roman Catholics?"

"Even most Catholics. You see, these young women all arrive at an age. . ."

"Twelve?"

"Sometimes thirteen, each is a little different, but God sees them all and causes them to change to prepare their bodies to be the wives and mothers that he means them to be. And certain other changes begin to occur too."

"Like falling off the roof once a month?"

"Yes, that and certain other things."

"Like needing bras?"

"And that too. Well, as I was saying, these changes are natural and beautiful and not to be made fun of or stared at. At some point a young woman needs a bra because a breast is a precious gift from God for a special purpose."

"So a bra is like the wrapping?"

"Yes, dear, but it's not to be toyed with, because it has to do with the way God made men and women different in order to be a picture of Christ and his bride."

"But I'm a boy."

"Yes. So you won't ever need one of these and there is no point in your staring at it. No good can come of it."

"I didn't mean that, Mom. I meant how can I be part of the bride of Christ? Boys are in his church, too, aren't we?"

"Yes, dear. It's a mystical thing."

"Do Jesus and his church have babies?"

"In a way, dear. We bear his fruit, the fruit of saving souls."

"Jesus has babies with the *boys* in his church?"

"Well, dear, that's not exactly how we put it."

"But if I'm a bride then it should be all right for me to look at Janet's bra, since I'm kind of a bride in Christ. That sort of makes me a girl, right?"

"*Calvin!*"

Mom shot me a shocked and angry glance.

"I meant in a spiritual way," I murmured.

"Calvin, I do hope you're not joking about the Things Of The Lord!"

I turned and looked up at the peaks of the Dents du Midi so that Mom would not see the grin I was trying to hide.

"No, Mom. I just meant that what with the church being a bride and all I thought that I could look at this bra and you wouldn't mind."

"Well, dear, I don't think we should talk about the church like that. And bras have nothing to do with that."

"Except that Jesus made everything," I said, turning back to Mom.

"Yes, of course he did."

"So he made breasts?"

"Yes, dear."

"And he knew Janet would need a bra someday?"

"Yes, he knows everything."

"So he knew I'd be looking at Janet's bra this morning?"

"Yes, dear. And we mustn't grieve him by sneaking between the sheets for ulterior motives."

"But if he knew I'd do it, then I could not have stopped myself, so in a way Jesus made me do this."

"Calvin!"

"But it must be the Lord's will to have me look at Janet's bra, Mom."

"Calvin!"

"Yes, Mom?"

"This sounds to me like you're being dreadfully levitous about the Things Of The Lord!"

"No, I'm not. I just wanted to ask about predestination and bras."

Mom frowned. I looked at her earnestly with a serious and unwavering expression. Mom stopped frowning. As long as she was convinced I was asking a "serious question" she would try and answer it. The trick was in not cracking even the tiniest smile.

"Well, dear, I see what you mean, but just because Jesus sees you and knows before you do what you'll do, doesn't mean you should do it."

"Well, how can he blame me, since it's all arranged already?"

"We don't want to grieve him, dear."

"Bras grieve Jesus?"

"Not when they're used for the right purpose. But looking can lead to certain thoughts, and certain thoughts are as bad as actions, dear. So we have to be careful of the laundry."

"Is that why you hang the bras between the sheets and pillowcases?"

"Yes, dear. We each have a responsibility not to cause another person to stumble, because Jesus said that if we cause even one little one—and by little one, he meant any believer—to stumble, it would be better to hang a millstone about our necks and throw ourselves into the sea."

"And drown?"

"Yes."

"I thought suicide was the worst sin."

"Well, dear, it is. Jesus only meant to show how very, very serious leading others astray is."

"So why do you hang my underpants right out in front, where everyone can see them?"

"Boys' underwear does not lead to the same problems, dear."

"It doesn't?"

"No."

"Why?"

"Well, dear, boys' underwear does not arouse girls' interest in the same manner as girls' underwear unfortunately arouses boys."

"So it's all right to let girls see my underpants before marriage?"

Mom frowned again. I gave her my most steady please-tell-me look. Mom smiled.

"No, dear, not that. I meant on the line, not on you."

"Don't girls like boys' underwear?"

"A girl is a more romantic creature, Calvin. A girl is never tempted by mere physical things like boys are."

"So girls are better?"

"In a way we are, dear, and that places a greater responsibility on us to dress in a modest fashion."

"And to cross your legs when you're sitting, the way you always tell Janet to when she sits like a boy?"

"That and many other habits and gestures the godly woman develops."

"Is that why you make Janet wear a slip?"

"Yes, dear. You see, the mere outline of the feminine form can arouse a sinful desire. And the woman who knowingly flaunts the precious gifts meant only for her husband is in part responsible for some poor man's sin, the sin of lust."

"So looking at this bra is a sin?"

"Lust is always wrong."

"I'm not lusting after Janet, Mom!"

"Of course not, dear. But still, the private undergarments of a young lady should be kept confidential."

It being Sunday, we had church. Every year Dad asked the manager for permission to hold a service in the hotel dining room. No one minded. The dining room was never used until lunch. The other guests were in bed having breakfast or out skiing. This year, because of the fact there was a piano for the band, church could be more like it was at home. Mom said that this was because the Devil "always oversteps himself." The piano was meant for jazz or worse but the Lord had used it anyway "to provide us a way to make a joyful noise unto him and bring good from evil."

On vacation, church was at ten A.M., just as it was at home. This was a terrible thing for a lot of reasons. For a start, it meant that I had to wait until about eleven thirty to go out to ski! I had to sit in my room or stare out the dining-room window and watch the English General and the other hotel guests go up and down the Riffelberg piste while I waited for church. Mom always said that we were "in the World but not of it." On Sunday mornings, while watching other people enjoy the slopes, I knew exactly what she meant.

A few weeks before the vacation, Rachael, Janet, and I had been talking about what we most looked forward to. Rachael said it was the opportunity to witness to people "not usually reachable by the gospel." Janet said it was the skiing, and I agreed with her. Then I said the thing I liked least was church in the hotel. Rachael looked shocked, though later she whispered that she felt the same way. Janet told me I was lucky; when she was little she would not have been allowed to ski at all on Sundays, even after church.

While I was helping Mom set up the chairs on the dance floor I asked her if what Janet had said was true.

"Mom?"

"Yes, darling?"

"Are you less strict with me than you were with Janet?"

"Each child is different."

"She says you never would have let her ski on Sunday when she was little."

"We were in St. Louis, dear. There is no skiing there."

"Well, what about other things?"

"Well, dear, as the years pass, one becomes more practical."

"You mean you love the Lord less than before?"

"Nothing of the kind! Now let's not discuss how we raised or did not raise Janet. How many times have I told you that the only sins you should worry about are your own? Janet is Janet and you are you."

I looked around the empty dining room and sighed. Mom and I had moved all the chairs into three rows on the dance floor facing the dais the band played from. Rachael walked in and started to help.

"But the Holy Spirit hasn't ever moved anyone to come in all these years," I said.

"Yes, he did, dear. The English General came two years ago, remember?"

"Oh, right. But he didn't get saved, did he?"

"No, dear, but perhaps a seed was planted."

"I think he only walked in to see if Eva had opened the bar because he heard singing. Maybe he thought we were in here drinking," Rachael said and giggled.

Mom ignored her. Rachael and I exchanged a grin.

"This year we have a piano and that might make all the difference, dear. We must always be ready, children. It's just like the father in the story of the prodigal son. He was ready for the prodigal to return. The home fires were kept faithfully burning, the fatted calf was—"

"Kept fatted?" sighed Rachael.

"Yes, dear."

"But it takes a whole suitcase to bring the hymnbooks, and Dad hates the luggage you bring. It made him swear at the Aigle station again, just like last year. What about his blood pressure?" asked Rachael.

Mom gave her a stern look. Rachael fell silent.

"You always say Dad should not eat salt and has to remember to take his pill," I said, coming to Rachael's rescue.

Grandpa Becker had died of a stroke. High blood pressure ran in the family. Each time Doctor Zwingli visited our chalet—which happened every few weeks because one of us, our fellow workers in the Vineyard of the Lord, or some of the young people, got sick—the doctor took Dad's blood pressure. We all stood around to see what it was. Mom told us to pray for one-twenty over eighty, or something like that. Sometimes it was and sometimes it wasn't.

Mom always said that if Dad started acting strange, had a sudden pain in his arm or head, was dizzy or fainted, or if the vein in his neck was pulsing so hard it looked like "a hammer on a drum," then we should remind him to take another pill, just in case. Mom said otherwise he might "blow a fuse."

"Mom, what could the result of a stroke be?" I asked after we had all the hymnbooks laid out.

"The symptoms could manifest themselves in a myriad of unpleasant ways, from death to the loss of the use of one's limbs, to sagging features on one side of the face, to dementia," said Mom. "Grandpa Becker died of a series of small strokes, each one more severe. If only someone educated had been present in your poor father's working-class family, Grandpa Becker could have been saved."

"How?" asked Rachael.

"Ignorance is a killer," Mom answered. "It is our duty to be informed. And with knowledge comes responsibility."

"How?" I asked.

"Well, let us suppose you had been with your poor, working-class ignorant grandfather when he first began to show symptoms. And let's suppose that as my son you had knowledge of what a stroke is because *your* mother, unlike your grandfather's dreadful working-class woefully ignorant and bitter wife—I'm speaking of your terrible grandmother—had told you what to look out for. And let us suppose you spotted the first signs, say dizziness or loss of the use of an arm, even a tingling in the fingers or general confusion. Then you would have done the right thing and called a doctor, maybe an ambulance, and gotten that dear man to some proper medical institution for professional care before it was too late. You know what that ridiculous woman did?"

"No, Mom," said Rachael.

"Your dreadful grandmother mixed up a batch of linseeds and boiled them into a mash and gave him *those!* Can you imagine?!"

"No, Mom," I said.

"Well, that's what she did. She murdered him right then and there!"

"But if she didn't know any better, how was it murder?"

"She chose to be ignorant of medical facts, just as she still chooses to be ignorant of the saving power of our Lord Jesus Christ. I explained both the dangers of high blood pressure and the doctrine of the Trinity to her several times. She is a dreadful woman." Mom shook her head and frowned. "As long as he takes his pills he'll be fine. I bring all thirty hymnbooks as an act of faith. Sometimes your father does not understand these things the way he should."

"Is that because he's not as close to the Lord as you are, Mom?"

"I wouldn't presume to say, dear. Only God sees the heart, but perhaps coming from the unfortunate background he does, these things just don't become as clear to him as they should. Remember, he never even *saw* a Bible until he was seventeen! And his dreadful mother, well . . ."

"Will I ever get to meet her?" I asked.

"You met her when you were three, before we got called."

"I don't remember her at all."

"Well, count your blessings!" said Rachael.

Mom began to gather the small flower vases off the sills below the huge plate-glass windows and arrange them around the base of the "pulpit" (one of the band's music stands).

"Mom?" I asked.

"Yes?"

"Janet said that when she was little, if she had come to Riffelberg you would never have let her go skiing on Sunday, even after church. How come?"

"Calvin, why are you so persistent?"

"I just want to know about things, I guess."

Mom sighed and perched on the edge of one of the chairs. Rachael and I sat down on a two bar stools to face her.

"As the years have gone by we have become a little more lenient, perhaps tried not to make faith as onerous to our children as it was to—" Mom stopped and pursed her lips. "You see, dear, Father and Mother raised me lovingly but in a way that was perhaps a little overly strict. So when I began to teach Ralph how to have a Christian home and family, and of course he had never been in one before, perhaps we followed my dear mother's rules a little too closely."

"Like what?" asked Rachael.

"Oh, well, for instance, on the Lord's Day we could read only the Bible or Pilgrim's Progress."

"But now you let us read C.S. Lewis and the *Chronicles of Narnia*," said Rachael.

"Yes, dear. He was an Episcopalian but still very close to the Lord, though some of his views are rather fuzzy."

"When I grow up I'm going to let my children read any books they want on Sunday," said Rachael.

"That could be very dangerous. It could lead to real temptation to break the Sabbath in word and deed. It is as bad as if you were, oh, I don't know, playing cards."

"Andy's parents let him play Old Maid," I said.

"Dick Keegan went to the wrong seminary. They are Real Christians but *not* truly Kindred Spirits, and I have to say that I'm praying the Lord leads them out of L'arche and that he leads someone more suitable to come and help us."

"But no one gambles playing Old Maid, Mom," said Rachael.

"Perhaps not, but it's a card game nonetheless and can lead to a bad habit and get you used to playing cards as a form of worldly distraction. Then it becomes easier to let down your guard and perhaps someday to be tempted into playing with the kind of cards they gamble with. And then you'd be playing some awful game of chance with real cards, gambling away precious resources the Lord has given you to be a steward of, while your children go hungry! And when your child says, 'Mommy, why have we lost everything?' you'd have to answer, 'Son, what have I done? I thought Old Maid was innocent but it led to real cards and that led to gambling and to alcohol! And now I have squandered the precious resources the Lord gave me because I failed to guard my heart against sin, and sin always begins in small ways but it is the first step that counts, the first step that leads to ruin!'"

"Yes, Mom," said Rachael meekly.

"So don't you two ever play cards with those Keegans!"

"They don't play cards, Mom, just Old Maid," I said.

"Calvin! Haven't you heard *one word* I've been saying? Now help me put out the hymnbooks," Mom muttered.

"We already did. And we'll have to collect them all again and I'll be even later getting out to ski," I muttered.

"Calvin! If the Lord calls just one of the hotel guests or staff to come to church, I want them to see they're welcome and expected," Mom snapped.

"But it looks so dumb," I said.

"Calvin! How *can* you say that? We put out the chairs and the hymnbooks as the Lord prepared the wedding banquet and sent his servants out into the hedges and byways to seek the guests! It is our job to be *faithful!* The Lord will bring in the harvest in his own marvelous and miraculous timing." Mom took a deep breath, smiled, and started talking in her cheerful voice again, but now it was a little higher than before and the lines on her forehead were still there.

"Don't you see, dear, that everything is for a purpose, even our vacations? There are no holidays from God! And this year we have a piano! And it may be that the English General or the Swedish ladies or other guests who once knew truth and fell away from the Lord— perhaps even the Germans—will hear the piano. And they will be in their rooms, perhaps even with a hangover from drinking and dancing the night away to fill the empty place in their souls, and they will hear the sound of 'Abide with Me' coming up the stairs as Janet plays the piano; and tears will fill their eyes and they will come down, haltingly, embarrassed that they have fallen so far from grace, and they will peek around the corner and see a chair set out for them waiting and a hymnbook lying on that chair and you singing from the bottom of your heart. And I will hand that poor lost sheep a book, opened at the right place, and point to the verse we're singing. And with tears streaming down his cheeks the lost sheep will begin to sing, at first in a soft quivering sorrow-filled voice, and later with a voice full of praise. And he will open his heart to the Word that is preached when Ralph is anointed and the angels will rejoice over that lost lamb brought back to the fold, and what was meant for satanic purposes, the piano, and the bandstand, and instruments, will have been turned to good and the prodigal will have returned and—"

"Mom?" asked Rachael.

"Yes, dear?"

"But the English General and the Swedish ladies and the Germans and everyone else are out skiing, so how will they hear the piano?" asked Rachael.

Mom got angry again and stamped her foot.

"Rachael! Will you just stop it?! The Lord may cause him to fall and hurt his leg so that he will be up in his room by ten," Mom said.

"You want God to break the General's leg?!" I asked.

Rachael laughed. Mom's brow puckered even more.

"Sometimes He has to chastise those of us He loves! I've always had a feeling that the English General gave his heart to Christ, perhaps long ago as a boy, and he has wandered from the truth. It is quite possible, you know. There used to be many Bible believing Christians in England before the liberals took over all the Anglican seminaries. Haven't you seen the way he looks so wistfully at us when I say grace before we eat at dinner?"

"I think he's just staring at us, Mom," said Rachel.

"So much the better. It is good to bear witness in all things!"

The fact that we had the piano for church did no good at all. No one even glanced through the windows no matter how loudly we sang.

Chapter 8

"YOU SEE, CALVIN," said Rachael, "I agree with Mom but think it's best to present these truths more cheerfully."

"I just think she likes to boss us," I retorted.

"That's awful! She does it for our own good."

Rachael and I were jammed face-to-face on the train. We were riding up to Gornergrat. Dad was taking a nap. Mom was sitting in the dining room writing letters. Rachael and I had squeezed into the first car just before it pulled out of the Riffelberg station. Rachael did not say so, but I knew she suddenly pushed into the first car, after Janet was getting into the second car, so we would not have to ride up the mountain with her.

"Do you want to take the long way or ski the fast piste?" I asked.

"Let's take the long piste," answered Rachael.

She smiled and glanced out the window, which was steaming up from all the skiers packed shoulder-to-shoulder around us. The train had been full when it arrived at Riffelberg. It reeked of cigarettes, perfume, and damp down parkas.

"Janet will be fit to be tied!" I laughed. "I thought you always asked yourself what would Jesus do."

"It wasn't un-Christ-like," Rachael retorted with a smile. "Jesus said we should be wise as serpents and harmless as doves! I'm practicing the wise as serpents part!"

We laughed. The other skiers were talking loudly. We had to shout to hear each other over the hubbub.

"You know," I said, "I think Janet and Mom are both plain nuts!"

"Mom isn't. Don't say that."

"Yes, she is. She makes all these rules and stuff."

"What 'stuff'?"

"The long graces, getting us home-schooled when everybody goes to a real school, no Old Maid, whatever."

"She has our best interests at heart."

"*And* she puts Dad in Moods!"

"Dad would be in Moods without her."

"She makes him."

"Mom does not! If it weren't for her prayers and long suffering, he'd be even farther from the Lord!"

"Why don't you ever agree with me?" I asked.

"She's a true woman of God. You know that."

"She's a true pain in the neck," I said, and laughed.

Rachael tried not to smile. Then she started to giggle so hard, a man next to us looked over and smiled.

The train pulled into Rotenboden station. There was a lot of jostling as the Rotenboden skiers got out.

"Uh-oh!" said Rachael.

I looked in the direction of her worried glance. Janet had gotten off the second car and was climbing onto ours, clutching her ski poles and mittens. She looked angry.

"You did that on purpose!" Janet said as she shoved her way toward us.

"Janet, the other car was full," said Rachael innocently.

"No, it was not! You two were just trying to escape adult supervision! You know perfectly well Mom put me in charge!"

"She didn't put you 'in charge'!" answered Rachael. "She gave us each our own ticket money!"

"Are you arguing?"

"It's such a lovely day!" exclaimed Rachael. "Look how white the snow is on the Mont Rosa! Don't you just *love* the *wonderful* shades of blue in the glacier crevices?"

"You're such a soppy idiot," muttered Janet, but she did look out the window.

Janet was still angry, but Rachael had managed to distract her enough so that when we arrived in Gornergrat no one got socked. Janet just strapped on her skis and sailed off without a backward look.

"She's sick, mean, and evil," I muttered.

"Janet just struggles a little," said Rachael sadly. "I really think she's getting better though. She's been quite kind to me this vacation. Do you know she let me have the bed by the window this year? She's never done that before. She usually makes me sleep by the door. She said I could have the view! I never knew how lovely it is to sit with the breakfast tray on my lap, looking out while I eat!"

"She just wanted to be in the bed by the door so she can sneak out," I said.

"What?"

"She sneaks out to dance when you're asleep. That's why she gave you the bed by the window."

"You shouldn't joke about something so serious!"

"Rachael, she really did."

"Of course she didn't!"

Rachael's eyes were filling with tears. All the other skiers who had ridden the train with us were gone. I sighed and shrugged. My sister's chin was quivering.

"I guess I was just kidding," I said.

Rachael frowned.

"There are some things you should never joke about. One of them is someone falling away from the Lord and doing something horrible like dancing or stealing or something. That was *not* funny!"

"I'm sorry."

Rachael leaned over and hugged me.

Chapter 9

EVA SAT NEXT TO ME on the bed. She had just put the breakfast tray down on the dresser. She did not open the shutters but sat right down in the darkened room. It was illuminated only by a twenty-five-watt bulb. I waited breathlessly for the kissing to begin. There was none. My heart sank. Eva looked at me for a moment before she spoke. In the darkened room it was hard to read the expression on her face, but she seemed a little nervous.

"Tu veux voir mes seins?" asked Eva.

I didn't know *seins* was the word for "breast" in French. So for a moment I had no idea what she meant. But when Eva stood up and took off her starched white apron and laid it on the bed, then lifted her sweater and a vast, creamy expense of lacy bra appeared, I got the idea that something very unusual was about to happen.

Eva reached behind herself with her pudgy hands and I heard a little snap. The next moment her giant bra sagged like a sail that has just lost the wind. Eva lifted her bra and sat back down.

"Tu peux toucher," said Eva.

The orbs of her breasts swam into my vision like two giant full moons shining out pale and lovely. They were white; so white that even the dim orange glow of the bedside lamp could not change their pale whiteness.

I could not breathe. Nor could I believe that I was in the room with two actual breasts! This event was beyond my wildest imaginings. I had been longing for a mere kiss and instead Eva had decided to give me the world!

The rest of Eva seemed to disappear into the darkness that enveloped everything but the breasts. Her voice seemed to come from far off, from someplace outside of the room. The breasts were the only thing that was or ever had been!

Eva cupped a huge quivering orb in one hand and presented it. I stared at the breast uncomprehendingly until Eva whispered, *"Tu peux toucher."* Then I lightly touched the side. It was warm and felt like satin stretched over a very full hot water bottle. Eva leaned forward. At the center of the pale pink circle the pea-size teat was hard as a little hazelnut. Eva leaned forward some more and sighed. My hand trembled.

"Comme ça," said Eva, and she flicked one of her fingers back and forth rapidly.

"Comme ça?" I whispered.

I tried it out. My hand shook. The nipple was rubbery. My arm felt almost too heavy to lift. I felt faint.

"Oui," said Eva.

Eva leaned back and rested on her hands as she shoved her chest toward me. She sighed. My hand was shaking. The breasts were getting warmer and I noticed they had goose bumps and that the flesh around the nipples was puckering up.

After a few minutes Eva pushed my hand away and reached back to fasten her bra. She snapped it shut, pulled down her sweater, and stood up.

"Voilà! Tu as tout vu," Eva said with a smile.

"M-merci," I stammered.

Eva left my room without another word. When I closed my eyes I kept seeing the breasts the same way you see the sun or a flashbulb after you've been blinded, then close your eyes and see the light again in the dark, a strange kind of imprint, like some kind of slide or movie projected on the inside of your eye.

The day of the breasts I fell a lot skiing. I would be zigzagging down the piste and forget to turn, my path blocked by Eva's breast, the snowbank becoming the vast lacy expense of her bra, the inside of my eyelid a screen on which Eva's small pink nipple was endlessly projected.

Eva breasts were everywhere! The memory of the feel of her nipple standing like a little tree in a storm, bending but snapping back rigid, saluting the day under my finger as I flicked back and forth overwhelmed me. I would plow deep into the snowbanks on either side of the piste and fall. I did not get up as fast as I usually did. I lay in the fluffy powder at the edge of the hard-packed snow, facedown thinking of the soft flesh, the heaviness in my hand, its weight, solid, liquid, heavy as the whole world and twice as big and, unlike the world, able to command my Little Thing to stand up hard and unbending. I lay grinding my pelvis into the snow until the cold seeped under my skin and I shakily stood up and brushed myself off.

Eva's breasts peeked from behind the Matterhorn. At noon they lay on the plate nestled between the pickled onions and the paper-thin slices of dark red meat, boeuf de grisons. I watched Eva's breasts float from table to table, levitate from behind the bar to the English General. I caught a whiff of Eva's unfortunate European aroma as she hovered nearby dishing out rice and émincé de Veau to my father. Now that I associated that smell with the breasts I found myself breathing it in deeply and appreciatively. Now that breasts had my full attention I came to realize that the world was mostly breasts, two per woman, going by, two-by-two, like the animals into the Ark, marching in long orderly rows from all over the dining room toward me.

"Oh please, let me see them again!" I silently prayed, as Eva's breasts sailed past while she collected our dishes.

As soon as I said so I was sorry. Once you got God's undivided attention, then there he was, right next to you checking everything! You might cut off certain thoughts midsentence—as I did when I caught myself praying to see Eva's breasts again—yet he still knew what I would have thought if I had kept thinking the things I wanted to think, before I remembered that he knew everything I was thinking.

Even though I cut off the thought and said to myself only: "I wish I could feel Eva's—" he knew that I meant to say breast. At the Last Judgment, in front of the whole host of Heaven, Mom, Dad, Janet, Rachael, and every Real Christian and even some Old Testament Jews (not to mention the angels) . . . in other words, everybody that counted would hear all my thoughts played back exactly as they happened, like a tape recorder.

There would be plenty of time to play every thought I ever had. Time was what there would be plenty of in Heaven! The Last Judgment could take eternity, for all God cared. God had all the time he needed to play back even half-finished sentences; thoughts that had stopped before they barely started, the smallest thought that grieved him or Jesus or the Holy Spirit or had caused anyone to stumble, even if I had not meant to do it.

I sat at lunch watching Eva the way a hungry dog watches a can of pet food get opened. I allowed all the bad thoughts to wash over me like the waves of the sea lapping at the foolish man's house in Jesus' parable while the sand just drifted away and the house of my soul got set to collapse and mighty was the fall of it.

Worse still, I encouraged the thoughts! Even worse, I did not care where they would lead. In fact, I *hoped* they would lead there! And now, worst of all, unimaginably bad, I had just *prayed* that God would help me sin some more!

"Dad," I said in a distracted voice as Eva's breasts served the braised endive.

"Yes?"

"Dad, if God made us the way we are, how come we get in trouble for being the way we are?"

"Are you asking about the original sin, Calvin?"

"I guess I am," I answered, and it seemed as if my own voice was far away and not really my own.

"Well, sin's our choice, not God's."

"So it's our fault?" I asked, as Eva's breasts floated past the English General, over to the serving cart, then back.

"Yes."

"What about the fall?"

"Original sin is the condition into which we are born."

"But we get blamed?"

" 'Blamed' is not the right word. We are accountable."

"But if we get born into original sin how come God punishes us for liking breasts?"

"What?!" yelled Janet, Rachael, and Mom in unison.

All their heads snapped to face me, their eyes wide and dark and staring at me the way they would when the tapes of my sinful thoughts got played back on the Last Day, which might well be sooner than later since the prophecy of the return of Israel had been fulfilled in our lifetimes and we were expecting Jesus' return at any moment, or at least Rachael was.

"What?!" they all exclaimed again.

I snapped out of my breast reverie and the dining room came into focus. My family was staring at me in horror. What, I wondered, had I just said?

"W-what I meant was, got blamed for our s-sin," I stuttered.

"You said *"breasts"!"* said Janet.

"No, I didn't."

"Perhaps he meant something else and it only sounded like that word," said Rachael.

"Calvin, I'm sorry, but you did," said Mom.

"I meant to say sin."

"Calvin," said Dad, "the point is that God will save some, the elect, so we do not need to dwell on the lost because we all deserve to be lost, but rather give thanks for the elect, we few who will be saved, for many are called but few are chosen."

"Why?" I asked. "I thought God liked people."

"Calvin!" shrieked Janet.

"The boy has a right to ask questions," snapped Dad. "Calvin, there are two kinds of sin. One is the human condition, the other makes us each deserve the damnation that we have inherited through original sin. Through our own individual sins we add to the original sin we're born with. That simply shows that given the same opportunity as Adam and Eve we all would have made the same choice to turn against God's will. So it shows we all deserve the eternal damnation that is the destiny of most of the human race, because we read in the Bible that only a few—the elect—will be saved. So we just need to make sure we each accept Jesus Christ as our personal Savior and live according to his will, not because keeping rules saves us—we aren't Catholics, and good works mean nothing—but because it's through living as Christians we demonstrate to others the saving power of Jesus and help bring them to the foot of the cross where they, too, can be forgiven if God has ordained that they are of the elect."

"How can we know?" I asked.

"Know we are saved?" asked Dad with a kindly smile.

"Yes."

"We know we are of the elect once we accept Christ. Otherwise he would not have drawn us to himself by the irresistible power of the Holy Spirit. We can no more resist his grace and save ourselves or choose not to be saved than those who are the Vessels of Wrath, chosen to be damned from before the beginning of creation, can change their lot."

"How do we know we've really accepted him?"

"Calvin, if you long for salvation, the very act of longing for it is an indication that your heart is tender for the Things Of The Lord," said Rachael.

"Then why do we have sinful thoughts?" I asked.

"What sinful thoughts?" Janet asked, and grinned.

"Janet! You just be quiet!" snapped Dad angrily. "The Old Man must be replaced by the New Man, Calvin, but we will not be made perfect in him until we are in Heaven. We all have sinful thoughts."

Mom leaned forward and smiled sweetly.

"Calvin?"

"Yes, Mom?"

"Is there some particular thing that is bothering you, dear?"

My whole family stared at me. Eva's breasts started collecting more of our dishes.

"No, Mom."

"You understand that you can tell us anything."

"Yes, Mom."

"You mentioned a certain unfortunate word a moment ago, Calvin," said Mom.

"I guess I was just thinking about that time with the laundry, about where thoughts can lead, about how I don't want to grieve the Holy Spirit."

Mom smiled and nodded. Dad stared at me in a sort of blank way. He almost looked disappointed. Rachael smiled sweetly and wiped away a tear. Janet shook her head; clearly she did not believe me. I gave her a hard look. That worldly dancer was in no position to judge me!

"He's not telling the truth," she said.

"Excuse me, dear?" said Mom.

"He's been looking at Eva all through lunch, staring and staring at her you-know-whats!"

"Janet, that is quite enough out of you!" barked Mom.

"Janet," said Dad, "you can just go to your room for talking that way. When someone has an honest spiritual question they're not to be hindered in seeking the truth. Do you understand, young woman?"

"Yes, Dad," said Janet. "I'm sorry."

Janet left the table and marched across the dance floor. The look she gave me, just before she stepped through the dining-room door next to the bar, was anything but sorry. And I'm pretty sure she mouthed the words "You wait!"

Chapter 10

I NEVER WOULD HAVE thought that I could be in Riffelberg on our annual ski vacation and that I would start to ignore skiing in favor of breakfast. Of course most of each day went the way of all days at Riffelberg, the way they had always gone. After breakfast there was skiing, then lunch, then skiing again, then dinner. After dinner we read out loud with Mom and my sisters in one of our rooms, usually Janet and Rachael's room (it was bigger than mine), then we went to bed. Dad did not join us for the reading. He stayed in his room catching up on his theological journals and sermon preparation.

I was not concentrating on the story Mom was reading that year at bedtime family prayers, though it was actually quite exciting. The story was filled with godless murdering Chinese who worshiped their ancestors and left their newborn daughters to die in special pagodas, until the Christian missionaries began to rescue the baby girls and teach the heathen Chinese that girls are children of God just as much as boys.

At bedtime we always read three chapters of the Bible: a Psalm, an Old Testament passage, and a New Testament passage; and a chapter or two from what Mom called a "devotional book." That year the devotional book—as opposed to our "regular story," which currently was *The Voyage of the Dawntreader*—was *The Life of Hudson Taylor*. It was about how this "splendid" nineteenth-century English missionary was "called to China's millions" to bring the light of Christ to them and how he grew a pigtail like a real Chinaman, the better to "reach the Chinese with the gospel." The book described his hardships, what Hudson Taylor gave up for the Lord, how he could have done anything in the World yet gave it all up "even though he went to Cambridge University and was a real gentleman," as Mom said.

None of this: Hudson Taylor's sufferings; the murdered girls; even some miracles in the Gobi Desert, when angels came to sing to some of Hudson Taylor's fellow missionaries to "embolden their hearts for the Lord," could hold my attention. I shivered right along with my sisters at the lurid descriptions of the Chinese as they abandoned their daughters, or bound their feet till the bones grew painfully deformed, but my mind wandered from the babies' "piteous cries." I felt sorry for the babies and very glad the missionaries came to save the little unwanted girls, but there was no question that if two lines were forming and at the head of one line was Hudson Taylor himself, along with all the missionaries of the China Inland Mission and all the baby girls they saved, and at the head of the other line was Eva, sitting on my hotel bedroom chair with her apron bib gently heaving up and down over her huge bosom, her cheeks flaming pink, that I would be in the line to see Eva! All the "great men of God" could wait and grow their pigtails till doomsday, for all I cared!

Breasts with breakfast was already more than any boy of fourteen could ever hope for in an imperfect and fallen world. On the fourth morning of the vacation, when Eva put down the tray and pushed my ski pants off the chair opposite my dresser, I was aquiver. She sat down on the chair and contemplated me for a moment in silence. I was a little taken aback. Eva was not sitting on the bed next to me. How were we going to kiss? How was I going to touch her breasts?

I could tell by how bright her eyes were, by the vivid scarlet splashes flaming up on her cheeks, that she had something interesting in mind. Only I could not guess what it might be and she was not sitting within easy reach. Eva was perched on the edge of the hard wooden upright chair. I was sitting in bed with my knees drawn up to my chin under the big white puff. Eva watched me and I watched her.

Even though her chair was against the opposite wall, between the sink and the old marble-topped chest of drawers, and I was sitting up in bed, we were still only about four feet apart. As usual Eva had on her white apron, knee-length black pleated skirt, crisp white blouse, Huguenot cross with a little dove over the cross, black stockings, and thick-soled shoes. She was so close, yet so far from me! I began to panic at the thought that soon Eva would have to go serve the other breakfasts and all she had done so far was sit across from me in silence, smiling, and blushing.

The shutters were closed, so the only light was from the twenty-five-watt bulb in the lamp on my bedside table. Eva's face looked even softer than usual, almost out of focus, as if she were sitting behind some thin gauzy veil. The light was next to me and opposite her. It cast enough of an orange glow so that when Eva opened her knees very slightly, and reached down and slipped the hem of her black, pleated waitress dress a few inches up over her thighs, the dim glow went right up under her skirt.

Suddenly I could see the tops of her stockings where the black nylon ended and pale flesh began. A moment before, my eyes had been glued to Eva's still clothed breasts. If someone had told me that I would lose interest in Eva's breasts and hardly bother to glance at them again for several minutes, I would have laughed at them. What else was there in the world to look at *but* Eva's breasts? What else was there to hope for but that she would soon take off her sweater and bra again?

It turned out that as soon as Eva shifted her weight on the chair, and as soon as I realized that she was sitting with her knees slightly apart, and as soon as it sank in that she had adjusted her skirt higher *on purpose*—rather than tugging it down the way every other woman I had ever seen did when I glanced at their knees if they were sitting across from me—I lost all interest in Eva's breasts. My eyes leaped to the dark shadow beneath her skirt. The dim light from my bedside lamp crept ever higher to places never seen and scarcely imagined, including Eva's stocking tops and what seemed like acres of white thigh beyond the sharp black border of the stockings.

I had seen the tops of stockings before, not often enough, but I had seen them. There was a picture on the package that Mom's new stockings came in that I had seen, even though she hid it by wrapping it in a bag when she threw it away.

I had wanted to look closely at the picture of the woman on the stocking package ever since I glimpsed it. Mom brought it home when she came back from a shopping trip to Monthey down in the valley, a few months before our vacation. As she walked into our chalet hall I caught a glimpse of the package sticking out of the top of Mom's big canvas shopping bag before she whisked it away. That was when I saw the drawing of a pretty young woman, with one of her long legs propped up on a step and her skirt hitched up as she adjusted her stocking and garter. She wore spiky high heels and the Eiffel Tower was in the background. Even though the picture was nothing more than a very nice pen-and-ink drawing, it was mighty realistic.

The package had a little oval cutout in the shape of the woman's leg top through which you could see the color of the actual stocking under the cellophane. I liked that package a lot!

A few weeks before we came to Riffelberg, Janet caught me looking in her drawer, hoping to find more stocking packages. She gave me a hard Indian wrist burn as a punishment for spying on her.

The method of giving an Indian burn is to grab someone's wrist, then twist with both hands in opposite directions while gripping it tightly. The person giving the Indian burn twists their hands back and forth so that the friction between their hands and the victim's wrist—especially where the skin bunches up between the twisting hands and gets caught between the knuckles of the person giving the Indian burn—begins to chafe, then burn. If someone with strong hands does it long enough, say nine or ten times, and if she is good at it and her hands are large and practiced, the skin on the victim's wrist begins to blister and will peel a few days later, as if the victim has had a sunburn. I agreed to receive the Indian wrist burn and not to tell as the alternative to Janet reporting to Dad that she had found me looking in her underwear drawer.

"Just be thankful we're not Mohammedans! Do you know that in their dark culture you'd be stoned to death for this, or beheaded?" Janet said as she twisted my wrists between her large strong hands until she raised white welts. "How I just hope I don't think of *you* pawing my underwear with your filthy little hands on my wedding night!"

So when the light illuminated the top of Eva's stocking, the fasteners of the garters, the little bit of ribbon covering them and running up under her skirt to the lacy part of the belt the garter hung down from, it was like some kind of deliverance from beyond all hope, some great miracle given to one who has despaired of ever getting a good look, an *honest look,* at a woman's stocking top.

Eva shifted and pulled her skirt a little higher.

"*Tu veux voir?*" Eva asked rather breathlessly.

"*Oui,*" I breathed, afraid that if I distracted her in any way she might change her mind.

Beyond the stockings, framed by the black stocking tops and the garters on either side, were Eva's thick white thighs. They curved in two plump generous circles into a perfect V of black panty that was framed on top by the garter belt and below by the little triangle of black skirt Eva was sitting on.

Eva slipped her dress higher. It was now well above her stocking tops. The garters, white thighs, and even a little of Eva's full, round belly were now right out in the room with me! I was no longer looking up Eva's skirt but was in the room *right out in the open with her panties!* And these panties were not tucked between pillowcases on some clothesline but on a real live woman who filled out their satiny black wondrousness and whose lovely full white belly framed the panty top and the garter belt!

Instead of snapping her knees back together and jumping up when she saw me staring, Eva just smiled a sweet smile. Then she sat stock still and let me look.

That a girl, let alone a woman, *a real woman* way older than my sisters, more like my mom, a Swiss woman, a Swiss with the unfortunate European aroma rising in an acrid cloud around her and no different than the women who rode the bus with their knees tightly pressed together and their skirts pulled down to the top of their winter boots, that *she* would do this thing was a revelation to me!

All my received wisdom about boys and girls exploded out of my brain to be replaced by a huge question: If *THIS* is what girls do, then what has Mom been telling me all these years about boys and our "special problem," as if *she* had nothing below her waist that bothered *her?!* WHAT DID EVA WANT?

Suddenly Eva snapped her knees back together, stood, and marched out.

I jumped up and locked the door. Moments later there was a record amount of pale yellowy-white splashes glistening all over my bed, the wall, and me. I sat dazed and breathing laboriously. The splotches were beginning to soak into the bedding like little miniature jellyfish melting in the hot sun on a beach.

A few moments later there was a knock at my door.

"W-who is it?" I gasped, still out of breath.

"Your mother."

"Just a sec, I'm in bed with the, uh, tray on my l-lap. Uh, what do you want?"

"What do you mean, what do I want? I'm bringing you a book of tickets for the lift, if you must know and I want to come in! *That's what I want!*"

I knew all too well that if Mom checked my sheets there would be horrible trouble. Usually I was careful and washed the evidence away. If she found my pajamas, bed, and wall covered in the always-hard-to-remove milky-yellow stains, she would go crazy. I knew she would find them, too! Mom checked my bed every morning, only usually not this early. Mom jiggled the handle.

"I'm just putting the tray aside."

"Why is the door locked?"

I cast about desperately for some idea.

"Last night the English General was drunk, I think, and he tried my door by mistake and walked in, so after he left, I mean he woke me and all, I thought that . . . and so after Eva left the tray, I locked it again without really thinking about it because —"

"Never mind that! Open the door!"

"Coming, uh, NO! Look what I've just done! Oooops!"

Mom had talked about the "little wet dream release of the Precious Seeds" as part of "God's great plan for all young men." I had never had a wet dream; in fact, I was sure Mom was making the whole idea up. Anyway I knew that if these dreams were real they never would involve the kind of powerful squirting that had just scattered my Precious Seeds as high as the top button of my pajama top and even hit the wall behind the bed.

That was why I had no choice but to dash the whole pot of chocolate over myself, the wall, and my bed. Mom would be angry at the mess but only the regular kind of oh-Calvin-how-could-you-be-so-careless angry. She would not be the oh-Calvin-how-could-you-grieve-the-Lord-by-giving-in-to-your-animal-desires-instead-of-waiting-for-a-wet-dream-which-is-God's-plan-to-help-young-men angry.

Chapter 11

YOU CAN'T SKI well when your Little Thing is poking out of the top of your underpants under tight ski pants. Quick turns, jumps, and schussing are out of the question. You have to keep stopping to make adjustments and hitch up your pants again and again.

After I fell for the sixth or seventh time, Janet made a christie stop on the slope right above me, sending a cascade of stinging snow into my face. Then she looked down at me with contempt and said, "What on *earth* is wrong with you this morning, Calvin Dort Becker?"

"Nothing, I'm fine," I said, hoping Janet would not notice the banana-sized bulge in my ski pants as I stood up and brushed myself off.

I stood, but not straight. I hunched over as if I had a heavy load on my shoulders.

"Don't lie, you little prevaricating twerp! You never fall. You've been falling all over the place. What's wrong? Are you going spastic?"

"I guess I'm just a little tired," I said.

"I'm telling Mom," said Janet as she skied off. She turned and called over her shoulder, "You might be developing epilepsy or a brain tumor!"

"Darling," said Mom as we began to eat lunch after she had said a very, very long grace, "Janet tells me you were falling a lot this morning."

"Just a couple of times," I murmured.

"What business is it of Janet's if he falls or not?" asked Dad through a mouthful of stew.

"Well, it *wasn't* just a few times," said Janet. "He fell *all the time,* as if he was doing it on purpose, trying to kill himself or something. Plus half the time he didn't even stand straight up but kind of skied hunched over. He looked strange, bent."

"Well?" asked Dad.

"Do you have a pain in your side?" asked Mom gently, with a coaxing smile. "I hope you're not getting appendicitis."

"I don't have any pain," I said.

"You're supposed to ski with your knees bent," said Rachael, and she gave me a kindly smile.

Janet turned on her furiously.

"He never really stood up all morning, even waiting for the lift he was bent like an old man the whole time. I'm telling you, *something is going on!*"

"Shhh! Janet, please lower your voice. Calvin, what are you up to now?" asked Mom.

"I was just pretending."

"What?" asked Janet accusingly.

For a moment my mind went blank. Normally I could come up with whatever story was needed as quick as breathing. I was hardly able to look at my sisters or any woman in the dining room—even my Mom!—without wondering mightily about certain things.

"Pretending *what?!*" barked Janet.

"Uh, pretending I was an old man trying to ski. That's what I was pretending," I said hurriedly.

"I don't believe you for one minute! Even if you aren't normal, you're not *that* stupid," said Janet.

"Janet, we do not call other people liars unless we're sure about something and it is a serious matter," said Mom.

"Maybe he just doesn't feel well," said Rachael. "Maybe he's feeling sick and doesn't want to say so because he thinks we'll think he's coming down with the typhoid from Zermatt."

"Oh, Calvin!" said Mom, "You feel well, don't you, dear?"

"Yes, Mom."

"When we changed trains you didn't touch anything at the Zermatt station, did you?" asked Dad between mouthfuls.

"No, Dad."

"Or drink any water at the train station?" asked Rachael.

"Of course not," I said.

"How long have you been feeling unwell?" asked Mom.

"I'm fine. I feel fine."

"But you spilled your whole pot of hot chocolate all over your room this morning and said you slipped. Are you sure you're all right?" asked Mom.

"Maybe he was having some kind of epileptic fit," said Rachael, and it sounded as if she was about to cry.

"This is just plain stupid," grumbled Dad. "Leave the boy alone."

"But, Ralph, I think we should see if he has some kind of difficulty standing. Perhaps he really does have a virus attacking his spine or maybe he hurt himself and isn't admitting it because he doesn't want to spoil the vacation," said Mom.

Eva cleared the table and served poached pears for dessert. None of us spoke until she was walking back to the bar.

"Oh well, go on, Calvin, just to please your mother, stand up," said Dad, and he winked at me and smiled.

"I don't want to," I mumbled, while willing, begging, commanding, abjuring my Little Thing to go down, to lose the rock-hard erection that it had been suffering from all day, ever since Eva had walked into my room. It had not lost its erection even after it squirted my Precious Seeds high and low!

My Little Thing was beginning to hurt. The ache started about mid-morning and just got worse the more I willed it to go down. This was some sort of record. It had been hard since about seven A.M.! It was now about twelve thirty! I felt frozen and bruised. The beef stew, served with rösti (a potato and cheese au gratin dish, only with more onions), had come and gone. I was staring down at my dessert and forlornly wondering if you could get gangrene from out-of-control hardness and if my Little Thing might just explode or drop off at some point. The pain was starting to make my legs go numb.

"Calvin, I agree it's dumb, but Elsa wants you to. Obey your mother," said Dad.

They all waited for me to stand. Eva was carrying plates of poached pears to the other guests. I glanced out the window at the blinding sun shining on the Matterhorn. A six-foot-long icicle that had been forming all week off the side of the dining room roof suddenly fell. It stuck into the deep snowbank like a crystal spear. Even this could not distract me. The ache and hardness persisted.

"Show us your spine is all right, dear," said Mom.

"Calvin, obey your mother!" ordered Janet.

"Go on, Calvin, why won't you just stand up?" asked Rachael.

"Calvin, let's get this over with," said Dad. "Obey Elsa, *now!*"

I stood up, but not straight. I bent to enfold the rigid pole. It stuck into my belly as if I were being prodded with a broom handle.

"*Look!* He can't stand up straight!" exalted Janet. "What did I tell you?!"

"Calvin, you're all bent forward. Is that the straightest you can stand?" asked Mom.

"Yes," I mumbled. "Yes, it is."

"But, darling, what's wrong?" asked Mom, as her brow furrowed into its most-worried triple ridge.

"Nothing," I muttered.

"Stop fooling around, Calvin. Stand up straight," said Dad.

"I can't," I said.

"What? Are you serious?" asked Dad.

"I guess I have a stomachache," I said.

"A 'stomachache'?!" exclaimed Janet. "But you ate your whole plate of salami, pickles, and dried beef same as the rest of us not fifteen minutes ago! And you ate some of Rachael's stew, too!"

"Well, my stomach hurts now and I can't stand any straighter than this," I said.

Mom and my sisters exchanged worried, grown-up glances. Janet shot me a smoldering, suspicious look. Dad seemed a little confused, but not angry, as he looked from me to the women and back.

The more I thought about my situation, the harder my Little Thing got. There was no way I was going to be able to walk away from the table after dessert without them all staring at me. (When I had walked in, I carried my ski jacket in front of me. Before I could stop her, Eva took it and hung it up by the door!) I wished Mom had bought me some new ski pants the way I had asked her to. The ones I was wearing were way too tight hand-me-downs from the missionary alliance box. They would have barely fit the year before and I had grown all summer.

There was no way I could get my mind off the stocking tops. Before Eva started bringing the special treats at breakfast, my Little Thing was soft most days, most of the time. It had been going hard only four or five times a day and it never lasted more than ten minutes or so, or until I snuck off to the bathroom and relieved my animal desires, which I did once or twice a day. After the Precious Seeds squirted, everything else arranged itself, at least for a while. Now getting my Little Thing to go down seemed to be impossible! I had relieved my animal desires four times already that day and nothing helped!

"Mom," I said.

"Yes, dear?"

"Maybe we should just take this matter to the Lord."

"Take what to the Lord, dear?" asked Mom.

"My not feeling well."

Janet shot me a furious glance. Even Rachael did not look pleased. It had been embarrassing enough at our first course when Mom had prayed one of her longest prayers. Now Eva had just arrived with Mom and Dad's coffees. If Mom prayed again, who knew how long Eva might have to stand waiting next to our table, with more and more people in the dining room staring at us the way they always did when Mom said grace.

"Well, perhaps we should," said Mom.

"Not now, Elsa," said Dad.

"But, Dad, I thought we should always go to the Lord, anytime we feel we need to talk to him," I said, playing for time.

Janet shot me a what-do-you-think-you're-up-to look. Mom smiled her happiest smile, the one she reserved for those moments when one of her children's hearts seemed to be growing tender for the Things Of The Lord.

"Ralph, if Calvin is moved to ask for intercession, I think we should encourage him, don't you? It's the first time he has ever asked me to pray for him in public. I think it would be a great witness."

"Elsa, not now!" snapped Dad.

Mom gave Dad one of her withering looks reserved for those times when it was "a matter of principle."

"Ralph, we are not to be ashamed of the Lord!" said Mom.

"Mom," begged Rachael, "can't we just wait until after lunch and *then* pray up in our rooms?"

Mom's cheeks had the spots of color on them that told you it was no use arguing.

"Rachael, the Lord comes first! It will be good for Eva and the other guests to see that Real Christians can pray at any time. It's just so exciting to enter the Throne Room, what does it matter whether it's in the middle of lunch or not?"

Without waiting for any more arguments, Mom bowed her head and began to pray in her best loud Monday-morning-prayer-meeting-voice. Of course the rest of us had to bow our heads too. Every head in the dining room turned in our direction, as if they were all on one hinge.

"Dear heavenly Father, we just come before Thee to ask Thee to bless us and to thank Thee for being who Thou art. And we ask Thee for dear little Calvin that he may be restored to full and good health and that he will be protected from illness and all physical health problems during our vacation that Thou hast so graciously provided for us. And we ask that Thy laborers in the Vineyard may take our rest from the labors Thou hast given us and return refreshed to the work that Thou hast led us to do for Thy kingdom's sake. And we ask that at this time of testing for Calvin, Thou wilt draw near to him and we thank Thee that Calvin has asked for his needs to be taken to the foot of Thy heavenly throne and that he has been growing in You, maturing, coming closer to Thee on this vacation and has now asked for prayer. So we just ask Thee to just bless Calvin's faith and to just reach down and touch him that he may just feel Thy presence in his life and just walk in Thy path and just grow closer to Thee in his daily walk, and we pray this in Jesus' precious sweet everlasting name, Amen!"

We all looked up and blinked. The English General was staring at us and chuckling. Rachael and Janet glanced his way and blushed. Dad's face had turned the color of a ripe plum and the vein was pulsing in his neck.

"There," said Mom brightly. "Calvin, I believe He will do a real work in your life."

I was almost as pleased as Mom. I am not saying I had been cured of anything serious like typhoid, but her long prayer did accomplish one thing: my Little Thing was gloriously limp! By the time she had said her Amen it had shrunk to the size of a small acorn and felt as shriveled as when I had just stepped out of Lake Geneva after we went swimming in Villeneuve.

"Thank you, Mom. I do feel much better. Look!" I said, standing up straight as a soldier on parade. "My stomachache is gone!"

Mom glared triumphantly at Dad, who shook his head and muttered something I did not hear.

Chapter 12

AFTER LUNCH JANET skied over and said, "Calvin, what on earth are you doing?"

"Just looking at the Matterhorn."

"When you were born you didn't get enough oxygen, you know," Janet said.

"Mom says I was fine, once I started to breathe," I answered.

"She tells you that to be kind. There was significant brain damage. We all know that."

"There was not!" I retorted hotly.

"Why do you think you have so much trouble learning to read? You still can't spell or read like other people. Do you think it's normal that you're only on the third McGuffey Reader and you're fourteen?!"

"Home schooling doesn't work, not when your teacher hits you on the head with a book!"

"You know perfectly well I only do it for your own good."

"I don't believe you."

"Are you calling me a liar, Calvin Dort Becker?"

"When you told Rachael she was adopted, that wasn't true either and she cried herself to sleep for a whole year before she asked Mom."

"I told her that for her own good. It was to build character. Anyway, she *might* have been adopted; she certainly is not like me at all."

"How do know *you're* not the one that's adopted?"

"When we get down to the hotel I'll give you an Indian wrist-burn you won't forget!"

There are times when it is best to give up and mollify your opponent. There were certain techniques to handling Janet. One was to take her into my confidence and ask her things of a scientific-medical nature that I pretended I was too embarrassed to ask Mom. Janet wanted to be a missionary nurse and prided herself on being a walking encyclopedia of medical knowledge. She also liked to play mother and do her own version of Mom's "private talks" with Rachael and me.

"Okay, I'll tell you what my problem is," I said haltingly, pretending that I was admitting something unwillingly.

"Ha! I *knew* there was something!" Janet grinned triumphantly.

"Janet, I have a very private question I wanted to ask Mom, but I don't dare because you are the only person I can be completely frank with."

I pretended to hesitate.

"Go on, Calvin," Janet said in her most motherly voice. "As your big sister it is my duty to help teach you all I can. Don't be afraid."

"I've been stopping and starting skiing while I think this issue over. I'm so glad I have you to talk to."

Janet's face softened further. She smiled.

"Very well," said Janet, "I'll tell you what you need to know, but if it's inappropriate you'll just have to wait until you're older for me to explain."

"Okay."

"Well, what's your question?"

"I was wondering about how babies actually get born, you know, come out and all."

"Calvin, Mom and I have explained all this to you before," said Janet, and she rolled her eyes heavenward, indicating that, as a dutiful older sister-in-the-Lord, she had to suffer my question patiently. "God chooses a man and a woman for each other from before the dawn of creation, and in a beautiful union, physical, spiritual, and mystical, the man and woman unite in a special way that is only appropriate for a man and woman God has joined together to become one flesh. You're too young for me to go into the details. After that, in certain women, who have certain female troubles you're *far too young* to know about, it takes more than one joining to conceive. But just for the sake of this discussion, let's say it works the first time and the woman's egg is joined to the man's seed in a marvelous, mysterious union that is a picture of Christ's Church on earth, and we who are the brides of Christ are ready to receive his spiritual seed so that we may bear fruit." Janet sighed, then in a severe voice added, "There! *That* is all you need to know till your wedding night!"

"I understand. I just meant *how* do babies come out?"

"You know perfectly well about the private, womanly gift! *That's* where the baby comes out of."

"But *how?*"

Janet looked at me hard and pursed her lips. For once mine was a sincere question. Ever since I looked beyond Eva's stocking tops to the little black V of her panties a thought had been growing in my mind: *It is so narrow down there!*

Of course, I had seen plenty of women in bathing suits, but somehow that was different. Why, I could not say, but I just never had paid as much attention to the dimensions "down there." Eva's narrow little strip of satin panty had gotten my undivided attention! It was burned into my brain! There was no way I could picture a baby coming out of that slender space between those two big thighs, no matter what was under the cloth! And that brought up yet another mystery: *Why* was looking up a skirt so much more interesting than seeing exactly the same view out in the open as a woman walked down the beach? Eva's panty had been less revealing than many a bathing suit but twice as exciting.

WHAT WAS UNDER THERE? The best I could guess was that it was something like the statue of Venus behind the Montreux Palace Hotel. Mom always hurried me past when we were on the way to the station (to catch the train back after a day-off walk by the lake). But I had seen the little stone *V*-shaped hummock between the stone goddesses's legs and wished a thousand times that she had not crossed her legs! All I could see was that it tapered to nothing down there. It seemed as if there was no opening at all! Now I had seen Eva close up, and all there was, was a strip of cloth no wider than a Band-Aid, even when her legs were apart! *How on earth did babies come out?!*

With my Little Thing, I could point to a certain spot and say, that's where it starts, or, that's where it ends. When Andy and I compared our Little Things, there was no dispute as to where they began or ended. (His was a bit longer when in the off position. Mine was half an inch longer when in the on position.) We measured each other by the same fair, from-just-below-the-Precious-Seed-Sack-to-the-tip standard.

With Eva I would have not known where to place a ruler if I had been asked to measure whatever it was under there. Everything seemed to flow into the next part. Eva's landscape had no beginning or end. The place melded into the white thighs on the sides and disappeared seamlessly into Eva's roll of belly above her panty. Below, it never even ended but folded away underneath between the crescents of Eva's large shapely bottom. WHAT WAS UNDER THAT PANTY?

Maybe, I thought, she is what Mom calls "one of those unfortunate women God has chosen not to bless with the ability to conceive." Eva, I thought, probably had what Mom called "female troubles." No baby I had ever seen could ever come out of that place!

I had always figured there was a flap or trapdoor down there. Andy Keegan said it was a sort of a pouch like kangaroos have that opened up and then closed up again after they pulled the baby out. The pouch, I thought, must be at least the size of a big coffee mug . . . and yet . . .

"Calvin, is this a sincere question, or are you just trying to get me to stimulate those unfortunate thoughts little boys have?"

"But Janet, I wasn't thinking anything bad, just wondering how big the hole is supposed to be?"

"*What?!*"

Janet stood looking at me with her mouth open. The bright sun was reflecting up off the snow. I could see the yellowy-pink roof of her big mouth lit as if from within.

"I mean, does the baby just fall out? Is there a pouch like a kangaroo? How big is the hole supposed to be in a normal woman, say as big as this?" I said, and held up my hands and made a circle with my thumb and forefinger about as big as a small watermelon. "Is it a pouch like a kangaroo? Is it a hole the size of a coffee mug? What?"

"Calvin! How *dare* you mock my sincere attempt to give you information about my most precious secrets, secrets that are hidden for all time except for the man God has picked out for me? Pouch like a kangaroo! Tcha!"

Janet lifted her ski pole in a threatening gesture.

"I was just wondering, Janet! Please, I really want to know! You are the only person in the world I can come to with my scientific questions!"

Janet lowered her ski pole. She looked undecided.

"Are you being serious or merely disgusting?"

"I promise I'm being serious. Please tell me. I feel I can talk to you so much more easily than to Mom. You know you're so good about giving advice and all that and know everything about science."

"Why on earth do you want so much specific information all of a sudden? Isn't it enough to know that a man and woman are like Christ and his church?"

"I was just wondering, you know, about God's great plan and all, his marvelous creation and all."

"I bet you were!"

"No, I really was."

"It's so hard to know how much to tell a boy of your age," Janet said at last. Janet shook her head and thought things over for a moment.

"If I can't go to you with my innermost scientific questions, who can I turn to? Who else has the medical knowledge?"

"If you promise to receive this information prayerfully and in a spirit of thankfulness to God for His wonders of creation and not to dwell on it, I will tell you." Her eyes were bright. "Do you promise?"

"Yes."

"Yes, what?"

"Yes, I will receive this information in a spirit of . . . of . . ."

"Thankfulness for His wondrous creation!"

"Yes, exactly like that."

"Calvin, don't tell Mother that I have told you this."

"I won't."

"I tell you not because you deserve to know but because knowledge is better than ignorance and superstition."

"Yes. I'm grateful."

"I can tell you because we are Reformed, evangelical Protestants who believe in the light of the Reformation and are not afraid of science or in the grip of old wives' tales and papal ignorance."

"Yes."

"I will show you in the snow."

"Okay, thanks."

Janet began to draw with her ski pole on the fresh snow next to the piste. With every stroke the snow sparkled so that her map of female anatomy looked as if it were studded with diamond dust.

"It's like this. Inside a woman there is a womb. See?"

"Okay."

"The womb leads to this passage called the va—well, never mind what it's called, it's enough for you to think of it as 'the Passage.'"

"Okay."

"Then down here is the opening."

"How big is the opening?"

"It's just a little slit."

"Where?"

"You know perfectly well where it is, Calvin! It's in the same place your silly Little Thing is!"

"I don't mean that. I mean how wide is the hole?"

"Don't you dare call it *that!* I told you it's the Passage and *not* a 'hole'!"

"The Passage, I meant. How big is it?"

"It's closed."

"Closed? Like this?" I asked, and I tugged off my mitten and made a fist and turned it sideways to show Janet the tight little slit between my thumb and forefinger.

"Yes, like that."

"On *all* women?"

"Yes."

"Then how does a baby come out?"

"This is far more specific information than you need at your age! In fact, until you're in your early twenties you should not think of this again. If I tell you, what will be left for you to discover when, on some distant night, or perhaps earlier in the day after the reception, you are to become one flesh with the young woman of God's choosing?"

"But *how* does a baby come out of a closed passage?"

"Is this a scientific question or mere prurience typical of your kind?"

"It's scientific, Janet."

"Very well. I only hope for your sake you've spoken the truth, because there is no such thing as a dirty thing, only dirty minds that make it so."

"Yes."

Janet thought for a moment before she spoke. When she did, it was in her best schoolteacher voice.

"Have you ever put on a sweater?"

"Of course."

"Not a V neck; I mean one of those turtlenecks."

"Yes. I have one on now."

"How wide is the neck?"

"What?"

"When you put it on? How wide is it?" asked Janet.

"It's tight and stretches out."

"Exactly!"

I thought for a minute. I pictured a baby's head. I pictured Eva's place and how narrow it was under her strip of panty.

"But Janet, *how* can it stretch out *that* much?! I just don't get it."

"How? I'll tell you how! 'To the woman he said: I will greatly multiply your conception. In pain you shall bring forth children.' Genesis chapter three, that's 'how'!"

"It must just split open! I mean it's so small!"

"Mom says it hurts so much that it feels like you've been torn apart between two moving freight trains!"

"Oh, wow."

Janet was breathing hard. She was no longer eking out the information as if each scrap was a precious pearl that I was unworthy to receive. She was joyfully gushing facts in one long breathless and excited rush.

"It's the Fall, Calvin! Man must till the soil! Woman gets stretched, split, pours steaming blood! 'I will greatly multiply your labor.' God said it, and he did! He made the passage too small! See, Calvin, before the Fall it was probably the right size, so the baby could get through with no more problems than, say, toothpaste being squeezed out of a tube. But then Eve was beguiled by Satan, and her punishment, besides Hell, death, and pain of course, was to have sorrow giving birth. God must have tightened things up as a punishment!"

"Is that in the Bible?" I asked, feeling somewhat shocked by just how mean God was.

"Not exactly, but that's how it must be because the sorrowing part has to do with stretching."

"Is it really that bad?"

"How would you like to have the piano in our living room pulled out of your mouth?"

I was speechless. Janet looked triumphant.

"*Now* do you get the idea? So the next time you get hit in your precious little sack of seeds, don't complain! That's nothing! Women suffer much more than boys!"

"I won't complain."

"*Now* do you understand?"

I nodded. Janet whacked at her anatomical illustration. The diagram disappeared in a spray of white powder that twinkled in the dazzling sun.

Chapter 13

AT LUNCH MOM ANNOUNCED, "The typhoid has been cured, praise God."

"They can't know that," growled Dad.

"They said the last case came back from the hospital in Sion yesterday," said Mom extra cheerfully.

"I wish you wouldn't contradict me," Dad said, and glared.

"Mom?" I blurted, trying to change the subject before they started to fight again, and before really thinking about what I was about to say. "I was wondering about why God punishes women by making it harder to have babies, you know, stretching them and all," I babbled.

"Calvin!" squealed Janet.

The English General heard her and glanced our way, then called out to Eva, "I'll have another spot if it's all the same to you, lass," and held out his whisky glass.

"Janet, will you please lower your voice?" asked Mom. "The General is looking at us again."

Eva's breasts sailed over to the General's table. Then they sailed to our table and hovered.

My heart sank. Janet was looking death at me and Mom was exchanging an unhappy what-is-the-boy-up-to-now-daughters-are-so-much-easier look with Rachael.

"You are weeshing for *encore du terrine?*" asked Eva.

"There must be something wrong with it. Don't take any," said Dad, and he looked at Eva darkly.

"Excusing?" asked Eva. She pursed her lips and her brow puckered up. "Excusing?"

Dad ignored her and stared out the huge picture window. I followed his gaze to the cloudless sky. There must have been a powerful wind way up above us, because a fine misty plume of blowing snow was spewing off the top of the Matterhorn in a long gauzy arc that looked like a comet's tail.

"Something wrong with the lovely terrine?" asked Mom. "Why did you say that, Ralph?"

"These stingy bums never give second helpings of meat," Dad muttered without looking at Mom. "It must be going bad. I thought mine smelled funny."

"Look how the snow is blowing, Dad," I said, feeling mighty relieved that everyone seemed to have forgotten about my bringing up the childbirth issue.

"Wouldn't want to get stuck up there today. Right, boy?" said Dad in a distant, almost dreamy voice. "Up there it must be blowing at over seventy-five miles per hour. Look at that snow and over there, too," said Dad, pointing. "Look at the Weisshorn."

I looked. An arc of ice crystals was spewing off the top of the sharklike white tooth in a long pale smear.

"Amazing how those winds rage and down here we feel nothing at all," said Dad.

I nodded. Mom and the girls did not respond. Dad smiled at me.

"Now I'm feeling sick!" said Rachael. "Mine tasted funny too!"

"Darling, darling," said Mom, shooting Dad a withering glance, "there's absolutely *nothing* wrong with this wonderful terrine. I expect they just made a little more than usual. What a *shame* that *someone* for reasons we will *never* understand, has poisoned your mind against this wholesome and lovely provision the Lord made for us!"

Dad clenched his jaw. He still did not turn from the window.

"Yes, please," Mom said in an extra loud and cheerful voice, while turning to Eva, "*I* will have some more!"

Eva gave Mom a bright smile. When she leaned over me to serve Mom, I think she leaned close on purpose because her breast definitely brushed past my cheek.

"You'll be sorry," said Dad, while staring out the window.

"I'll be just fine," said Mom brightly.

"You'll be up all night vomiting," Dad said, and winked at me.

Mom gave Dad a look and began to eat all the terrine and all the little cubes of beef jelly and slivers of pickle that went with it. Dad never looked at her once the whole time but kept gazing up at the peaks. The rest of us watched her in silence.

"Darling?" asked Mom, turning to me as she finished the last bite and delicately touched the corners of her mouth with her napkin.

"Yes, Mom?" I answered.

"Darling, what was that you mentioned about God 'punishing' women?"

My heart sank. Why, oh, why had I blurted that? What was wrong with me that I would get some idea swirling in my brain and think and think till it just spilled out?

"I thought I heard once, uh, someplace, that before the Fall it was easier to have babies. Isn't that in the Bible?" I mumbled.

"Well," said Mom, "the Bible does tell us that a woman's travail and sorrow has been increased when she gives birth. So in a way the Fall did result in this special kind of challenge for women."

"Women don't have anything to complain about. Suffering increased for everyone," said Dad.

Mom flicked her eyes pityingly toward Dad.

"Even for animals?" asked Rachael.

"Of course," said Dad.

"Why? What had they done?" asked Rachael.

"Nothing, they have no moral capacity," said Dad. "But I know what you're wondering, you're wondering if it's fair. Is that it?" Dad spun around to glare at us all. "Everyone always wants to know if things are fair. FAIR?! What's *that* supposed to mean? Is it *fair* that cats eat mice? Is it *fair* that we swat flies?"

"It says Jesus knows about each sparrow when it falls from the air," said Rachael in a quivery little voice. "God c-cares about e-every little creature, doesn't He, Dad?"

"That's right, dear," said Mom reassuringly. "Suffering grieves the Lord because it's not what He intended, but we spoiled everything when we fell, right, Ralph?"

"We fell?" asked Janet. "Who's '*we*'?"

"Janet, you know perfectly well what I mean. Don't *you* be difficult!" snapped Mom.

Rachael gave Janet a sorrowing look. For a moment Dad said nothing. Then he sighed and spoke in a tired voice.

"We are creation's stewards," said Dad sullenly. "When we fell we took the whole of creation with us, because as the ones who got to name each creature, we were their keepers. When Man fell, all the creatures in his domain suffered. At least so they say. There is no such thing as 'fair.' "

"Do mice get stretched, too, when they give birth?" I blurted.

Rachael shot me a little smile and shook her head as if to warn me that I had better be quiet.

"Calvin!" exclaimed Janet.

"I do wish you'd stop shrieking like that," said Mom.

"Janet, what's wrong with you?" asked Dad.

"Nothing, Dad, only it's lunch and Calvin is being so disgusting!"

"Calvin has the right to ask questions," said Rachael.

"There is nothing wrong with discussing original sin at lunch," Dad said bitterly, and smiled darkly. "What else is there to talk about?"

None of us knew how to interpret Dad's Mood. There was some sort of current, some sort of underlying bite in his words that we had not heard before. He sounded less angry than fed up. Obviously Mom did not like whatever it was Dad was doing.

"That's right, Janet," said Mom with a reproving glance at Dad. "The Fall is a perfectly edifying topic at mealtimes. My dear father often discussed the Fall and questions of predestination at table . . . in his calm, rational, and scholarly manner."

Dad banged the table. A fork flipped up and spun in the air before it fell to the floor. I might have been wrong but I thought I saw a little smile flash across Mom's lips before she got her aggrieved look. The English General glanced our way, chuckled, then raised his glass as if toasting Dad. Rachael blushed. Janet shot me an angry see-what-you've-done-now glare. I gave her a quick what?-I-didn't-do-anything look.

"Oh, Ralph," said Mom sorrowfully.

"Don't 'oh Ralph' me, Elsa!" roared Dad.

Every head in the dining room swiveled toward us.

"Yes, dear."

Dad said nothing for a moment. He was staring at Mom hard. Then she smiled ever so slightly. Dad exploded at that smile.

"And don't 'yes, dear' me, either!" shouted Dad.

The English General laughed out loud and said, to no one in particular, "The bloody Yank's gone off his bally rocker! Splendid!"

"Dad?" I asked hurriedly.

Dad was glaring at Mom. He looked as if he was about to start throwing things. I had to do something.

"But, Dad?" I asked urgently.

"Ask your mother! She knows everything! She's so perfect like her dear, dear, dear, mother and father!"

"Dad?" I asked.

"What?" Dad said as he turned his furious gaze away from Mom and glared at me. "What? *What?* WHAT?!"

"I was j-just wondering if God sinned when he made it so women got stretched and screamed when their babies got born. Dad, is God mean?"

"Calvin!" yelled Janet.

"Oh, Calvin!" wailed Rachael.

"Don't blaspheme!" wailed Mom.

"Calvin can ask anything he goddamn well wants to!" shouted Dad.

Eva stopped halfway across the dance floor, a serving dish of steaming pommes nature held in front of her, wreathing her rosy face in steam.

"Oh, Ralph!" whispered Mom in her most shocked voice.

My sisters were looking at their plates. I was wishing that I lived with any other family in the dining room, even the English General.

"God, Calvin, is not as mean as he seems sometimes," said Dad in a quiet but tense voice. "Anyway, He's beyond our human judgment, even Elsa's. He's the 'I AM' and that's damn well *that!* He does what he damn well wants and we just *damn* well live with it, because *that's* the way it is!"

"But, Ralph, He sent forth His Son to die for us," exploded Mom in an urgent whisper. "Reassure the children!"

"Elsa, did Calvin ask *you* anything?" barked Dad.

Mom looked down at her plate. Her neck was beet red. The girls' faces were too. I was trying not to meet any of the many curious eyes looking our way. I stared out the window at the plume of snow blowing off the Matterhorn and thought about my family and how, when I had been little, I was always on Mom's side. But recently I was starting to see that in her way, her nice, smiling, little-innocent-comments way, she was as bad as Dad. He yelled and pounded the table, but maybe Mom was worse. At the end of a fight she always looked cool and collected, but Dad was red and sweaty and people stared at him and pointed and sometimes laughed when he "went right over the edge." When they looked at Mom, they felt sorry for her as she sat, eyes cast down, biting her lip, twisting her napkin or handkerchief. No one ever felt sorry for Dad . . . And yet who really started their fights?

"No, Ralph. He didn't ask me anything, I admit," said Mom quietly.

"Then will you just shut up and let me answer?" Dad snarled while breathing hard.

"Yes, Ralph. I will obey you in all things, even when it troubles my conscience," said Mom in a cool calm voice.

Dad turned to me. It took him a moment to focus on my face before he could speak.

"Calvin?" Dad asked at last.

"Yes, Dad?"

"God is not mean. He just is the way He is. The regular rules don't apply."

"Okay, Dad."

"As I said, He is beyond our judgment and understanding and His creation is groaning under the weight of our sin. That's why there is suffering."

"And too much stretching in childbirth?"

I could not stop myself! Janet once read something out loud to me about a new invention called the "subconscious." Mom said it was a secular idea and that Real Christians had only the Holy Spirit dwelling within them. But I figured it must be that subconscious thing doing this blurting.

"What?" asked Dad.

"When the baby comes out, like a piano being pulled out of their mouths," I babbled.

"That's an awful analogy!" moaned Mom. "Oh, Calvin, *who* has put such an *awful* mental picture in your head?"

I pointed to Janet.

Mom gave Janet a shocked look. We all stared at Janet. She shot me a terrifying now-you're-dead glance.

"He wanted to know about the Fall and childbirth, the passage in the book of Genesis," said Janet through clenched teeth.

"What does that have to do with *disgusting* word pictures that will defile what ought to be a beautiful image of Christ and his bride bearing fruit, young lady?" asked Mom.

"It wasn't like he said," Janet replied in a sulky voice.

"He's an innocent little boy!" said Rachael. "How could he make up something that awful?"

"Just calm down," Dad said in a friendly voice.

We turned to him. He was smiling. His Mood had evaporated. Dad was smiling not in an angry sarcastic way but in the way he did when he was relaxed and happy.

"Boys aren't like girls, Elsa," said Dad cheerfully. "Now all of you stop acting so shocked by everything, for goodness' sake." Dad turned to everyone in the dining room and grinned. The other guests looked away hurriedly, all except the General, who gave Dad a cheery thumbs-up. "The way you all get shocked so easily is really starting to annoy me. Now, Calvin, what do you really want to know? What's eating you, boy?"

"I just wanted to know about babies getting born, so I asked Janet and she tried to explain. I guess I got what she said mixed up a little," I said meekly.

"Just be glad *you're* not going to have to squeeze out a puppy or two!" Dad winked at me, then laughed. "The women bake the rolls, right, boy?"

Dad laughed. Mom shook her head sadly. Rachael went bright pink.

Eva arrived with the second course. It was tongue with caper sauce along with the pomme nature. Janet groaned.

"There is nothing wrong with tongue, dear. It is just another cut of meat," said Mom.

"I love tongue!" said Rachael. "Especially the caper sauce."

"But remember, God is not mean, Calvin," said Mom.

"It's just the women you've got to watch like a hawk!" said Dad.

Dad chuckled and winked. Mom stared down at her three thin slices of tongue.

"What are capers?" I asked.

"I need a little mustard, Eva," said Mom.

"Show me how to use my knife and fork," said Dad. "Is this how they do at Princeton . . . ? Is this how Hudson Taylor did it when all the missionaries were real gentlemen? David Livingstone even dressed for dinner when he was out in the bush in Africa, didn't he? Tell them."

Mom did not take the bait or look up. I glanced at Dad and saw he was still smiling in a friendly way. He was just teasing Mom a little. Dad was not angry anymore. There was no figuring his Moods.

Janet glanced at me and made the Indian wrist-burn motion with her hands. Rachael sighed. She was starting to fade back to her normal pale white from rosy pink. Mom began to eat with tiny delicate bites, her hands holding her knife and fork perfectly.

Dad wolfed down his food while forking whole slices of tongue into his mouth. I wondered if he was chewing with his mouth open on purpose to annoy Mom. Then I wondered if Mom was cutting up her food in such dainty little slices and eating so slowly and politely to annoy Dad.

"Capers are the buds of a small plant in Spain," said Mom quietly.

I hate this family, I thought.

Chapter 14

JANET SHUT THE DOOR of the ski room with a soft click. The other guests were already back out on the slopes or up in their rooms for a nap. We were alone.

The ski room was a windowless stone structure about the size of a large garage, built on the back of the hotel. The interior walls were made of big uneven rocks cobbled together with cement and glistening with ice. They were lined with wooden racks studded with large pegs, between which the hotel guests stood their skis in rows and on which they hung their ski poles. The cement floor was crunchy with snow tracked in from the outside. There was a single naked lightbulb hanging from a wire lighting the room. When you walked under it, the bulb cast a looming shadow on the wall.

My back was turned. I did not hear Janet come in. By the time I heard the crisp crunching squeak of snow under her ski boots, it was too late. She was between the door and me, casting a huge black shadow on the wall.

"You know what I need to do?" asked Janet.

"Yes," I said.

"And you know you've never deserved it more?"

"Yes."

I pushed up my sleeve and stuck out my right wrist. I could still see the faint marks from the last Indian burn Janet gave me. I felt resigned. I could take it. I always did.

Janet knew she was not allowed to do wrist burns on me. But what was the point of telling? She would just do something worse later. It was best to get these things over with and move on. Janet gripped my wrist firmly, with both hands held close together so that the skin of my wrist bunched up in the space between her thumbs and index fingers. Letting Janet torture me seemed like a normal, if unpleasant, fact of life. It had always been this way. But that afternoon was not like any other time. For once I thought I had an angle.

"Janet?"

"Yes?"

"Before you start, can I say just one thing?"

"Okay, but don't waste my time begging. I want to get out there and ski, the same as you do. So don't be selfish."

"I won't, but I just have this one thing to say before you start."

"What?"

Janet held my wrist, ready to begin twisting. Her mighty arms were flexed, the muscles of her forearms taut. I could feel her hard fingers twitching in anticipation. But she waited. Part of our time-honored ritual was that Janet always allowed me to say some last words. When we were both younger she sometimes would ask, "Does the prisoner have any last words before the sentence is carried out?"

"Janet, I saw you dancing in the dining room," I said a bit breathlessly.

Janet tightened her grip and said nothing. Her face flushed. The steamy breath that had been pouring out of her nostrils suddenly stopped. I felt her hands tense on my wrist. My heart was pounding. I was not used to standing up to Janet.

"I'll tell, and you know they'll take us home if they know you're sneaking down to dance."

"I never danced," Janet said quietly.

She did not look at my face but kept staring down at my wrist. She did not begin to administer the burn. I felt hopeful.

"I bet the cook will admit it. Sergio doesn't know it's sinful. He's a Roman Catholic and won't think anything of it. If Mom asks him if he danced with you, he'll tell. I'll tell Mom to ask him, and if you deny it, then you'll get punished for lying on top of everything, and I bet you don't even get to go to Lausanne and shop, let alone go anywhere with anybody again until you're married or something. I saw you *press* against him!"

Janet's face darkened from the color of sliced fresh tomato to the color of raw liver. One thing she hated to do above everything else was ever admit she liked boys, let alone had flirted with one. Janet tightened her grip. She still would not look me in the face, though I was holding her with a steady gaze. My heart felt as if it were about to pop out of my mouth.

"Let go," I said, and my voice shook.

Janet would have made a great general, probably a Nazi general, but still a great general in somebody's army. She was able to think strategically and swiftly.

Janet moved so fast that it must have happened in the twinkling of an eye, because one instant both her hands were holding my wrist, and the next, one hand had a handful of my hair and the other hand had my "Precious Seed Sack" gripped so hard, it felt like a big pair of pliers had just fastened onto my left testicle.

"Calvin?" asked Janet in a calm steady voice.

"Yes?" I whispered between clenched teeth.

"Will you please believe me when I tell you something?"

Janet tightened her grip.

"Yes! I'll believe you!" I grunted.

"Calvin, I will rip away your Precious Seed Sack as King David cut off the Philistines' foreskins from the enemies of the Lord and gave them unto King Saul as a token of his love for Saul's daughter. Do you believe I will do this?"

"Yes," I whispered.

"I shall squeeze all your precious seeds out like Mom making fresh orange juice when you're sick in bed. I will crush your pathetic little grapes as though they were poached eggs under the heel of this ski boot! I will feed them to the birds of the air! Do you believe me when I tell you that I will do this thing?"

"Yes!"

"Do you want me to rip them off?"

"*No!*"

"Are you ever going to tell Mom or Dad that I danced?"

"No!" I yelped.

"You solemnly promise as you hope to see salvation?" Janet asked calmly.

"Yes!"

"Because if you *do* tell or even *think* about this ever again, I will be in so much trouble it will not matter to me what happens. Like a cornered beast, I will have nothing further to lose and I will grab these sad little grapes of yours and hold them in the palm of my hand and I will keep twisting and pulling and squeezing like *this* . . ."

Janet gripped, yanked, twisted, and pulled.

"Ow! *OW!*" I shrieked.

The room seemed to grow dark.

". . . until they come right off in my hand, one at a time, like a loose tooth does when it's been hanging by a thread. But you won't get fifty centimes under your pillow for these! There is no testicle fairy, Calvin!"

"*I promise!*" I wailed.

Janet let go. I slid to the icy floor. She was panting as she stood over me. The steam from her breath made a huge cloud of white around her flaming red cheeks and a rainbow halo around the lightbulb.

"Now stand up and hold out your wrist," said Janet.

"B-but you already squeezed my Precious Seed Sack!" I moaned.

"That was to prevent blackmail. We still have to attend to the matter of what you said at lunch. The law is the law! Hold out your wrist!"

Chapter 15

GOD'S HAND MUST have been in it, or rather on me through Janet. How he works is always a mystery. He always gets what he wants. "His ways are irresistible," as Dad says.

The morning after Janet became the instrument of the Lord's chastisement, I locked my door so that Eva could not get in with my breakfast tray. I did not want to be stimulated in any way. I was in enough trouble. I could hardly pee.

Eva knocked several times. I heard the clink of the dishes as she put the tray down and her footsteps leaving. I still did not unlock the door in case she had just pretended to leave.

For the next two mornings I kept my door locked. Eva left the tray outside the door. She stopped giving me extra rolls. When I saw her later in the dining room at lunch and dinner she would not look at me. I went skiing, slowly, and made sure not to fall.

The swelling was gone by the second night after Janet attacked me and by the third morning I felt almost well. Janet never spoke to me or even looked at me. I do not know if she felt bad about what she did but at least she left me alone.

There was a snowstorm on the first night of my convalescence. The second day, the General fell and twisted his ankle in the deep new snow. He sat in the lobby with his foot propped up while reading three-day-old copies of the *Financial Times,* drinking whisky, and calling out cheery greetings to everyone.

The band played and the Swedish twins danced. Sergio, still wearing his kitchen gray-checked trousers and white jacket, walked over to our table to ask Janet if she would be around when the dinner service was over. She gave him such a fierce look that he retreated before Mom or Dad suspected anything. Later Mom said to Janet that her response had been "very appropriate." We finished dessert and Mom hurried us out as fast as she could before the dancing got going or the cook could come back and make "further dreadful advances," as Mom said.

On the third morning after the attack I not only unlocked the door but opened it wide, right after I pressed the service button. I opened the shutters, too, so there would be no doubt in Eva's mind that I was up, awake, and ready to see her. I also got up and wetted down my hair and combed it and put on fresh pajamas. Then I waited, sitting up in bed and trying to look natural.

I worried that Eva would never be as friendly as she had been before the attack on my Precious Seed Sack. But on that third morning—it also happened to be our next to last day at the hotel—when Eva turned toward me, after putting my tray down on the dresser, she was smiling. I noticed her face was flushed pink. There were three extra rolls on the tray and I took this as a good sign.

"*Demain tu pars?*" asked Eva brightly.

"*Oui, demain c'est la fin de nos vacances,*" I answered.

"*Tu veux le petit service?*" asked Eva, and, without waiting for an answer, she closed the door and locked it.

My heart raced and I felt my Little Thing leap up and do its telephone pole imitation in less than ten seconds. As soon as it did I felt a slight twinge of pain but it was not bad enough to distract me.

"*Oui, merci, je le veux beaucoup!*" I said breathlessly.

A moment later Eva's big lacy white bra, garter belt, stockings, panties, skirt, blouse, apron, shoes, and pink fluffy sweater were piled neatly on the end of my bed one after the other. She did not undress fast or slow, just at a normal speed. She did not look at me as she undressed.

When she was stark naked (all except for her Huguenot cross), Eva slowly turned all the way around. She did this several times and each time got up on her toes like some sort of ballet dancer. She was smiling at me. I was staring and staring at her.

Eva did not look like the statue behind the Montreux Palace Hotel. The statue was slender and tall and had no hair under its arms or on its most private place. Eva was a lot more compressed, as if somebody had sort of squashed the statue of the goddess—Venus or whomever she was supposed to be—down by a few feet and everything had gotten fatter and thicker and bulged more. Eva's face was flushed, but the smooth skin on the rest of her body was the color of cream and just as spotless. Now that she was standing up, naked, her breasts bulged like big oval water balloons almost ready to burst.

Eva's round belly protruded out far enough that as she turned around and around she looked like some sort of an *S*-shaped Christmas tree ornament slowly twisting in the hot air rising from the candles. Eva's bottom was large and shapely as a big summer peach, the kind I never saw in Switzerland but that showed up in Italy on the table at the pensione once in a while for dessert. Eva's legs were heavy in the thighs but tapered down till they looked as dainty as the legs on Mom's stocking package. Eva had a small waist even though her belly was nice and round. That waist combined with her huge breasts and large bottom made her as curvy as a mountain road.

I could have sat watching Eva's full, short body forever. My only problem was how to decide what part to stare at! I looked at her most private place till my eyes almost popped with the intense strain of trying to *see* what lay under her thick fuzzy triangle of hair. Then I realized that I was wasting the rest of her! So I stared at her breasts. Then she turned, and at first I was saddened and longed for her to face me again till I noticed just how great and wonderful her big bottom was, how vast and shapely, how perfect in its peachy roundness! When she turned sideways I was sad to see that glorious bottom drift away but delighted to see Eva's breasts again, now in pointy silhouette profile against the blinding light reflecting off the dazzling snow.

"You liking?" Eva asked as she turned.

"*Oui,*" I breathed.

Eva stared at me and took three steps to the bed. She pulled off the puff with one swift twitch and then lay down.

Eva was heavy! Her wide hips covered mine completely, past them on each side by a good six inches. Her large breasts pressed down on either side of my chest and flowed over me and seemed to fill the bed. I touched her bare back. Her skin was silky soft.

I wished that I did not have on my pajamas, yet was sort of glad that I did since, wonderful as this all was, it was also mighty embarrassing! I was so stunned, so amazed, so overjoyed by the inexplicable turn events had just taken that I was not breathing and suddenly had to gasp for air.

All that heavy flesh was molding itself around me, pressing me down deeply into the soft mattress and flowing over me and onto the bed each time she pressed herself on me. The only thing I did not like was that I could not see Eva well enough! Even though I kept straining my neck to look up and over her shoulder, all I could see was her wide, lily-white bottom looming between me, the window, and the Matterhorn.

My Little Thing was being pressed between Eva and me. I knew she must feel it, know it was hard. My face grew hot. I tried to pull back and hold still. Eva did not seem to mind that it was hard and poking her. She pressed down on me again and again. I felt a stab of pain. My recovery from Janet's attack was not so complete after all! I cried out. Eva must have misunderstood my shout, because she pressed down even harder and began to groan. I yelled "OW!" again. She pressed harder and harder.

My bed began to squeak and bang against the wall. It was rocking back against the wall so hard that a picture of the Old Man of the Mountains—

in the picture he was carrying a gun in one hand and had a deer he had shot slung over his shoulders—crashed to the floor, the glass shattering. Eva was moaning loudly. Another involuntary "Ow!" burst out of me as my injured testicle, jammed into my pajamas and crushed between Eva's heavy pelvis and my thigh, was mercilessly rolled to and fro.

"OW! OWWWW!"

"Calvin?"

It was my mother's voice! Eva did not notice and kept banging her hips down on me.

"*Calvin Dort Becker!* What are you doing in there?"

This time Eva heard Mom and leaped off me. I struggled to sit up and scrambled for the puff. Mom tried the door handle.

"Open this door this instant!"

Eva was frantically tugging on her skirt.

"Open this door! What's going on?"

The door handle jiggled furiously. Mom started to bang on the door. I was glad Eva had locked it when she walked in!

"I'm getting your father!"

I heard Mom's footsteps running up the hall.

"*Vite!*" I gasped.

Eva did not need me to tell her to hurry. She grabbed her apron, pulled on her sweater, and unlocked the door. In an instant Eva was gone. She ran out barefoot, carrying her thick-soled shoes with her.

A few seconds after I heard the door to the staff stairs close behind Eva, my door opened and Mom charged in, followed a moment later by Dad. Mom was in her bathrobe and Dad in his pajamas. She had on slippers. His feet were bare. Dad looked as if he had been asleep moments before and had marks on his face where it must have been pressing into his pillow. Mom was still clutching her toilet case. (She must have been passing my room on the way to the bathroom at the end of the hall when she heard Eva and knocked on my door.)

"Calvin, *what* has been going on?!" asked Mom in a high-pitched distressed voice.

"Hi, Mom, hi, Dad, uh, what do you m-mean?" I said, while trying to keep the shake out of my voice.

"Calvin, your door was *locked!* I heard bumping or hammering and a shout. What *has* been going on?"

"Nothing, Mom. I was just eating my breakfast."

Mom and Dad's eyes darted to my untouched breakfast tray sitting on the dresser. There was a thick skin over the hot chocolate which by this time was no longer steaming. I followed their glance. At exactly the same instant the three of us all saw Eva's garter belt, bra, panties, and stockings lying on the floor in a fluffy tangle next to the chair at the foot of my bed. All three of us gasped.

"What on earth?!" Dad barked.

I closed my eyes. When I opened them, Mom was standing over me holding the underwear in front of her at arm's length. She was staring at the lacy fistful with her mouth wide open. Dad was the color of a sunset. The vein was pulsing in his neck.

"Calvin Dort Becker," shrieked Mom, "what on *earth* have you been doing in here?"

"Nothing, Mom," I muttered.

"How did those get here?" asked Dad.

"I don't know, Dad. They were just there when I came in last night. I don't even know what they are. What are those things, Mom?"

Dad turned to Mom.

"Are they Janet's?" Dad asked.

Mom held up the bra and examined it.

"Most certainly not! Look at the size of this thing!"

Mom spotted the shattered glass where the picture had fallen down behind the bed.

"What on earth?" yelped Mom, pointing to the broken glass that had skittered over the floor. She sniffed. "This room smells of unfortunate European aroma!"

Mom held the bra up to her face and sniffed.

"This is where that smell is coming from!"

Chapter 16

THERE ARE TIMES when an outright denial does not work. Then there are times when the best way to lie is to say something so bad about yourself that no one would make it up, because it means you will get a big punishment, but that's still going to be a smaller punishment than you would get if the truth came out. This was clearly one of those times. Fortunately for me, Mom handed me my lie on a platter by jumping to conclusions.

"Calvin, you've been touching yourself!"

Suddenly Mom grabbed my puff and pulled it off. She stared at me for a moment, then pointed to my pajamas with a shriek of dismay.

"Look!" gasped Mom.

Dad stared. I glanced down. Only then did I realize that I had squirted my precious seeds while Eva was on me! I had been in such pain that somehow I had not felt it happen. My light green pajamas were stained dark and were soaked with big sticky patches.

I waited a moment and thought out my lie as carefully as I could. Dad was looking at me in a tired sort of way. Mom was all aquiver and seemed to be vibrating.

You have to keep your head in these sorts of circumstances. There is no margin for error when you are discovered in a hotel room with your pajamas soaked with telltale stains, a broken picture behind the bed, and your mother and father standing over you, looking at you while your mother's hands are full of women's undergarments, including an extralarge lacy white bra smelling of unfortunate Europeans.

"Where did these come from, Calvin?" yelped Mom.

"Out of the hotel laundry hamper next to the, uh, kitchen," I said meekly, while trying to make it sound as if each word was being dragged unwillingly out of me.

I tugged the puff back over me. Mom wrenched it off again.

"Why did you bring these things up here?" said Mom as she shook Eva's underwear in my face.

"To . . . to . . . uh, look at them. I wanted to . . . to . . . okay I admit it! Mom, I gave in to temptation and looked at these!"

"Jesus Christ!" shouted Dad.

"Ralph!" shrieked Mom.

Dad sometimes swore, but even he almost never reverted so completely to his working-class roots that he took the Lord's name in vain. He said "God damn it" sometimes, but I had never heard him use Jesus' name that way before. I had heard him blaspheme as badly only once before, when the mission board decided to send someone that Dad hated to be a fellow worker in the vineyard, and he had appealed their decision only to have them reprimand him. That time Dad had said, "God damn Jim's moldy little ass to hell!" but even then he had left the name of our Lord and Savior out of it.

"Jesus Christ!" shouted Dad again, and then added, "the boy's been jacking off on women's underwear Elsa! Jesus!"

Then Dad walked out, having denied his Lord three times. Mom burst into tears and ran from the room clutching Eva's bra, panties, and stockings.

From somewhere down the hall, Dad called out, "Calvin, you wait! Don't move! I'll be back once we've decided what to do about you!"

Chapter 17

IN THE OLD TESTAMENT they stoned incorrigible youths to death. Dad always said how, to us, because we were Reformed Calvinists, the Old Testament was "just as relevant to our lives as the Gospel." We were not a bunch of freewheeling Pentecostals talking incessantly about the Holy Spirit, healing, and how much Jesus loved each one of us. Old Testament wrath of God was part of our lives, and yes, Jesus had died for our sins, but there was still plenty for God to be angry about, and touching your Little Thing *while* holding women's underwear was obviously at the top of the list!

I was alone in my room for more than an hour. Of course I never even thought of going out skiing. I knew without being told that the vacation was over. Obviously Mom and Dad had to work out how to punish me in some extra-big way that I feared would be far more Old Testament than New Testament. Obviously I had driven Dad not only over the edge but maybe to the very gates of Hell, or at least to the edge of madness. Real Christians never took the name of the Savior in vain, not ever.

Killing your son was illegal in Switzerland, even in the Roman Catholic part, so I felt fairly certain I would survive whatever was going to be done to me by Mom and Dad. Usually I was punished by one or the other. Sometimes Mom would turn me over to Dad for an extraspecial punishment. But I could not remember a time when I had been caught by them *both* at the same time doing something so serious they needed to go back to their room to *collaborate* on a plan for my punishment! And with Dad swearing, and with Mom so upset at both of us, who knew what the harvest would be?

Perhaps a long hard strapping with Dad's Bavarian braided leather belt, the one with the John 3:16 belt buckle—he got it as a prize in a preaching contest—would be my punishment. The most he had ever struck me before was six strokes with the belt. I wondered if a dozen or maybe twenty strokes would be appropriate. Or maybe some kind of incredible task would be set, like copying out the whole Bible or at least all of Leviticus five times.

When at last the door opened, *Mom and Eva were standing there!* I was expecting Mom and Dad. This was worse! When I saw Eva, my chest felt as if a hundred pounds of rock had suddenly been dumped on it. I assumed that somehow Mom found out what had really happened and that now whatever calculation I made about my punishment, for touching my Little Thing while holding women's underwear, was irrelevant! What awaited me now would be as close to being killed as a father and mother could do to their son without actually getting arrested by the Swiss and sent to prison.

"Calvin Dort Becker?" said Mom in a heavy, quivering voice.

"Yes, Mom?" I answered, in a tone as full of meek repentance as I could muster.

"You are going to be punished severely, but first you will apologize to Eva for stealing her most intimate garments out of the laundry and defiling them in an unspeakable manner. Perhaps the humiliation of this will teach you that what is hid will be known and that your sin will be revealed to the whole host of Heaven on That Great Day when the Lord returns. Count this as a rehearsal for the Last Judgment!"

Eva gaped at me. Her cheeks were crimson. I could smell her from where I was trapped in my bed, even though she was still well out in the hall behind Mom. I felt stuck under the puff and was getting hotter by the moment. Eva did not have any idea about what was going on or understand about Mom and the Last Judgment. Eva looked confused, and very scared. I was sure she thought that *I* had told Mom what had happened and *that* was why Mom brought her to my room!

I was having problems breathing. The Matterhorn seemed to be wavering out in the frozen wasteland beyond my window. My cheeks were hot and my feet and hands felt like refrigerated lumps of clay. If I had not been in bed I would have fallen.

"Eva," I said, "I am very sorry for taking your underwear." I paused. Eva's eyes were open so wide I could see the whites all the way around. "Mom, I don't think she knows what I'm talking about and I don't know the word for women's intimate garments in French."

Mom held out the stockings and garter belt and panties. Eva let out a startled yelp and covered her mouth with her hand when she saw them. She turned an even deeper shade of scarlet than I had ever thought was humanly possible and put out her hand to steady herself on the door post. Mom nodded approvingly at Eva's shock and gave me a see-what-you've-done-now look.

"Calvin took these out of the laundry, Eva. He took them for lewd purposes. He has given in to the worst possible kind of temptation and we as a family are sorry. Of course he will be severely punished."

"Mon Dieu!" exclaimed Eva.

"Calvin, apologize!"

"Yes, Mom. *Eva, il faut m'excuser,"* I mumbled in a raspy voice.

Mom handed Eva her undergarments. Eva was still not certain what was going on. She backed out of the doorway gulping for air and clutching her stockings, panties, and garter belt to her bosom. Then she turned and fled down the hall.

"Now, Calvin," said Mom in a sad calm voice, as she walked into my room and sat down heavily on the chair, "there are many things about this tragic incident we will be talking about over the next few years. Many, many, many things! As you know, you have defiled the Temple of the Holy Spirit."

"Yes, Mom," I whispered.

I looked at the Matterhorn.

"Look at me!" snapped Mom.

I looked at her.

"Worst—well, I don't know if it's the worst, there is so much about all this, there *is so much* that is so awful about what you have done—you have undone all our good work over the last few years in trying to reach out to dear little Eva."

I nodded and tried to look sincerely repentant.

"Do you think she'll ever come to our church service or listen to the Gospel or visit the mission now that you have done this terrible thing?"

I sat, wishing my bed would swallow me up and sink to the center of the earth. It did not. So all I could do was try and look Mom in the eye and be as repentant as possible. Mom surveyed me dolefully and then continued.

"She is a dear, sweet, simple girl, and every time I ask her to pray with us in the morning, when she brings us our breakfast tray, she sits right down on the edge of the chair at the end of our bed and bows her little head and folds her sweet hands so prettily that it makes me think that she must have had a good Christian upbringing, or at least a praying mother at some point in her life."

Mom looked at me expectantly. I opened, then shut, my mouth several times. I could think of nothing to say.

"Eva is a Swiss Lutheran, which is not a Real Christian, but still she has always been open to the Things Of The Lord when I have witnessed to her. I showed her the Heart of Salvation last year and I'm quite certain that she was on the verge of accepting Christ as her personal Savior before I even turned to the last page and showed her that it was gold, for the streets of gold in Heaven. Her eyes lit up at the thought of eternal life and now, and now, well I had *hoped* that this vacation we would be able to lead her to the Lord! Now Eva will never listen because of what you have done! Her soul is on your head, Calvin!"

"Yes, Mom."

"What you have done is so awful, the vacation is, of course, at an end."

"Yes, Mom."

"We will catch the train down to Zermatt and then go on from there and try to get home before the last bus up the hill. I will be telling the girls what you have done. Of course I will spare them the most degrading details, which are unfit for human, let alone any young women's, ears. But they will have to know that a defilement of the most tragic sort is involved." Mom crossed her arms over her chest and shivered. She gazed at me sadly for a moment. "We are all going to have to be vigilant from now on with you, Calvin. When we get home, both the girls' undergarments and mine will have to be hidden. From now on you are never to go into your sisters' rooms unaccompanied. Do you understand? No more sneaking around!"

"Yes, Mom."

"Or my room."

"Yes, Mom."

"Calvin, how could you?"

"I don't know, Mom."

"And that horrible shout you let out. It sounded positively demonic!"

"I guess I got carried away in my defilement, Mom."

"What were you really doing, Calvin? And as God is your witness, don't you dare to lie!"

"Rolling on the underwear," I whispered.

"Oh, Calvin!"

"Rolling and shouting out and touching my Little Thing and rocking back and forth and shouting bad words," I said in a louder and more confident voice.

"Oh, Calvin!"

Mom stared at me. Her cheeks were flushed. She was beginning to breathe hard, gasping out her "Oh, Calvin's," and her eyes were bright. She was leaning forward. I could see my confession was working well.

"I gave in to the temptations of the flesh, Mom!"

"Oh, Calvin!"

"I felt some dark presence in the room. I felt as if some voice was whispering to me, 'Calvin, Calvin, defile your Temple! Come with me. The pleasures of the flesh are beckoning! Calvin, taste the . . . the . . . uh, sweet fruit of evil!'"

"Oh, *Calvin!*" wailed Mom.

"That's when I began to rock and thrash and sway and the room seemed dark and filled with smoke."

"Oh, Calvin!"

"I'm sorry!"

"How did you open yourself to this satanic attack?"

"It was the dancing, Mom!"

"You mean in the dining room?"

"Yes. You know how they all started dancing early?"

"Yes."

"Before you could get us out?"

"Yes."

"Well, I was watching."

"And?"

"It was that pounding beat, how it throbbed in me and . . . and made me want to move and sway and to . . . to . . . to *dance* with naked women and see their underwear because of the way the twins danced and moved and how the General touched them and . . . and . . . and where he put his hands and—"

"*Enough!*" Mom commanded as she leaped to her feet.

Mom raised both her arms over her head as Moses must have when he parted the Red Sea.

"*ENOUGH!*"

Mom sat back down. We sat in silence for a moment.

"Perhaps you have, at last, learned the lesson about where these things can lead. I believe that this tragedy began at home when I caught you sneaking between the sheets looking at things not meant for your eyes."

"Yes, Mom. That's the day it all began."

"Did you desire to see more intimate apparel?"

"Yes. I went down there with the idea there might be underwear in the hotel laundry. It was underwear I wanted to see, Mom. And there it was, so I took it and brought it up here so I could take a good look. And all night I prayed to be delivered of my temptation and wept before the Lord, but I could hear the band still playing and I knew they were dancing even though we had left the dining room a few minutes after they started. And I thought about how the Swedish twins moved and what they must have on, underneath. And this morning I woke up and looked and then . . . then I started to do the bad thing."

"You even broke the picture. What on earth?"

"I got carried away. I pretended I was downstairs dancing."

"Dancing with the underwear?" Mom wailed.

"Yes! I clutched it to me and danced on the bed . . . naked! I held the underwear and thought of Eva and all the other women!"

"What were you dancing to?" asked Mom between sobs. "The drums?"

"The music I heard throbbing in my head, the music that started when the band began to play just before we left the dining room."

"And you were on the bed and that's how the picture fell down?"

"Yes," I said in a meek small sorrowing voice.

"Did you feel you were full of lust?"

"That's right, lust."

"And then what happened?"

"I fell back on the bed and touched my Little Thing. That's when

I called out and at that moment you knocked on the door. And I was—"

Dad walked in. He shut the door softly behind him. Mom blew her nose and shook her head.

"Calvin has apologized to Eva," said Mom. "And he has explained how it started and what led to it. It was the music, Ralph."

"I'm sorry, Dad."

"It's time you get out of here, Elsa."

Mom stood up.

"I will be praying for you, Calvin, as you receive your punishment," said Mom tearfully.

Mom shut the door. Dad sat on the end of my bed. He looked at me. His face was blank. I tried not to look as if I was looking, but I glanced at his hands. I wanted to see if he had the belt with him. He did not.

"Calvin?"

"Yes, Dad?"

"We need to talk," he said in a flat, conversational voice.

"Yes, Dad. I told Mom how I got tempted by the music and how it led me to have thoughts I could not control and get on the slippery slope to sin and how—"

"Calvin?"

"Yes?"

"Shut up."

"Yes, Dad."

"Save your bullshit for the women."

I stared at Dad with my mouth open. For a moment I did not think I could have heard what he said correctly. He did not sound angry, just tired.

"What?"

"I said, save your bullshit for the women. I never should have allowed Elsa to be the one to talk to you about sex in the first place."

"You mean her talks about the Physical Things?"

"I said SHUT UP!"

"Okay."

"Not another word!"

I nodded.

"Now you listen to me."

I was feeling thunderstruck. Lying to Mom was easy compared to this. Dad had never talked this way before. His voice was so matter-of-fact. He was not shocked or angry. I had no idea what to do or even what lies to tell.

"Your mother is a woman. So is Rachael. Janet is, of course, Janet. She's just Janet. I am busy in the Lord's work with the young people. You are being raised by three women."

I nodded some more while feeling numb and yet trying to strategize all at once. Mom had been easy. I knew what she would say to every word I spoke. Talking to her was like pulling the string on Rachael's talking doll. But what on earth was Dad doing?

"Women are fine in their way, but they're not realistic about some things. I was an only child. At least, I didn't have sisters and my mother wasn't saved, so I pretty much found out what I found out from other boys. Do you understand?"

I nodded, though I did not understand at all.

"Boys don't call their penis a 'Little Thing.' Boys don't talk about 'unwrapping Christmas presents' or the 'woman of God's choosing before creation.' Boys don't call their balls a 'Precious Seed Sack.' "

I nodded.

"Women talk like that and they giggle when they have their period and call it 'falling off the roof.' It's as if it's all some cute secret."

I nodded.

"Well, son, we men aren't cute! Got it? Don't be cute!"

I nodded.

"Don't look so damned surprised. And shut your mouth before something flies in. You look like a fish!"

I shut my mouth. Dad winked at me. I hoped he wasn't going to turn violent. He was clearly insane and I was watching him to see what he would do next, ready at a moment's notice to spring for the door and take off down the hall.

"Women, in a way, are idiots, Calvin."

I nodded.

" 'Jack off' is a much better name for it than touching your little whatever the hell. All boys do it. And it's none of your mother's God damn business! From now on just do what you have to do in the bathroom, like everybody else, so she'll stop checking your sheets for stains! I'm sick of all this nonsense! I'm sick of Elsa coming into our room crying, saying that she's found stains on your sheets! Do you understand? One time she said she knew what they were because she'd sniffed them! *God!*"

Dad stood up, turned around, stalked out, and slammed the door.

Chapter 18

I STAYED IN MY ROOM through the morning until early in the afternoon when Dad knocked and shouted through the door, "Why aren't you skiing? Don't let that fool woman scare you! Get out and *ski!*"

I did ski, sort of. While riding the T-bar, I saw Janet and Rachael out on the piste, too. They did not respond when I waved. I figured Mom must have told them about what I had done. They would not look my way. As for Mom, she seemed to have disappeared and so had Dad. There were not many skiers on the slopes and hardly any were using our lift; most just sailed past as they skied down from Gornergrat on their way to Zermatt.

The sun was shining through a high scrim of pale gauzy cloud. The sky had a yellowy tinge to it and the mountains appeared washed out and far away. I looked down to the far end of the Zermatt Valley, and sure enough, there were heavier clouds brooding over the peaks. The weather was changing.

I hung around at the top of our lift near the one-room chalet-hut the attendant sat in next to his wood-burning stove. In front of the hut the attendant kept a deep tunnel-like path cut to the door past his neatly piled stack of firewood. All winter he cleared enough snow away so he could watch the lift-top out a small window. (His job was to hit the emergency *OFF* button if someone got the strap of their ski pole looped around the T-bar and was being dragged, or some other problem occurred like the cable coming unhooked off the pulleys.)

I skied past the hut, then, putting my skis parallel to the steep slope, climbed up the mountainside on the sharp edges, one sideways step at a time till I was at the top behind the hut. Then I skied the few feet needed to get to where the stovepipe came out of the little chalet's wall, level with the top of the snowbank.

The hot pipe poked out about six feet above the ground, rather above where the ground would be in the summer when not blanketed in eight feet of deep snow. Now the pipe emerged at my feet from the wooden wall just below the apex of the roof. It poked out through a galvanized steel plate, then bent and went up past the roof, where it was held in place by a couple of wires. There was deep snow piled on the roof of the hut and it had melted in a semicircle near the stovepipe.

The stovepipe was level with my face. The fire was burning so hot that there was very little smoke. When I looked across the top of the pipe the view of the mountains shimmered. I could tell when the attendant added a log to his fire. A shower of bright sparks shot out of the pipe, looking like a swarm of fiery bees.

I shuffled this way and that on my skis to warm my back, then my front, then my sides from the heat radiating off the pipe. Once I scooped up some snow and melted it on the pipe. When I pressed the icy chunk to the searing hot metal it hissed and squealed and I could smell scorched wool from my mitten.

Because of the stovepipe I was able to hang around the mountaintop for several hours. Only my feet began to ache with the cold. I did not have the willpower to ski. I felt blank, washed out; featureless as the snow I was trampling into flat icy mush next to the stovepipe. It was a comfort to stop thinking about what had happened or would happen and just concentrate on staying warm, melt chunks of snow, and wait for the next shower of sparks.

Gradually the high clouds thickened over the mountains. The piste began to look flat and shadowless. The clouds moved lower. The tops of the peaks disappeared as if sliced off by a knife. The wind began to blow. Loose snow started to pour across the slope in a cascade of stinging crystals that followed the contours of the mountainside. Soon the piste looked like a fast-flowing river of hazy white mist. Then the mountains disappeared altogether.

I got too cold to stay where I was and slowly skied back to the hotel, now barely visible. I was so cold I could hardly get my ski bindings unfastened. On the way inside I noticed Rachael's, Janet's, and Mom's and Dad's skis were in the rack so I knew they were inside. Everything seemed far off. I was feeling so dazed that, for a moment, I could not remember which room I was in and walked up and down one of the halls on the wrong floor.

When I came in, I had not bothered to slip on the huge slipper-like felt overshoes provided by the hotel. (They were there so you could walk to your room with your ski boots on without scuffing the floors.) I knew that if the manager's wife caught me in the hall with just my boots on she would scold me. I did not care.

I met no one on the stairs or in the halls. I sat in my room idly watching the storm while warming up under the puff. My feet stayed numb for a long time. When sensation returned I wished it had not. It felt as if someone hit my toes with a hammer. Eventually the pain changed to pins and needles and finally settled into a dull hot ache.

The snow was being driven in horizontal lines across the window. Somewhere a loose shutter was banging. There were cheery voices in the hall as the guests came inside and changed, took baths, rested in their rooms, or gathered in the lobby or dining room to play cards, drink, or talk. I stared at the white-gray blur of snowflakes flying across the window until it seemed as if my room was spinning.

Suddenly I felt desperately hungry. Then I remembered that I had missed lunch and breakfast.

Because of the storm, night fell early. By late afternoon it was so dark that the only light outside my window was coming from the wall of blowing snowflakes reflecting back a little of the glow from my bedside lamp.

One of the Italian maids knocked and walked in. She had come in to turn down the bed and shut the shutters. When I heard her knock I grabbed up my Bible and pretended to be reading. I thought Mom was at the door.

A few minutes after the maid left Dad called through the door, "Calvin, don't sit in there moping, boy, dinner in ten minutes. Be there!" His voice sounded normal, even cheerful. I jumped when he called my name. He did not open the door.

When I got to the dining room, Mom was already at table. She had changed into her evening gown as usual. She had her thick well-worn Bible with her and was reading it and furiously underlining passages with a big red pencil. Her lips were moving and I knew she was praying. I noticed that she had not bothered to put on any lipstick. I had never seen her without lipstick at the dinner table. She looked pale and did not speak to me when I sat down.

Dad walked in a few moments later. He was smiling. Rachael followed Dad. A minute later Janet walked in. The girls would not look at me and did not speak. Mom nodded to them but did not say anything until she said grace. Her prayer was unusually short. Rachael's eyes were red and puffy. Anytime I glanced in her direction they filled with tears and brimmed over. Dad studied the menu as if it was the most interesting thing he had ever seen and did not look up until Eva started serving.

Janet had not been crying. She looked darkly triumphant, as if she finally had something on me so big, so fine, that she could use it just about forever to keep me in my place.

Soon Dad was shoveling in his food. Mom looked disappointed and confused every time she looked in Dad's direction. He would not meet her eyes. From the way Mom sighed and kept glancing at me and shaking her head, it was clear she was still mightily upset and thought a lot more should have been done to me. She kept looking at Dad sorrowfully as if he had let her down, not only with me that morning, but also for having such a hearty appetite. Mom did not touch her food.

Eva crept around our table as if we were a family of ghosts and she was trying to leave food for us the way pagans left food in front of scary idols. Eva did not even issue the usual warning—*"Attention! C'est très chaud!"*—about how hot the plates were when she served us.

Halfway through the meal when Dad asked for more roast beef, Eva jumped. (There was none.) Mom took Eva's jump, her pale face, and her nervousness as a further sign of just how badly I had driven her away from the Things Of The Lord. I could tell Mom thought this because of the way she gazed at Eva, shook her head sorrowfully, then looked at me and sighed. Rachael also looked at Eva and sighed even louder than Mom did. Janet wasn't sighing. She stared at me and mouthed the words "You wait" and made a squeezing and tugging motion with her hand.

"Rachael, will you quit sniffing!" Dad barked.

When Dad broke the silence, Rachael jumped about a mile and her fork flew out of her hand. Dad had hardly said a word up to that point besides "pass the salt." He had been sitting, hunched over his plate eating, and making no effort to start any kind of conversation.

"Oh, Ralph, she's upset and understandably so!" exclaimed Mom in a petulant rush, as if the words were bottled up and she had been longing to say something, anything to reprove Dad.

"Elsa, you cut it out too. No one got killed, did they?" snapped Dad without looking up from his food. "And Janet?" he said as he fixed my sister with a hard direct stare.

"Yes, Dad?" Janet said in a quavering voice.

"If you look at Calvin one more time that way or threaten him again with all that stupid Indian wrist-burn crap, I'll give him permission to hit you back, even though you are a young woman. Understood?"

Janet opened her mouth, then shut it. Then she turned beet red.

"And I mean it!" said Dad. "Has it ever occurred to you that Calvin could beat the ever-living piss out of you if he wanted to?"

"N-no, Dad," stammered Janet, and her voice shook.

"Well, he could." Dad turned to me. "Calvin?"

"Yes, Dad?"

"If Janet touches you again, beat the ever-living piss out of her. Got it?"

"Yes, Dad," I muttered.

"Oh, Raaaalph!" moaned Mom.

"Don't 'oh, Ralph' me!" Dad glared around at the girls and Mom. He took a bite, chewed, and swallowed. "I've had it up to here with all of you *women!*"

"Yes, Ralph," said Mom meekly.

"And leave Calvin alone."

"Yes, Ralph."

"And leave *me* alone!"

"Yes, Ralph."

"Rachael, will you quit crying into your roast beef?"

"I'll t-try, Daddy," choked Rachael.

We were all dumbfounded, and not just because Dad had said "ever-living piss" and "crap." His whole demeanor and tone had changed. Dad seemed like some stranger. He did not even appear to be in a Mood. Dad was talking matter-of-factly, not angrily. He did not even look flushed or pale and no vein was pulsing, even though he was using many bad words. He just seemed like a regular sort of man, eating supper, who happened to use swears in everyday conversation.

Mom, on the other hand, turned ashen while Dad talked. She was almost as white as the concave drift of snow piling in a swirling veil of shimmering flakes against the lower corner of the windowpane next to us and lit by the cheery light streaming out of the dining room. I knew Dad sometimes talked to Mom, yelled at her, in ways we children never heard about. But the way he was talking was so strange, it made me more frightened than if he had just strapped the stuffing out of me the way I had expected him to do that morning. And judging by Mom's face he was scaring the daylights out of her too.

"Well, ladies, what are you all so upset about anyway?" asked Dad. "What's your problem with willie-whacking?"

Dad chuckled. Mom dropped her glass on the floor. Eva crept up to the table and mopped up, then tiptoed off to get another glass. Rachael whimpered and stared at her hands, which were twisting and untwisting the napkin on her lap. Janet was bright pink.

"All boys do it," said Dad with a big grin.

Rachael choked. Mom jumped up. Janet began to shake so hard, her knife and fork clattered on the plate in front of her.

"Ralph!" whispered Mom urgently. "Ralph, *stop* it!"

"Be quiet, Elsa!" shouted Dad. "And SIT DOWN!"

Mom sank back into her chair, almost flopped into it as if she were some kind of puppet and somebody had just cut her strings. Everyone in the dining room turned to stare at us. The English General smiled and held up his glass. Dad smiled back and held up his glass in return. Eva was hiding somewhere behind the bar, trying to stay out of sight.

"Boys aren't like you girls. See, you all have your plumbing hidden. Ours is right out there swinging in the wind. You can pretend you don't have anything down there at all, but that's not true. It just makes you hypocrites feel more holy, as if somehow you have a right to look down your nose at men. But a penis is a fine, stand-up sort of thing. No fakery about it! I mean we all know where we stand. Right, Calvin?"

Rachael fell off her chair and landed on the floor with a plop. It was a moment or two before she managed to climb back up with the help of Eva, who rushed across the dance floor when she fell. Meanwhile Janet was stuffing half her large white linen table napkin into her open mouth. Mom began to sway back and forth and looked as if she too was about to slide to the floor. I felt as if I was going to wet my pants, as if the world had suddenly flipped over and we were all tumbling to the ceiling.

"But I ask you girls: Who was the man after God's own heart?" Dad waited. No one spoke. "I'm talking to you, Elsa," snapped Dad, and he stopped smiling.

"King David," whispered Mom.

"Ha! And was he some kind of eunuch? Did he talk about his 'Little Thing' and his 'Precious Seeds'? No! Damn your stupid euphemisms! He charged, dick out straight into the Philistine throng, then speared himself everything in a skirt that moved! They were still bringing him virgins to warm his bed when that horny old bastard was a wrinkled geezer and lay dying! And Solomon was just like the old man. What did he have, Elsa, a thousand wives and concubines? Don't forget the concubines, Elsa! We're not talking about chopped liver!"

Dad smiled and took a long gulping drink of water. He nodded meaningfully at my sisters and grinned as if to say that he now had something really good to tell them. Mom shuddered.

"God," continued Dad, "made sex, girls. It's all in the Bible. He gave Calvin the same equipment he gave King David. All Calvin did was look up and say, 'Hey, what's this? This feels good! Hey, I'll do that again real soon!' And so what? So damned well *what?!* You want *me* to strap the boy for having a penis? And you girls, I wonder what you all get up to under those nice big thick covers? You can fool Mom but you can't fool me! Just because you don't leave anything on your sheets for this crazy woman to sniff, like some kind of nutty sex bloodhound, doesn't make you any better than Calvin!"

At the start of dinner I thought I had a problem. But by the time Dad called Mom a "sex bloodhound," my particular problem was forgotten. Clearly Dad had finally blown a fuse. Clearly Mom's worst fears that Dad would someday revert to his working-class, unsaved ways had been fully realized. Dad had obviously lost his marbles, and judging by my sister's and Mom's squealing—they started to squeal, as if they were imitating train brakes the moment Dad said "sex bloodhound"—the world might as well have just ended.

As for me, I was beginning to be truly sorry for what I started. It looked like what I did had basically ended our family. Dad was saying things that could not be explained away even by Mom, things no one ever said. Judging by their high-pitched squealing, Mom and the girls were apparently losing their minds, too.

Mom leaped to her feet.

"Children, stand up!" commanded Mom.

The girls stood unsteadily. I had a hard time getting my legs to work, so I stayed seated.

"Yes, Mom," Janet and Rachael gasped.

Everyone in the dining room was still staring at us. Dad burst into laughter, then roared, "You all sit right back down this instant!"

I said nothing. I studied the roast beef fat congealing on my plate and wished we had never come on this vacation, or that I had been born into a family of lapsed Anglicans or even agnostic Jews.

"Walk slowly out of this dining room," commanded Mom, "then go up to Janet's room. I want you to wait there. Lock the door and do not open it to anyone but me! Wait there for me."

We stared at Mom and then at Dad and then back at Mom.

"Go!" said Mom.

"And I said sit down!" bellowed Dad.

The women hesitated, then sat. At that same moment I saw the hotel manager herding the members of the band ahead of him through the door. They were pulling on their gold jackets. One had a napkin tucked into the collar of his shirt. Another had a fork in his hand and was still chewing. They did not even stop at the bar to pick up their drinks. Obviously the manager had hauled them out of the staff dining room and hustled them into our dining room to start playing dinner music earlier than usual.

"Children," said Dad calmly, "I'm free."

We all looked at Mom for instructions. She did not meet our look. For the first time in my life I felt as if something had happened to which Mom might have no answer. The band started to play. Dad looked at all of us one at a time till we met his eyes. Then we all looked away. The scariest thing was that he was smiling pleasantly.

"Did you hear what I said?" Dad asked, and smiled.

I nodded. No one else moved.

"I said, I'm free!" laughed Dad.

"Free from what, Ralph? Free from me? Free from the Lord?" asked Mom in a quavering, small voice.

"All of the above," said Dad and he smiled.

The other diners had begun to eat again once the music started. Eva sidled up to our table with a big copper serving dish full of braised endive. We all stared at our plates. She wordlessly served us more endive even though no one except Dad had eaten anything.

"Am I to understand that you have renounced your faith?" asked Mom, after Eva crept away.

"Stick a sock in it, Elsa!" Dad laughed. "I'm not 'renouncing' anything and you won't ever understand what I just said, so just stick a sock in it! And don't say things like 'am I to understand' anymore. Jeez! Who do you think you are, Winston Churchill?"Jeez! Who do you think you are, Winston Churchill?"

Mom opened her mouth, then shut it. Dad ate all his braised endive and all of Rachael's untouched beef. Then he sopped up the juices with a chunk of crusty bread. He sighed, smiled, and sat back with his arms folded over his chest.

"Ralph? Why are you being so unkind to me?" asked Mom in a quiet icy voice.

"Elsa, why should I be kind when you're already so kind to yourself?" Dad asked. "Try listening for once. If you girls aren't eating, do you mind?" Dad said as he forked Janet's untouched beef onto his plate. "Elsa's folks were real bluebloods, all right." He chewed his massive wad of beef for a moment. "But they never gave up their table manners, right, Elsa?" Dad bellowed with sudden barking laughter, wiped his mouth, and tossed his napkin into the center of the table. "Elsa was already in college, and this was back before the GI bill, when college meant something. I listened to Elsa when she told me what I needed was to grab hold of Jesus so I could be like her. Of course, Elsa already had him by the balls!"

When Mom screamed, "Satan has taken him!" the band faltered. The manager motioned to them to continue. They started up again, but kind of halfheartedly. Everyone in the dining room was staring at us.

"Satan has not taken me," Dad said calmly, and smiled.

Mom had picked up her Bible and held it up between Dad and her as if she were warding off a dog with a stick.

"Then I got 'called' to Switzerland's teeming millions by your mother's relatives, who just *happened,* by God's grace, to control the board of the mission, and we set up shop. I mean, *I* would've liked to stay in our church where I was pastor. But *noooo,* that was not the Lord's will for our lives! The Lord always told *Elsa* what his will was for *me!* It was *Elsa,* always *Elsa* who was the true high priest of our household and the Lord's work. It was *your mother* who had a direct line to God and the mission board and wrestled in prayer night and day while I just did the work, preached the sermons, and tried to learn to eat with my fork held backward like some . . ." Dad paused, then screamed, "FUCKING ENGLISHMAN!"

When Dad screamed, he had not been looking at any of us but up over our heads, as if he were talking to the tops of the windows across the dining room. Mom closed her eyes. Her nostrils were flared. Her eyelids fluttered. The girls were staring at Dad with open mouths. I was holding on to the table edge, glancing at everyone while trying not to catch anyone's eye.

When Dad had yelled out, everyone looked at us again and the piano player hit a whole string of wrong notes and even the drummer faltered. Then Dad continued talking in a conversational tone. It was a while before I began to listen again because I had a rushing sound in my ears as if there were a stream running through my brain. ". . . and I tried," Dad was saying when I tuned back in, "I really did, kids, but then something began to happen and I started to see how this woman, who had driven me nuts, was going to drive you kids nuts too.

"Well, it was already too late for my daughters." Dad glanced at my sisters, then looked back up to the window tops. "Elsa had you girls wrapped around her little finger. Then I started to watch Calvin. At first I saw Elsa and you girls were only trying to turn him into a pietistic idiot. I figured what the hell. But after that the 'Talks' started. And suddenly I realized what Elsa was trying to do was to turn Calvin into a *girl!*" Dad looked at Mom and his voice got loud and harsh. "Yes! Don't deny it! You wanted him to be a girl because women are the real leaders of the Protestant churches and have been since that bitch Carry Nation started driving men out of bars with an ax! Oh sure, you let a man preach from the pulpit, but who drags all the men to church every Sunday? Who runs the show? Who does the preacher have to please unless he wants to get kicked out?"

Mom's eyes flew open. She stared at Dad. She looked more than angry. She looked at Dad as if she hated him. Dad stared right back at her, steady and unwavering. Then Mom's eyes narrowed to slits. Her mouth pulled into a thin, tight line as if there were strings sewn into her cheeks pulling her mouth taut. Then she looked away.

Eva floated in with the dessert. No one even glanced at her. She floated away. Dad was still talking. Mom shut her eyes again.

"This morning Elsa happens to be in the hall and thinks she hears 'something going on' in Calvin's room and comes running into our room yelling about Calvin 'defiling his Temple' because she hears a 'strange horrible banging on the wall.' So we kick down Calvin's door and sure enough he's been taking his monkey for a walk and Elsa has kittens." Dad paused. "Well, something finally snapped, Elsa. You've ruined my life, but you sure as hell are not going to turn Calvin into a simpering fool! You've got the girls! Calvin is mine! Do you hear me? And from now on you, Elsa, are to damn well do what I say. Elsa, get up and dance with me. If you don't, I promise you, you can kiss this marriage good-bye and I'll take Calvin with me back to the States and become an engineer the way Mother wanted me to before you ruined my life. Dance with me *now!*"

The whole time Dad had been talking I expected Mom to leave the table or argue back. She had mostly sat as still as if she were carved of marble. When Dad finished, Mom sat for another long moment without moving a muscle or looking up, then she opened her eyes and spoke.

"Ralph," said Mom quietly, "I shall never dance with you or anyone else. I will not be party to setting that sort of example for my children!"

Mom stood and took a step away from the table. The girls tried to stand.

"Janet dances with Sergio!" I blurted out.

They all stared. Dad laughed. Mom looked from Janet to me and back again. Rachael's eyes welled over.

"Janet," said Dad, "so you have a soul after all."

Dad laughed some more. The band began to play another number.

"Is this true?" asked Mom.

"Yes, Mom," whispered Janet.

"Well, Janet, since you're a dancer, how about you dance with your old man, or do you just dance with Italian cooks?" Dad asked, and he stepped around the table and grabbed Janet by the wrist.

Dad led Janet out onto the parquet floor in front of the band. There was nothing Janet could do. For a moment Mom, Rachael, and I stared at them. Then Mom stalked out of the dining room. Rachael followed her on wobbly legs. I sat rooted to my chair. Janet and Dad danced; rather Dad did, sort of. Janet shuffled miserably around after him clutching on to Dad as if she was about to fall.

Chapter 19

WHEN I WENT TO BED after the horrible dinner, I did not fall asleep for several hours. Mom hadn't come in to pray with me, let alone read out loud. As I lay awake tossing this way and that I could faintly hear the sound of Dad shouting at Mom. Once she screamed back. Hours later I heard the manager's voice telling them to be quiet. By then I felt as if I was out in the storm floating on the wind, racing with the snow over the mountains.

No one believed me when I told them Jesus killed Mom. I would have just lied to Dad, told him whatever he expected to hear. But with Jesus having killed Mom, it was different. I could not lie. I knew God killed a lot of people in the Bible, and in a way killed each one of us when he took us home to be with him. But I did not know he *killed* you, not killed you dead directly and personally with the tip of his index finger after crashing through your bedroom ceiling.

"How do you know it was Jesus?" screamed Janet.

"I know, that's all," I said.

"What did he look like?" Rachael whimpered.

"Like Jesus," I said.

"But we don't know what Jesus looks like, no one does!" shouted Janet.

"I do. He looks exactly like he's supposed to," I said.

"I'd like to kill *you*, Calvin!" yelled Janet.

"Go ahead. I'm not afraid of you, I have seen the Lord!"

"Calvin!" screamed Janet, and then she rushed me.

"Guess who's just arrived?" Rachael said.

"Who?" I asked.

"Eva," said Rachael.

"Eva?"

I could hear her stockings rubbing where Eva's thick thighs rolled together like big pieces of dough. Eva's face had changed. It still looked like her but only in the middle, as if she were pushing her face through a balloon.

"You're *so* fat!" I exclaimed.

I heard a tearing sound and Jesus stepped through the wall, right through Rachael's Bible-quiz blue ribbons, and tapped Eva on the shoulder. She turned, fell to her knees, and started to boil. Eva boiled as if she were a pot of water, only without the pot, just clear see-through water shaped like Eva. The room filled with steam.

Jesus turned to me.

"Fat is mostly unfortunate European water," said Jesus.

Eva rolled over and heaved up to her knees. Her clothes hung loosely from her pencil-thin body. Then she fell sideways and lay still.

Jesus nervously puffed on his cigar. My bed poured over the edge. I could see through the wall, out past the Dents du Midi, past the forest, past the earth's atmosphere where the sky turned black, past the stars that poured in streaks like shreds of foam on the glassy inside curve of a huge breaking wave.

"Boo!" said Jesus.

Dad lifted his arm as if to ward off a blow, staggered, and almost fell. Jesus steadied him.

"I'm going to give you a sign, Ralph," said Jesus.

Dad nodded. Jesus puffed on his cigar till the tip looked like the inside of a glass blower's furnace. The room filled with smoke. Dad coughed.

Jesus grabbed Dad's hands and held them apart. Then Jesus bent down with his cigar clamped between his teeth and touched the glowing tip to the palm of one of Dad's hands, then the other. Dad let out a terrible howl each time the cigar touched him. The cigar burned its way right through each palm and poked out the other side in a shower of sparks and ash, just as if the cigar were a red-hot poker being shoved through a sheet of newspaper. Dad was crying.

"Hurts, doesn't it?" Jesus chuckled. "But luckily for you, Ralphy, I can say, *Ralph Becker be healed!*"

The holes in Dad's hands stopped burning and the wounds closed up with a swirl and a click, just like the iris of a camera.

"Oh!" Dad groaned.

"Better?" asked Jesus as he let Dad's hands go.

"Yes," whispered Dad.

"I can't hear you!" Jesus roared.

"Yes, sir!" Dad shouted.

"I can't hear you!" shouted Jesus, and the mountains quivered and all the pine trees on our hillside fell down.

"Yes, sir!" Dad yelled at the top of his lungs.

"Better," chuckled Jesus. "You'll bleed for forty days and forty nights."

It took only one drop of Dad's blood oozing from the wounds in his hands to heal them. The recently blind ran around in traffic, dodging cars so people could see that they could see. Everyone was flexing muscles that had been all shriveled up moments before. The patients grabbed everything they had: money, watches, jewelry, skis, fur coats, whatever, and threw it at Dad's feet to show their gratitude. Those coming to Dad for healing who wore a brace or prosthetic limb screamed in pain as their new limb expanded out into the brace and filled it in one instant.

"This is it?" asked Dad in a quivering voice.

"Cheer up, Ralph!" said Jesus. "We all gotta go sometime, Ralphy!"

Jesus laughed and reached out to kill Dad with the tip of his finger.

"Wait!" I shouted. "Can't I say good-bye to Dad first?"

"Come away in the name of Jesus!" said Jesus, in a strange high tone that sounded like Mom's voice. "Oh, Calvin, come away!"

Mom stood hovering over my bed. I could not see the expression on her face. It was wrapped in such deep shadow that she looked as if she was hooded in black. I could smell Mom's breath clearly enough though. It reeked of anxiety, was stale as the stench of asparagus pee. It was her breath that convinced me that I was awake.

I woke up with a jolt, opened my eyes, and saw Mom standing over me. She was moaning something over and over. I was so surprised that Jesus smoked cigars that, for a moment, I did not pay attention to what Mom was saying.

The room was cold. I turned my head away from Mom's breath and could smell the icy, faintly tangy scent of fresh snow. As Mom came into focus, and images of Jesus puffing his cigar slowly faded, I realized that Mom was begging me to leave with her. This seemed as strange as the dream and I shut, then opened, my eyes several times trying to figure out if I was awake or not.

My shutters were tightly shut. I did not know if it was day. The only light was coming from the bulb out in the hall.

Dad shuffled into my room as Mom was begging me to "come away in the name of Jesus" for the tenth time or so. He stood at the open door and told Mom to leave me alone. Dad's voice was tired. Janet and Rachael were with him. Mom and Rachael were dressed in their ski clothes. Dad was in his pajamas. Janet wore her long red flannel nightgown.

Mom just kept moaning, "Oh, Calvin, come away with me in the name of Jesus, come away." Rachael was in tears and seemed to be hiding behind Dad. Janet stood at the door next to him and the hall light illuminated her face in profile. She turned. Our eyes met and, incredibly, Janet gave me the faintest of sweet smiles. Everyone seemed to be a lot more awake than me. Mom and Dad must have woken the girls first, then came to me.

"Choose Ye this day whom Ye shall serve, me or that nut," said Dad.

The way Dad paraphrased the Bible verse sounded like some sort of bitter joke, but he was not smiling. His voice was dull and angry.

"Children, come away with me!" Mom begged in a high-pitched wail, all the while still looking down at me.

"I'm staying with you, Dad," Janet whispered.

Mom burst into tears.

"I abjure and implore you in the name of Jesus to come with me!" sobbed Mom as she spun around to face the others.

Janet would not look at Mom, and turned away. Dad pivoted on his heel and stamped back down the hall, his slippers making a slapping sound on the linoleum. Janet hesitated, then followed him.

"Then we aren't sisters anymore!" Rachael sobbed after Janet.

"Rachael, you're as nutty as your mother!" Dad called back from somewhere down the hall.

I heard a door slam. Mom knelt by my bed and tugged on my pajama sleeve. Rachael was crying.

I wanted to crawl back into my dream. Mom's breath was making me feel sick. I had liked the smell of Jesus' cigar.

Chapter 20

I DO NOT KNOW WHY I stayed. Maybe it was because I was starting to see things more Dad's way than Mom's.

Mom and Rachael took the first train to Zermatt. It was the return trip of the train that brought up the fresh rolls, bread, and milk before dawn. By then all the talking was done. It was just before sunrise. Mom and Rachael left in silence.

I had gotten dressed, but not in my ski clothes. Dad was still in his pajamas. No one looked at anyone else. There were no other guests up yet. Rachael had huddled against Mom. Mom had bent her head toward Rachael and did not look at the rest of us as we stood in the semi-dark in the lobby while waiting for the assistant Italian maids to fetch the sled for Mom's luggage.

The big shock—besides being woken up at four in the morning by Mom—was the fact that had Janet stayed with Dad and me! Either Janet wanted to dance or something in her snapped like it had with Dad.

It was low season, so even though our reservations were used up our rooms were still available. After Mom left with Rachael—their luggage piled on the big sled pulled up to the station through the fresh snow by the two Italian assistant maids, who had been rousted out of bed by the manager's bemused and sullen wife—Janet, Dad, and I each went our own ways. As Rachael was walking out the door she turned to me and gave me a hug and whispered, "Oh, Calvin!" Her cheeks were wet with tears. That was it. Mom did not say a word.

"It's been a rough night. I'm going up to take a good long nap. See you kids later," said Dad, after a somewhat embarrassed silence.

Dad went up to his room. Janet hugged me, then, without a word, went to her room too. I sat in the lobby alone. Had the world ended?

With a sudden jolt of excitement I realized that it was breakfast time! Our family might be ended, maybe even the world was ended, but Eva would be bringing the trays to the rooms at any moment! I ran back upstairs and my spirits began to rise.

As I flew up the old stone steps I was thinking that with Mom gone there was the band and Sergio for Janet and Eva for me. Now Dad could eat any old way he wanted to.

When Eva knocked on my door I was back in bed with my pajamas on. Eva set the tray on my dresser, then flung open the shutters with a smack. There was fresh snow on the Matterhorn. The sky was gray with high clouds. The room filled with frigid air. Eva shut the window and turned.

"You are departing today also?" asked Eva.

She was smiling. My heart was racing. My Little Thing was so hard, it ached and seemed to be tugging me out of bed, as if it wanted to jump on Eva all by itself. This time I wanted to feel something besides pain when Eva got on top of me!

I was alone with Eva! It was a fine morning! There were warm rolls on my dresser and a charming round little waitress would soon remove her clothes next to my bed! My mother was gone! Dad was sleeping in his room! My older sister had suddenly and inexplicably become nice! Soon I would ski down the dazzling diamond carpet of fresh snow after Eva rolled on me! Maybe later still Dad and I would take the Schwarzsee cable car and do our father-son day out after all!

"No," I answered, "I'm staying a few more days."

I smiled at Eva and waited for her to lock the door.

"*Votre maman*, she has gone now? Zey telling me thees *dans la cuisine*."

"Yes, my mother and my sister Rachael have left."

"Et puis votre papa?"

"We're staying on. Only Mom and Rachael left."

"Pourquoi?"

There was no quick answer as to why Mom and Rachael left. So I threw the eiderdown aside. Eva smiled and shook her head no. She reached out and tugged the big white puff back over me. I frowned.

"Eva, come sit down," I said, and I patted the bed next to me.

"Non, I do not weesh. Eef your fasser, he come een and I will lose my working at *l'hotel."*

"Mom's gone and Dad's in his room asleep. Everything's changed. Mom's gone. Now we can—"

"What ees eet changing?" asked Eva, and her brow furrowed.

"Come sit with me and I'll tell you."

Eva sat down on the edge of my chair. Sadly, her knees were tight together. I patted the bed again. She shook her head and smiled. Eva was looking determined, even stubborn. Her little pink mouth was set in a pout. I sighed and decided that I would have to explain things before Eva would oblige. But how to explain? I sighed again.

Should I start by telling Eva about the China Inland Mission and Mom's parents? Should I start with Dad meeting Mom and accepting the Lord? Should I just tell Eva about what had happened since Mom caught me with Eva's underwear?

"Et bien?" Eva asked, and tapped her foot. "Why your fasser, he shouting last night?"

"Eva, have you ever noticed that my family is kind of religious?" I asked.

"Yes, I have seen zees theeng. Een zee keetchen we call you zee 'leettle popes.' "

Eva giggled.

"Well, we're not Catholics."

"Excuse?"

"The point is, something has happened to us. You know about being born-again, accepting Jesus as your personal Savior?"

"Votre maman, she already speaking zees many times each year you are coming. I do not know why I must do zees theeng."

"No," I laughed. *"I'm* not witnessing to you! I'm just trying to explain what happened to Dad."

"Oui?" Eva said, while looking more and more puzzled.

I sighed. How could I ever explain my family?

"It was just an example. When you get born-again and accept Jesus as your personal Savior you change from lost to saved, from light to dark, from the Old Man to the New Man."

"Yes. Eet ees as your mother, she has explained zees many times weeth zee strange book een zee shape of zee heart, not so many pages *seulement les couleurs."*

"Oh, she must have shown you the Heart of Salvation."

"Oui!" Eva giggled. "Eet was zee book in the shape of . . ."

Eva traced a large heart shape in the air with her two stubby index fingers and smiled.

"Well," I said, "the Heart of Salvation shows how it works. The first page is black with sin, then there's the red page for Jesus' blood, then the white page for your heart once it's washed in the precious blood, then a green page for, I forget what the green page is for, but last there's a gold page for Heaven and the streets of gold where everyone who's born-again will go."

"Calvin, why are you tell me thees also?"

"The point is, when you become a Christian you change instantly."

"Oui?"

"Well, I just found out it can go the other way too!"

"Comment?"

"You can get lost-again in an instant too!"

"Excuse?"

"For instance, there was Connie."

"Who ees zees?"

"Connie. She was an opera singer. Then she came to L'arche, our mission, and got saved. And the second she got saved all her worldly desires for fame and opera evaporated and she wanted to stay and become a missionary with us and learn to lead others to Christ instead of singing songs about depraved Italians and all that other stuff. Do you see? I'm talking about how people change, only now it worked the other way with Dad. That's what I'm getting at. He's lost-again. Do you see?"

Eva pursed her lips and her brow wrinkled.

"The point is, you change instantly," I said, and sighed. "Now won't you come sit next to me and . . ."

"Non! First you must telling me why zey go!"

I felt a kind of sinking feeling in my chest. Why couldn't she understand? Eva was sitting there frowning at me while I was trying to explain something I did not even want to be talking about. I wanted Eva to stop looking so worried and just take off her clothes!

"See, it's the same with alcoholics," I added in a rush. "We don't get many of them at our mission but Mom reads me stories about other missions, where they get fewer students and more alcoholics. One minute they're a hopeless drunk lying facedown in a Chicago gutter, stained with sin deep within, and the next minute they're in the mission eating soup and singing 'The Old Rugged Cross' and crying and accepting Jesus while their desire for alcohol just melts away as the Holy Spirit does work in them, and they learn to play the piano and lead others to the Lord. Do you understand? *Change* is what we're talking about. Only Dad changed, but it went the other way. See?"

Eva stopped frowning and gave me a long silent look I did not understand. I wondered if I had said something wrong, because all of a sudden she seemed so serious and sad. There were tears in her big blue eyes.

Eva started to cry. I sat bolt upright in my bed as if I had suddenly been shocked by a live wire. This was all going very badly! *Why on earth was Eva crying?!* What had I said to make her so upset?

"What? No, I didn't mean that!" I said. "Eva, stop crying!"

"Eet ees so sad to remembering!" Eva said, and started to cry harder and harder.

I leaned forward and tugged at the hem of Eva's skirt till she stepped over and sat next to me. Then I put my arm around her plump shoulders to comfort her.

"My fasser, he dreenk *le vin et puis le Pernod* every night *dans le café.* He beating *Maman* and me also *comme ça.*" Eva made a punching motion with her fist. *"Tout les nuits!"*

Eva cried for a good long while. When her shoulders stopped heaving up and down, and all she was doing was sniffing, I tried to get things back on track.

"Eva, I'm sorry! Forget it! I just wanted to explain how Dad has gone and gotten himself lost-again. He's unaccepted Jesus. Could you please take off your clothes now?"

Eva shook her head no. She frowned. Apparently more explaining would have to be done if there was to be any hope of getting this breakfast to a happy ending.

"He's converted to Satan or something. He's thrown off the New Man and put back on the Old Man, just like Connie left opera. *That's* what I was saying. I was just talking about the Heart of Salvation and all that as an *illustration* of how people can suddenly change!"

Eva tugged a lacy handkerchief out of the sleeve of her fluffy white sweater and blew her nose.

"I do not understanding."

I tried to touch Eva's breast. She batted my hand away. I sighed.

"Explaining to me!" commanded Eva.

"Mom got disgusted at Dad's backsliding and left. She said she wouldn't be in the same building with him until Dad repents and comes back to the Lord. Janet and I stayed with him. I don't know why. I mean I know why I did, because you're here, but not why she did. But see, Eva, Dad says he does not love Jesus anymore."

"But your fasser, he ees zee priest, no?"

"Yes, he's a minister of the Gospel. And, by the way, we Real Christians do not use the word 'priest.' We are Reformed, Protestant Presbyterian, not Catholics."

"I am not understanding."

I put my hand on Eva's lap. Eva pushed it away.

"Weell be deevorcing?"

"No, not divorce . . . She left Dad to think about his sin and repent. Dad has done the unforgivable sin, I think. Now *please* take off your sweater!"

"But my fasser, he ees steell dreenking and my poor *maman* . . ." said Eva, starting to cry again.

"Eva, I'm sorry about them but . . ."

I held her close. Eva tugged away from me and stared at me angrily through teary eyes.

"*Non!* I do not weesh! My poor *maman!*"

Eva started to cry harder.

"I should never have told you about the drunks getting born-again," I muttered sadly. "I didn't know your father had that problem. I didn't mean to bring him up. I'm very sorry."

"My fasser, he dreenk, then he beat me and my poor *maman*. She say no and he beat her again. That ees why I am somebody so weecked, Calvin! He touch me *like thees!*"

Eva motioned with her hand to her breasts and to her most private place.

"You understanding?"

"But they're not here now, Eva. It's just me!" I said in the most cheerful voice I could.

It was no use. Eva's face was all puckered up and her eyes were full of tears. Her little chin was quivering.

"*Non!* You! You *man!* You are all zee same theeng! You are like my fasser! You are *dirty!*"

"*What?!*" I exclaimed.

"You are always wanting to see, to *toucher tout ça!*"

"Eva! But it was you who . . ."

Eva jumped up and stood over me, looking down angrily.

"Non! Votre maman she ees correct! I will find *Jésus! Jésus* will wash me as een zee strange book she show in red, in zee heart! White like zee snow! Yes! I weel asking *Jésus* to come into my heart as *votre maman* has say to me many times I must do!" Eva sighed a long end-of-crying kind of shuddering sigh. "Calvin, telling me how to change my heart from *noir* to *blanche!*"

This was worse than the nightmare about Jesus. Eva sat on the chair and waited.

"Are you crazy?" I asked. "I just told you Dad has *reverted* to his working-class background and thrown Jesus *out* of his heart! And I've stayed with him and so has Janet. *I* can't lead you to the Lord!"

My voice was starting to shake and had gone up to a sort of squeak. I swallowed hard a couple of times.

"*I'm* not the person you should talk to if you want to ask Jesus to be your personal savior! You should've asked Mom or Rachael before they left!"

"But, Calvin, I have been very kind to you, *non?*"

Eva looked at me. Her eyes were wide.

"Yes, I guess you have," I muttered, and looked away.

I pulled the puff cover off. Eva pulled it back into place.

"How many time young boy, they have zees opportunity?"

"Not much I guess," I mumbled.

"I am asking you ees seemple small theeng and you are refusing when I have let you *toucher mes tétines?*"

"Look, I just meant that I was never the one who was very good at witnessing. You should have asked Rachael. That's all."

"Calvin, please you are telling me zees!" Eva said in a begging voice.

I sighed deeply several times.

"You want to know the Sinner's Prayer and get born again?" I asked with a rising sense of hopelessness.

"Oui! Zee story of the drunken *en* Chicago. Eet touched me *ici!*"

Eva pointed to her heart. I got a very sad feeling. I had brought this on myself. It was my stupid story that got Eva interested in the Things Of The Lord by mistake! Now Eva wanted to accept Jesus! It seemed as if Mom's witnessing had borne fruit on the very morning when Mom stormed out of the hotel. Either that, or this just proved once and for all that God's Irresistible Grace is truly irresistible!

"Eva?" I said with a tremor in my voice.

"*Oui?*"

"How about we . . . you know, one more time, *then* I'll lead you to the Lord?"

Eva stared at me angrily.

"*Non!* Telling me zee words to saying. Your mosser, she telling me but I forgetting."

"At least show me your breasts first!" I said sternly. "*Then* I'll tell you how to be saved."

"*Non!*"

". . . Please?" I asked in a sad voice.

"*Non!*"

I sighed.

"Okay. Pray after me."

"*Comment?*"

"Say what I say. Would you like to kneel?"

"Excuse?"

"Forget it. Just say after me, 'Dear heavenly Father.' "

"Dear heavenly Fasser."

"I come to you to ask for you to forgive my sins."

"I come to you to ask for you to forgeeving of my seens."

"I'm a sinner in need of salvation and you're the Lord, the creator, and have come to save me by being nailed to a cross and dying and, on the third day, being raised again from the dead. I ask you to wash my heart clean as snow and write my name in the Book of Life. In Jesus' precious name, Amen! There! That'll do, it I guess."

Eva opened her eyes after she finished her prayer. I sighed.

"How do you feel?" I muttered.

Eva smiled.

"Well?" I asked.

"Très bien!"

"I was afraid of that. Is there a kind of bubbling up, a kind of inexplicable joy?" I asked dejectedly, all the while feeling sadder and sadder.

"Excuse?"

"Do you feel rivers of living water rising up in you?" I said in a hollow voice.

"Oui!" exclaimed Eva, loud and happy.

"Are you filled with unspeakable joy and peace?" I muttered.

"Mais oui!"

"Have you been healed of all your bitter thoughts and sad memories? Are they but a distant shadow now laid away like lavender in a bottom drawer, a sweet sorrowful memory, nothing more?"

"Excuse?"

"Do you feel better about the things your dad did and all?"

"Bien sûr! Now I weell going 'ome and tell my fasser of *Jésus* also!"

"Oh, boy," I muttered.

"Excuse?"

"Never mind," I said, and took a breath or two. "Eva?"

"Oui?"

"Do you have a Bible, so you can grow in the Word?"

"Non."

"Well, you might as well, to do it right." I sighed in despair. "Take mine. It's right there."

Eva's face lit up in a big happy smile. I reached out to the bedside table and handed her my big black King James.

"Calvin, you are doing zees for me?"

"Yes. Take it. I won't need it anymore. I'm sick of the whole thing."

"Merci infiniment, Calvin!" said Eva, and she gave me a quick shy kiss on the cheek, grabbed my Bible, and hurried out.

Mom would have said Eva's face was shining with the inner light of peace and joy.

Chapter 21

WITH EVA SAVED there was nothing left to do except ski. My testicles were feeling fine now, but that did not cheer me up. What was the use?

The weather had changed. The sky remained overcast. The temperature dropped. When it snowed, the flakes were small and dry and drove into my eyes in a stinging mist. I could see only the bottom half of the Matterhorn. The top was shrouded. The other mountains ringing the valley had disappeared.

The ride up the Riffelberg T-bar drained all the heat from my body, while the light flakes of snow stuck to my wool hat and clung to my eyelashes till my face was numb. I could not help but wonder if this change in the weather had something to do with Mom leaving. When saying grace at table she always prayed for good skiing weather, explaining to God, as she always did, that as his servants we needed rest from the "labors in Thy vineyard" and so to please "give us the mercies of glorious weather that we might enjoy the full bounty of Thy glorious creation."

The piste looked flat, featureless as a white sheet. When I hit a bump the first I would know of it was when my knees buckled and my body was jarred so hard I would almost fall. If I wore my goggles the piste looked even flatter, so I took them off.

I skied while squinting, as the snow on my lashes blurred my vision. Sometimes with the snow blowing in my face I would think I was skiing when I was actually standing still. Other times I thought I was standing still when I was moving.

With the exception of Eva, everyone was avoiding Dad, Janet, and me even more than usual. The other guests all knew about what had happened. Most of them must have overheard the final night's fight and they certainly must have wondered what all the noise was at four A.M. the day Mom stormed out. Even the English General would not look in my direction and busied himself with the menu when I glanced at him.

Dad stayed in his room. For some reason the Italian maids still set our table for five, as if they expected Mom and Rachael to come back. Janet and I sat at our usual places. This put us at opposite ends of the table. We ate but did not talk much.

Dad stayed hunkered down for two days and nights. At lunch and dinner Eva took him a tray. At night Janet danced with Sergio. I could not watch her for long. She did not look happy. It was embarrassing to see her plodding around the dance floor looking depressed. I sat alone like some kind of orphan.

The second night after dinner, I huddled at the bar with my back to the dance floor and answered Eva's questions about God. She was the only person in the hotel speaking to me and all she would talk about was God! I felt as if I had been condemned! Mom was gone, Janet was dancing, and yet the Lord's hand remained heavy upon me, as if I were some sort of Old Testament prophet who was running from God only to be cast into the deep like Jonah.

"I weell serve *le Général son Baba au Rum,* zen I am asking you a question," said Eva with an eager happy smile.

"Fine," I muttered miserably.

"Your seester, she ees a good dancer, *non?*"

"I don't think so."

"Your fasser, he ees still *malade dans sa tête?*"

"I don't know if he's crazy. He's in his room. I haven't seen him all day. I haven't seen him at all."

"I weell taking heem a nice soup."

When Eva got back from taking Dad his soup—it was the same consommé with tiny slivers of carrot we had all been served—she started right in with a kind of Bible quiz. I sighed.

"Jésus, he ees zee son of God, non?"

I nodded and wished I had not given Eva my Bible. Apparently she was reading it cover-to-cover and could read English well enough to ask a lot of questions.

"And he ees also zee one who ees making everyssing, *non?*"

I nodded.

"Zen why ees he making us to do the *les méchantes choses,* so he ees having to die?"

I thought about not answering her and just bolting from the room. Maybe, I thought, this is how old people feel, sick of everything. Maybe Mom is on her knees praying against me this very moment! What was this? We weren't still on vacation but we weren't at home either. I didn't know what sort of days these were. I sighed.

"I don't know. It's kind of complicated, but the main point is, it's all our fault and not God's. He let us choose between good and evil and we chose evil."

"Comment?"

"But if he made it so we couldn't choose, then we'd be animals and then what would be the point?"

"Excusing?"

"He knew we would sin, but he let us sin anyway so he could save those he had chosen from before creation to save."

"Oui?"

Eva's mouth was open and she was staring at me with blank incomprehension. I began to fiddle disconsolately with a couple of beer coasters. One of the band members sidled up to the bar. Eva filled his glass with something that looked like water and smelled like licorice. Then she added a splash of water and the drink turned milky. The band member, a small bald man with dark skin and acne scars, winked at me, smirked at Eva, lit a fresh cigarette, clamped it between uneven teeth, and turned back to the band. As he walked away I noticed he had a rip in his gold jacket and the lining was hanging down.

"Please?" asked Eva. "You are continuing?"

"He does what he wants, Eva. It might seem complicated to us but it's not. It's simple to him and he has his reasons." I thought for a minute, tried to make the coaster stand on edge, then muttered, "And sacrifice is important."

"Comment?"

The band started playing loudly. Eva was leaning over the bar. Her brow furrowed with concentration. She cupped a palm to her ear and leaned toward me.

"Please repeating!" shouted Eva.

"Sacrifice!" I yelled. *"Through the Old Testament things get sacrificed as the picture of the Lamb of God—that's Jesus—who'll get killed for us all so we can come back to him again and be the ones he chose before he made us to be the lost in order to get saved!"*

"Je ne comprends pas!" Eva bellowed.

There was a break in the music. The last of Eva's shouted words hung out in the air. Some heads turned. Then the band started to play a slow number with a lot of wire brush on the drums and breathy sax. Sergio clutched Janet close. Her face was beet red and she was wobbling with the strain of trying to dance and lean away from the cook's limpetlike body at the same time. I shuddered and turned hastily back to Eva.

"All the rest are Vessels of Wrath created for the purpose of being damned so God can pour out his wrath on them. See?"

"Non."

"God is angry!"

"Pourquoi?"

"I guess he knew we'd do bad things and it put him in a Mood before he even created us. How would you like to be God and be able to do anything and somehow wind up creating people who do things you don't like, when you tried to make everything so nice, and yet, because you're God, you knew that they would fall all along? I mean maybe he feels stuck or something. You know, like when you order off the menu but later you'd rather have what somebody else got but it's too late and you just have to eat it but aren't happy about it?"

Eva was looking confused. I made a what-can-I-say-don't-blame-me gesture, a combined shrug and outstretch of my hands palms up. (I had learned this gesture from the Italians when we were on vacation in Portofino.)

"I do not understanding."

I made the gesture again. Eva looked worried and disappointed. I felt sorry for her. I wanted to add something to cheer her up.

"God's also merciful. At least he's merciful to his chosen," I said. "So you'll be fine because you said the Sinner's Prayer."

Eva pursed her little pink lips into their tightest rosebud pucker and watched the dancers for a moment. She shook her head bemusedly.

"How are we knowing who ees zee chosen?"

"Ah, *that's* the problem! Mom says we elect know we're the elect because we have a 'desire for the Things of the Lord,' which you do, Eva, because you're asking all this stuff. So don't worry."

Eva shivered. The band began to play some kind of folksy polka dance number that included an accordion the drummer pulled out of an old suitcase. When the accordion came out the whole German family got up to dance. The Germans organized everyone into a circle and made them link arms. Everybody's face was shiny and red and there was a lot of unfortunate European aroma floating around. Janet got stuck between the English General and Sergio. They seemed to be having a contest to see who could bump and rub up against her more vigorously.

"Teach me zee songs of *Jésus*," Eva said, right out of the blue.

I sighed. Eva's hunger for the Things Of The Lord was so intense and so persistent, it reminded me of something out of one of the missionary stories Mom read to me about how some little Chinese boy wanted to learn about God so badly, he walked through the Gobi Desert because he found one page of the Gospel of John and wanted to read the rest.

When the Lord drew somebody to himself, as he was doing to Eva, he sure got a tight grip! One look at Eva's bright eager eyes let me know she sure was "on fire for the Lord," as Mom would say. I sighed again.

"Okay, but I'm not going to sing loud, so you have to lean close. I'll teach you 'Jesus Loves Me, This I Know.' How about that?"

"Jésus love bees?"

I laughed and shook my head no.

"It's 'Jesus Loves Me, This I Know'!"

I sang it as best I could in spite of the accordion polka music. The band played. The guests danced. Janet ran out of the dining room after the General felt her bottom a second time with his withered old hand. Eva and I settled down at the bar and sang children's hymns, the ones I knew by heart.

I kept feeling stranger and stranger in the pit of my stomach, as if my guts were in the spin cycle in Mom's washing machine. I almost had to admit to myself that Mom was right about how empty "fleeting worldly pleasures" turn out to be. Here I was free to listen to godless music, even free to dance if I wanted to, and yet I wasn't enjoying myself at all.

Chapter 22

NOW THAT EVA was saved, all she did was leave the breakfast tray and tell me how much she loved Jesus. I even think she was wearing a longer waitress skirt and looser sweater. The situation was hopeless.

The third morning after Mom left I could hear Eva coming up the hall singing "Jesus Loves Me" in her thick accent. *"Jésus* loves me, zees I know, for zee Beeble tell mee zo. Leetle ones to eem belong, zey arrrre weak but Eee ees strrrong. Yes *Jésus* loves meee, yes, *Jésus* loves meee . . ." And so forth. My heart sank. There would be no breasts for breakfast, no rolling on top of me, not even a kiss!

Eva set the tray down on my lap and flashed me a cheery smile. As she opened the shutters—it was still overcast and snowing lightly and the mountains were completely hidden—she quoted some Bible verse, from Mark, I think. " 'And zay sought to lay hold of Heem, but feared zee multeetude, for zay knew He ad spoken zee parrrable against zem.' " Eva smiled, then added, " 'Eef he sanctifies hees field from ze Year of Jubilee, according to your valuation eet shall stand.' "

I was almost done with breakfast and eating the last bites of a roll and butter curl while pondering Eva and the Bible. I was trying to figure out how she was selecting verses to memorize. Eva was learning just any old verse with no rhyme or reason. And she was quoting verses no one ever paid attention to.

John, 3:16: "For God so loved the world . . ." *that* was the sort of thing you were *supposed* to quote when you got saved, along with the nicer parts of the Psalms, not stuff like, "If he sanctifies his field from the Year of Jubilee, according to your valuation it shall stand."

That particular verse was from Leviticus, chapter twenty-seven. I recognized it because I happened to learn it as a punishment the week before we started our vacation. (I had let some mice loose in the girls' dormitory over at Andy Keegan's chalet.) But you didn't quote such stuff, not under ordinary circumstances.

Mom always said that if a Bible washed up on a desert island, it had "everything in it the natives need to be saved, presuming the poor dears could read." She said we "need no manmade traditions like the Greek Orthodox, we need only the Bible, not liturgical mumbo-jumbo." Mom often said, "I thank God every day for *Sola Scriptura!*"

Seeing how Eva was just learning any old thing, and quoting it, made me wonder if Mom was right. How was Eva supposed to know the difference in importance between how to mark out boundaries of your fields if you were a Jew living three thousand years ago, and the way of salvation? Say Eva thought she had to do all the stuff in the Bible and started to stone to death youths who disobeyed their parents? What then?

"Dad wants us to come to his room," said Janet in a small, frightened voice.

I looked up and stared at her absently. Janet was standing in my doorway. She must have opened the door quietly, because I did not notice her till she spoke.

"Janet, have you ever wondered who decided what was supposed to be in the Bible and what got left out? If our faith is based only on the Bible, like Mom says, then what did the Early Church believe in, you know, *before* the Gospels and Epistles got written? And if there were no Real Christians *before* the New Testament got written, then who was Paul writing to in his Epistles?"

Janet stared at me. Then she stepped over to the bed and grabbed me by my shoulders.

"Will you pay attention? I said Dad wants us to come to his room, *now!*" she said, and gave me a couple of shakes, till the dishes on the tray on my lap rattled.

"What does he want?" I asked.

"I don't know. You'd better come," she said. "He sent me a message by Eva when she brought my tray."

I got up and followed my sister. She looked worried. I was in my pajamas. Janet was dressed in ski pants and a huge sweater.

"You look Norwegian in that sweater," I said.

"If Dad becomes violent, you dive for his legs while I jump on him. Then I'll hold him down and you run and get Sergio to help."

"Help with what?" I asked.

"I told him Dad's had a nervous breakdown and that we're staying here while he is in convalescence."

"Is he?"

"Is who what?"

"Is Dad having a nervous breakdown?" I asked.

"He's having something. I don't know what you call this. I wish I had gone with Mom while I had the chance!"

We stopped halfway down the hall and were talking in whispers a few doors from Dad's room. Suddenly Janet reached out and hugged me.

"I love you," said Janet.

"I, uh, love you too," I said, feeling mighty surprised.

"If this is good-bye, then I am sorry for everything I did. I have been an awful sister."

"Oh, you're not that bad. What do you mean 'if this is good-bye'?"

Janet hugged me tighter but did not answer. Most of the guests were still in their rooms asleep. You could tell because they had not yet collected their ski boots and other shoes from the little orange rubber mats that sat next to each door, where we guests put out our shoes and ski boots to be polished.

"Does Sergio polish our boots?" I asked.

"What?" asked Janet distractedly. *"What?!"*

"Does he do the shoes?"

"He's the cook," whispered Janet, all the while still hugging me.

"But Dad said in small hotels, you know, everyone does everything. Like Eva serving breakfast trays and doing the bar."

Janet let go and took a step back. She stared at me.

"Cooking is a high profession. Cooks have dignity, Calvin. A cook is not just some waitress."

"Janet, shouldn't we go see Dad?"

Janet looked at her watch.

"It's still a little early. He said eight. It's only ten till."

"Then why are we standing in the hall whispering?"

"I want to listen awhile before we go in, just in case."

"Listen to what?"

"Shhh! To banging or yelling or incoherent raging. Maybe we should get a butcher knife from the kitchen, the big one Sergio uses to cut chops. He's strong, you know."

"Dad?"

"No, Sergio."

We stood in silence for a moment. From far off and floating up the staff stairs I could hear Eva's voice singing "This Little Light of Mine."

"What on earth's that?" whispered Janet.

"Janet, do you want to know something interesting?"

"What?"

"I led Eva to the Lord. She's singing hymns now."

"Calvin, why do you choose a time like this to tell stupid lies?" said Janet, and she glared at me.

I found Janet's glare comforting. Anything familiar was reassuring.

"It's perfectly true. She prayed the Sinner's Prayer. I guess Mom was right about that after all, about having church in the dining room all those years." I grinned. "Maybe you should ask Sergio if he wants to be saved, too, so he won't pinch your bottom."

Janet glared at me. Her face flushed.

"Calvin, I'd pound you into a spot of quivering jelly right here in the hall if it wasn't for the fact it would wake the guests. I know you're lying. You never witness to anyone."

"You just said you loved me."

Then Janet surprised me again. She smiled and her eyes filled with tears. I shivered. Janet's eyes *never* filled with tears! Everything seemed so upside down! I would have welcomed an Indian wrist-burn if it meant we could get everything back on track.

"Janet, you know you're being a lot nicer to me than you have for a long while."

"Maybe," said Janet in a sad voice.

"I did lead her to the Lord. Though it was kind of in a roundabout way—kind of, you know, backward."

Janet smiled. There were still tears in her eyes.

"So are we Real Christians anymore or not?" Janet asked.

"I don't know what we are. I guess Mom and Rachael are but I don't know about Dad. What about you?"

Janet looked at her watch. She took a deep breath.

"Time to go, and don't say anything stupid. Dive for his legs at the slightest provocation. They say lunatics have insane strength!"

Janet opened the door to Dad's room.

Chapter 23

"DAD?" WHISPERED JANET after she tapped on the door and opened it a little.

"Come in," said Dad in a quiet voice.

He did not sound enraged. Janet and I exchanged relieved glances and took a couple of deep breaths. We had not seen Dad for three days. He was sitting up in his bed. He was unshaven. The room smelled of stale tea bags. In fact, there were old tea bags sitting in a saucer on Dad's bedside table. They were dry and as shriveled-looking as long-dead mice forgotten in some trap under the refrigerator. Dad's breakfast dishes were on the dresser. The shutters were shut, and judging by the thick cheesy air, had been shut the whole time Dad was cloistered in his room.

The room smelled faintly of urine, too. I was sure that Dad had been peeing in the sink. I glanced at the sink. Sure enough, I could see some telltale yellowy dried splashes on the rim.

Pieces of paper and stationery from the desk (with the name of the hotel on each sheet) were scattered everywhere. It looked as if Dad had used up all the paper in the room. Everything was scribbled on in his scrawling, jagged, pointy handwriting. Even the little square pieces of paper that hung over each hotel bedroom sink (for wiping razors on); even the little waxy envelopes with the blue cross on them that sat on the glass shelf over the sinks (for women to put used pads in); even the envelopes from the dressing table, all the stationery, and the wrapping paper used to line the chest of drawers: all these different pieces of paper had writing all over them and were spread around the bed!

As my eyes adjusted to the dim light I saw that Dad's big old black fountain pen had leaked. His fingers were inky. There was a blotch of ink on the bridge of his nose. I noticed an empty ink bottle on the nightstand with the cap off. There was a smear of ink on Dad's pajama front. Janet and I exchanged a nervous glance.

"What have you been, uh, writing?" I asked.

"I'm in the middle of a very important course of study," said Dad. He pointed to all the pieces of paper. "Do you have more paper in your rooms? I've run out."

"I can go down to the front desk and get some when the manager wakes up," I said.

Dad grinned.

"You think I've gone crazy, don't you?"

"No, Dad," whispered Janet.

"I have not," Dad said with a chuckle, and smiled broadly. "I have finally come to my senses. I now know that I was confused before; what I'd dimly suspected is now clear to me."

"What's that, Dad?" I asked.

"That your mother's the Antichrist," said Dad calmly.

Janet choked and nudged me and took a step back toward the door. I could tell she wanted me to start thinking about springing for Dad's legs. But he was in bed, so the idea seemed silly.

"S-she is?" I asked in a voice that cracked and quavered a little.

"Not literally!" Dad chuckled.

"Oh," said Janet.

"I speak in parables, children."

"Oh," said Janet.

"Stop looking so worried. A man and woman need a little distance to take stock of each other from time to time. That's all. Everything will work out fine."

"Oh," I said. "So we're going home to see Mom soon?"

"And by 'work out' I don't mean go home. I don't ever want to see the mission again. I mean we will all survive somehow."

Janet nudged me again.

"You two will just have to relax," said Dad.

Dad pointed to the foot of his bed. Janet and I took two steps and sat gingerly on the edge, as far from Dad as we could get. Papers slid to the floor. Janet surreptitiously squeezed my hand.

"I have studied all night and found that I do not believe in the Word of God any longer."

Janet gasped.

"My mother was right to warn me. Elsa *is* a 'pansy-ass fake,' just like Mother said."

Janet and I held hands and braced for the attack. That Dad had gone completely nuts, snapped in the worst possible way, was clear.

"You both look so surprised," said Dad, and he stared hard at our faces, then burst out laughing. "You know, the question is, can you be saved?"

"But, Dad," whispered Janet, "I thought you just said . . ."

Dad barked with laughter. I jumped.

"Not saved from *sin!* Saved from being completely ruined by Elsa, saved from that nonsense we've been cramming your heads with! I've thrown away my life on the Wizard of Oz and now I'm trying to get back to Kansas!"

Dad roared with laughter. Janet was clutching my hand. My heart was pounding.

"I want to live! Do you realize how many women there are in the world, Calvin?"

I opened my mouth to try and speak but nothing came out, so I shut it again.

"Calvin, did you know before I fell in with bad company I was a regular sort of guy?"

I shook my head no.

"Well, I was! I was a *regular guy!* When I got up in the morning I never said, 'let's pray about what the Lord would have us do today,' I just said, 'good morning' like everybody else. Then she came along!"

Dad tapped his teeth with his pen. The nib made a click, click sound. Otherwise the darkened little room was quiet, except for the faint far-off cry of ravens.

"Like some starstruck kid! Look, I was just a jerk who fell off a fish delivery wagon. Your mother looked like some kind of goddess. I *could* sell fish, though! Did you know that?"

"Yes. Mom has told me all about your humble beginnings," I said.

"I bet she did!

Dad fell silent. His face suddenly got stormy-looking.

"Bitch!"

Then Dad's face cleared. He grinned. Then he frowned. Watching the expressions change on Dad's face was like watching the clouds scudding over the mountains on a windy day. One minute everything was dark and stormy, the next moment the sun came out and the mountains would light up and seem to shine.

"Back then, the fanciest thing I had ever seen was the Atlantic City boardwalk. So here comes your mom with those little hands holding that well-worn Bible and . . ." Dad's face went from smiling to brooding and back. "I would listen to my mother complain because Dad hadn't gotten her one of those new clothes ringers she wanted. So she would scream at Dad and I would think about all those nice tea sandwiches and the classical music at your mother's house and reading aloud . . ."

Dad fell silent and he stared at the window.

"Dad, would you like me to open your shutters?" I asked.

He said nothing, so I got up and opened the window and pushed back the shutters and fastened them. Dad gazed out the window and blinked at the light, as if he had never seen the view before. I followed his gaze and watched the ravens wheeling in the vast open space between our hotel and the Matterhorn, or rather the place where I knew the mountain was, since the sky was so overcast she was nowhere to be seen.

"Which line would you rather be in, Calvin?" asked Dad with a sigh.

"What line, Dad?"

"Especially if this very pretty girl, the one with the narrow waist, was at the head of one line saying, 'Jesus loves you and has a wonderful plan for your life and if you believe in him, *I'll* be part of that plan, Ralph!' and my-hank-of-hair-and-a-bone old mom was at the head of the other saying, 'Ralphy, you brazen brat! You get your skinny ass down ta the cellar an' fix my wringer or I'll take-a-belt-ta-ya!' "

Dad picked up a sheaf of inky papers. He carefully shuffled them for a moment, turning them this way and that till he had them arranged. The he began to read what he had written out loud.

" 'Every belief is religious in nature,' " Dad read off the back of a sanitary-napkin-disposal envelope. " 'We take everything we are told on faith. Words are the way we humans try to capture the essence of things. Everything is belief, everything is longing for meaning. Unbelievers, believers in so-called rational inquiry as opposed to religion, are deluding themselves when they speak of "facts versus faith." What they mean by "facts" are merely the words they use to describe the parts of existence they come in contact with.' "

Dad peered over the top of the paper at us. His hands were trembling. The edge of the sanitary-napkin disposal-envelope shook. Dad cleared his throat.

" 'All we know for certain,' " Dad continued reading " 'is that there is something there rather than nothing. We live knowing that in the grand scheme of things, if there is a grand scheme, all inquiry may well be futile. The big rule is, we know nothing. The smaller rule is we will act as if we do know something so that we can function.' "

Dad turned over the sanitary-napkin-disposal envelope and began to read from the side with the blue cross printed on it.

" 'Once we surrender to this lesser rule, and begin to live within the framework of the second and lesser rule, we can say we "know" things as long as we do not really claim to KNOW them. We can speak of Shakespeare's being a "better writer" than, say, P. G. Wodehouse. We can speak of standards and say that the *New York Times* is the "paper of record" and not have that statement appear farcical. It is, of course, only the "paper of record" in the sense that we accept our ability to communicate some meaning, even though overall meaning, if there is any, is unknowable.' "

Dad shuffled his scraps of paper until he found what he wanted. He started to read again, pausing now and then to decipher his own nearly illegible scribble.

" 'This is religion: Trust in the experiences of others communicated to us in human words. We have a—' " Dad peered intently at the paper—" '. . . a *hierarchy* of values. The second, lesser reality of knowing is one in which we have invented a whole ritual of life to give it a shape, to feel secure within ourselves. The secular Jew believes most of what he reads in the *New York Times* and the fundamentalist Christian believes most of what he reads in the Bible. Neither one can objectively "know" anything because life is too short to test all hypotheses. We trust others. We trust order. The *Times* is no more the "paper of record" than the Bible is "the truth"—no more and no less, for both describe a reality to readers who are only reading anything to begin with as a religious attempt to reach out and grasp for a sense of meaning.' "

Dad choked up. It seemed as if he was about to start to cry. He continued to read in a shaky, breaking, edge-of-tears voice.

" 'Life is beautiful and words describe something we all long for. Maybe that means something.' "

Dad looked past us, blinked away some tears, and smiled. He laid his papers aside. He stared at us for a moment.

"Now I suppose you two kids want to know what we're going to do," he said in a matter-of-fact voice.

I closed my mouth with a snap. It had been dropping farther and farther open as Dad read.

"Here's a plan!" said Dad in a loud cheerful voice. "We'll ski some more! Try to pick up women! Eva's pretty cute, in a round too-many-chocolate-chips kind of way."

I shuddered.

"What's wrong, Calvin?" asked Dad. "Don't you approve?"

"Calvin says he led Eva to the Lord," whispered Janet.

"Damn! Why couldn't you leave well enough alone? And I thought she gave me a look, you know, kind of direct. Now you say she's saved? Talk about the last guy getting killed in a war! Oh well, maybe I'll give her Bible studies." Dad chuckled and winked.

I shuddered again and took Janet's hand. It was ice cold.

"Look, kids, you can just stop staring at me. Get used to it! You never met me before! This, *this* is me! The other guy was some goof. How do you do, children, m' name's Ralph Becker!"

Dad stuck out his hand. He held it out until Janet and I each reluctantly shook it.

"Janet?"

"Yes, Dad?"

"Will you go down to the front desk and see if they've got cigarettes? I want to smoke."

"Oh," whispered Janet.

"And Calvin?"

"Yes?"

"Later we'll all go skiing. We'll take the train up to Gornergrat, ski down to the other side to Sunnegga, then take the lift up to Schwarzsee and if we can even get a run in on the Schwarzsee glacier."

"It's snowing, Dad," I said.

"So? Maybe we'll stay at the Zermatterhof for the night, and catch the train back up in the morning. You can dance and try your luck, too! Swear a little from time to time if you feel like it."

"Excuse me?" I asked.

"Swear a little."

"Why?" I asked.

" 'Why'? To get rid of that goody-two-shoes taste in your mouth! That's 'why'! Try it!"

"What shall I say?" I asked.

"Say, hey, Dad, that's a goddamned good idea!"

"Okay. Hey, Dad, that's a goddamned good idea," I muttered.

Dad clapped his hands with a loud smack.

"Bravo! Your turn, Janet!"

"That's a damn good idea," whispered Janet.

"No! Say, 'hey, Dad, that's a *goddamned* good idea!' You gotta run it all together, let it roll off your tongue!"

"That's a God damn fine idea, Dad."

"No cigar! Try again."

"Do I have to?" asked Janet in a shaky voice.

I squeezed her hand to encourage her and she squeezed back.

"Hey, Dad, that's a goddamned good idea," Janet said meekly.

"By God, she's got it! Now, children, look up."

Janet and I stared at Dad, uncomprehending.

"I said look *up!*"

"Where?" asked Janet.

"At the ceiling, of course!"

We all looked up.

"What do you see?" asked Dad.

"Pine boards," I said.

"Seem pretty solid, do they?"

"Yes," I said.

"No holes? No smoke? No fire?" asked Dad.

"No," I said.

"What do *you* see, Janet?" asked Dad.

"Pine boards, same as Calvin."

"No fire?"

"No."

"You may both look at me now," said Dad.

We did.

"Now," said Dad, chuckling, "what did we learn?"

Janet and I exchanged glances. She was pale. I was feeling as frightened as my sister looked.

"That nothing happened!" shouted Dad. "We were not struck by lightning! No bolts of lightning. Nothing happened! Isn't that great?"

I nodded. Janet had stopped moving and sat frozen.

"Oh, I know what's worrying you! Don't bother about *that!* We've got all the money we need! I've got the mission checkbook *and* the building fund checkbook right here! We have plenty to go along on before anyone tries to stop us! So you don't have to be anxious, children, the Lord will provide! Maybe we'll go to Spain, even Morocco!"

I could hear Dad laughing fit to bust as Janet and I walked, hand-in-trembling-hand, down the hall.

"Our family will be like the beggars in the Milan station!" Janet said. She looked all slumped down and tired out. She shook her head sadly. "Now go away. Oh, I'm sorry, Calvin, I didn't mean that," Janet said, then sighed deeply and hugged me. "You're so young to be launched into the world penniless," she added.

She hugged me again.

"You're the oldest. *You* do something!" I said.

"Now let thy servant depart in peace," Janet said with a sigh. Then she went into her room and locked the door. Knock and plead as I would, I could not get anything useful out of her for the rest of the day.

"All I see is darkness." Janet groaned when I came back later and tried to rouse her to action. She would not come out or help come up with a plan. Once she said, "It's hopeless." Then I heard the sound of crying.

Chapter 24

IT WAS LATE AFTERNOON of the day Dad called us into his bedroom and read out loud from his papers. The hotel was so quiet, I could hear the sound of Eva's cloth squeaking on the glasses she was polishing before I even stepped into the dining room. In the distance Sergio was singing opera in his loud tenor, which Mom always called "semiprofessional," as he clattered the pots and pans. From the other side of the huge picture windows came the low hum of the ski lift motor and the tinkling rattle of the T-bar hitches bouncing over the pulleys.

I had been working on a plan to get Dad home. I did not like living at the mission, but preaching the Word was the family business and all Dad could do. Anyway, I loved my Dad and it seemed as if every blood vessel in his brain was about to up and kill him. Something had to be done. He needed a doctor.

I stepped up to the brass-edged, glossy mahogany board and breathed in the scent of lemon rind, beer, old cigarettes, and the stale grapy odor of wine leavings. I had a lot on my mind, but out of habit sniffed up the deliciously worldly bar-stink with relish. Eva turned and smiled. My heart sank.

How, I wondered, had Eva learned the born-again smile so fast? It was so different from the friendly grin she shot me back in the good old days when she brought breakfast. Now she cast her eyes downward and tilted her head slightly to the side. Eva's teeth did not show anymore when she smiled. The corners of her mouth tightened, along with her little chin; sort of flattened out into a prissy taut line but her mouth stayed shut. Eva's old toothy smile used to end in a giggle. Her new smile ended with a rueful little shake of the head. She must have picked up the smile, and the little shake of the head, from watching Mom and Rachael over the years. Either that or the Holy Spirit was working some sort of record-breaking change in Eva's life.

I heaved myself up on a bar stool. At the very instant I sat down the light turned from pale cold gray to brilliant gold. Eva's pink round face, the deep red-brown wood grain in the bar, the bottles, the dining room, and the picture windows framing the Alps were all suddenly suffused with a golden rosy glow. The sun had just pierced the clouds a moment before setting and was blasting through a slit between the cloud cover and a jagged ridge above the Zermatt Valley.

I was facing the bar, staring into the huge mirror at the reflection of the dining room and mountains, as well as at the row of brightly colored bottles. The amber, red-brown, yellow, and green liquors glowed in the sun. Long shadows cast by the dividers between the windows shot out in thick dark stripes across the honey-colored parquet dance floor. The familiar shape of the Matterhorn—only partially visible between the rent in the clouds—was crusted with fresh snow and weirdly backward in the mirror. Even the uppermost craggy cliff of her chunky square summit—so steep and windswept that usually no snow stuck there—was crusted powdery white. The rock, the snow, and the swirling clouds were all tinged a warm rosy pink. The beauty made everything seem worse. How, I thought, could everything be so lovely, so perfect, and yet our vacation and family be such a mess? I sighed.

"Eva?" I said, while staring past her into the mirror at the wispy shards of cloud peeling away from the mountain's face.

"*Oui?*" said Eva.

"Let me tell you about how nice our ministry is."

"*Bien.*"

"I'm sure you would love to go there and study the Word."

"Perhaps eet ees so."

Eva smiled her new tight little smile. I tried to smile back. What I planned to say was giving me a sinking feeling in the pit of my stomach. I decided to play for more time.

"Uh, when my parents began the work of L'arche they were alone."

"Ah, oui?"

Eva held up a bottle, then another, and another to check the contents. She replaced several that were almost empty with ones she took from the locked cupboard under the bar.

"My sisters have memories of America and the church where Dad was pastor before coming to Europe."

"You were leeving een America, *non?*"

"No. I've been here since I was little."

"Oui?"

I knew I was stalling, but I was looking for the courage to say what I planned to say. So far I just could not work up the nerve.

"Uh, a few years after God called my parents to Europe he began to bless the Work, so Mom got to buy a second chalet, one right next door. It's Mom's prayers that get answered for things like chalets."

"Ah oui?"

Eva replaced a bottle of some kind of drink called Bolls. The bottle looked as if it was made out of gray pottery. Eva started polishing glasses again.

"Yes, she's definitely the spiritual leader of our family, which is another reason that you should think of coming to L'arche soon."

"What ees eet you are doing zere each moment?"

My spirits rose a little. Eva was definitely helping to steer the conversation in the right direction.

"Well, let me see. On Monday mornings, when we all sign up on the prayer chart for our weekly day of prayer, Dad takes only half an hour of prayer time, whereas Mom puts a line through lots of one-hour boxes and goes off to wrestle before the Throne for hours and hours."

"Oui?" said Eva. She looked confused.

"Mom loves talking to God. She'll teach you how if you want."

"For zee praying to *le bon Jésus?*"

"Right, I guess he—*le bon Jésus* I mean—likes Mom because he mostly does what she tells him to do, so the work grows and the Thermometer of Blessing has thirty thousand francs marked on it in red crayon and Mom's picked out the third chalet she wants to buy because married couples have no place to stay when they come to fellowship."

"I do not understanding."

"The point is, Mom and Dad are a team. So we need to get him home in order that . . . that . . . uh, the Lord's work goeth forth."

"She ees also priest, your mosser?"

"Oh no. Mom can't preach, because the Bible says women shouldn't."

"Pourquoi?"

"Eva, the point is, we need to get Dad back home! And you need to come too."

"You are weeshing me to accompany you?"

"Yes."

"What eef I am coming shall we doing?"

"You'll love it!" I exclaimed with all the false enthusiasm I could muster. "Monday: day of prayer; Tuesday: Bible study and chores around the chalet; Wednesday: morning Bible study with Mom chores and counseling sessions—young men with Dad, young women with Mom; Thursday: group activities—hot dog roasts in the summer and Bible study and hot chocolate with marshmallows in the winter. The marshmallows come from the mission board because you Swiss don't know about them; Friday: a lecture by Dick Keegan, our fellow worker, for now anyway—Dad and he don't agree on predestination as much as they used to, so he's not really Kindred—or a lecture by Dad on Christian answers to modern questions; Saturday is our day off. And you'd like the dorms. In our chalet we have five rooms for the young people, mostly four to a room, but next door the Keegans have four rooms for the young women and two face the mountains and have only two beds, so it's almost as good as a hotel or something."

"What ees eet you are doing for zee working?"

"Our family's work is to witness to Christ!"

Eva stared at me uncomprehendingly.

"We hang around, or do something like going for a walk, but what we're really doing is waiting for a young person to open up."

"Excuse?"

"Opening up means that the young person might say something like, 'Tell me about Jesus,' or, 'Sir, what must I do to be saved?' or, 'I see the love of Christ so clearly in your family—tell me how I can have this inner peace too.' Anyway, that's the way it's supposed to work when the young people open up."

"For I 'ave ask *Jésus* to saving me weeth ees blood?"

"Exactly! Then we pull out a Bible or repeat a verse we've memorized— "For God so loved the world"—whatever, and let the Holy Spirit do his stuff. Sometimes we're the midwife at the new birth, as I was with you, and lead them in praying the Sinner's Prayer as the newfound lamb enters into the Kingdom, whatever. That's it. That's what we do."

"*Et puis* you are all doing thees *tous les jours?*"

"Sure, people get saved all the time."

"*Mais pour l'argent,* for zee money, what ees you are do?"

"We pray and the Lord provides through the gifts that people send in. And *that's* the point! See, with Dad having his stroke, things will not work out and everything will get ruined. The Lord can't provide if there's no ministry going on! Besides, if all the funds get spent on skiing and all, then . . . then . . . well, it's just going to get awful, that's all!" I took a deep breath. "Eva, what I'm trying to say is that Dad isn't well. We need to get him to Dr. Zwingli before he spends all our money and makes us beggars or his brain explodes, whichever comes first! Have you ever been to Milan station?"

"Excuse?" asked Eva, staring at me in wide-eyed confusion.

"There are beggars in Italy. We see them each year when we go on vacation to Portofino and change trains in Milan."

"Ah oui. Zee Gypsies. Zey are very naughty to *les animaux,* make zee bears dance. Zey are evil, zee Gypsies. Here een *Schweiz* such theengs are not permitted!"

"Well, my dad will turn *us* into beggars if he keeps going! I don't know how much of his brain is left or what he'll do next. The point is, Eva, you have to help me get him home where my mother can take charge of him again. He needs to have pills or shots or something till he feels better and stops acting crazy. Janet says a blood vessel has burst in my dad's head and it's flooding his brain. That's what a stroke is, Eva. The brain cells are dying by millions. Soon he'll be a dithering cretin."

"Un fou?"

"Oui, crazy."

"Ah, je comprends. 'You shall not sow your vineyard weeth different kinds of seed, lest zee yield of zee seed wheech you have sown and zee fruit of your vineyard be defiled.' "

Eva smiled beatifically. I began to feel despair. Between my chickening out and Eva's spouting any old Bible verses for no reason, I just could not seem to say what I had planned to say. Eva started to polish glasses again.

Chapter 25

BEFORE I COULD GET OUT what I had been working my way up to say to Eva, the manager's wife walked into the dining room and told her to take a tray of drinks to the Germans in the lobby. My Last Ditch Eva Plan, as I was thinking of it, was not working out very well. I had been laying the groundwork, but all Eva did was quote strange Bible verses and smile with sweet sorrow. Before she hurried off to carry the tray of schnapps to the Germans I asked Eva to lend me two francs in fifty centime pieces. Then I went to the stuffy little pay-phone cubicle in the lobby and called Mom.

I did not call my mother because I really wanted to talk to her, but because of what Dad said about the bank accounts and because of the vein pulsing in his neck, and because I had lost my resolve to say what I had been planning to say to Eva. This way, I thought, maybe Mom would come up with some idea.

As soon as Mom heard my voice she started to cry in an angry hic-cupy sort of way. She kept sobbing and saying that since I had betrayed her and stayed with Dad I was a "Judas." She said that there was nothing for us to talk about until "you cast yourself before the Mercy Seat of the Lord and repent!"

Mom's voice was shrieky and loud. I held the big black phone away from my ear for a few minutes. I put in another fifty centime piece when the phone beeped its running-out-of-money warning.

When Mom finally ran out of breath I jumped in and told her about Dad saying he had the two checkbooks with him. At the mention of the checkbooks Mom quieted right down. All I could hear was sighing and a lot of heavy breathing. I described Janet's and my meeting with Dad. Then I told Mom how worried I was that Dad was having a stroke. Then, to kind of smooth things over I told her that the reason I stayed was that I believed someone had to "keep watch over Dad for the sake of the gospel." I even put in a plug for Janet. "She's fully repentant and in her room praying for forgiveness," I said.

There was a long silence. At last Mom spoke, and when she did it was in her smallest and saddest voice.

"What makes you think it's a stroke?" Mom asked.

"He made us swear."

"Swear what?" asked Mom, and I noticed her voice was gaining in strength.

"Say bad words."

"Oh, no!" Mom exclaimed, and she sounded more like her usual confident self.

"Oh, yes," I answered grimly.

"Oh, he is such a wicked, *wicked* man!" Mom wailed. "Wicked, wicked, *wicked!*"

My spirits rose a little. It seemed as if Mom had forgiven me.

"He made us look at the ceiling, Mom."

"What?"

"He made us look at the ceiling to show us that we had not been struck by lightning and that there is no God."

"He did *that?!*" Mom gasped.

"Yes, Mom."

The phone started to beep. I put in another fifty centime piece.

"Has he lost feeling in his arms or legs?" asked Mom in a calmer voice.

"I don't know, but he sure is acting crazy, demented—like you said is a symptom."

"You have done the right thing to call me. What did he say he would do with the building fund?"

"He said he had a checkbook so we could use it to do whatever we wanted. He talked about Spain and finding . . . finding . . ."

"Finding what?"

"Never mind."

"Calvin!"

"Okay, finding women."

"Women?"

"Women."

"*What!*"

"Women and cigarettes. He wants to smoke and drink alcohol and find women, he said. He wants to teach us swear words and go on long ski trips, too. I guess the ski trip part is okay, that must come from the part of his brain that hasn't been destroyed by the stroke, right?"

"He's gone out of his mind!"

"That's what I think, Mom. And Mom, you better call the bank or something, because he's planning to ski down to Zermatt and use the checkbooks. There won't be anything left in the Thermometer of Blessing."

I heard Mom whispering something unintelligible. Then she took a couple of deep breaths.

"Calvin, you are wise beyond your years. The Lord has given you great insight. It is a gift. Now I see it was His will that you stayed behind. I'm sorry I called you a Judas Iscariot."

"Never mind, Mom, but please don't tell Dad how you found out about what he's doing, because he'll kill me."

"I expect so," Mom said.

"What should I tell Janet? What should we do?"

"Where is Janet?"

"In her room crying, like I said."

"She is a broken reed," said Mom glumly. She heaved a sigh, then in a loud rush exclaimed, "Calvin, I'm so proud of you! You seem to be the *only* one I can count on right now!"

"But what can I do? *You* need to come back and get Dad!"

"No. That's impossible. I will not give in to that man. I told him, until he repents I will not be under the same roof, and I mean it!"

"But, Mom, he's not well in his head, so it's not really his fault, is it? He needs to see the doctor."

"We cannot negotiate with unrighteousness, Calvin! No, the only thing to do is for you to tell your father you want to come home."

Mom's voice had taken on the tough tone I knew so well. If I was ever going to talk her into coming back and getting Dad, she would need to be a lot more worried. I took a deep breath and decided to go for broke.

"Mom, the Lord's hand is in all this, I think. I led Eva to the Lord."

"Oh, Calvin, that's *wonderful!*"

"She must have been listening to all those hymns and been secretly touched, in her heart."

"And you reaped the harvest!"

"Yes. But the reason I'm telling you is that Dad said he wants Eva, too, so I fear that all the harvest will be lost and Eva driven far from the Lord!"

"Wants her for what?"

"Wants her!"

"You don't mean . . ."

"Yes."

"Oh, Calvin!"

"I think you better hurry back and get him."

There was a long silence. My hopes began to rise. Mom sighed a couple of times before she spoke.

"No, I cannot. It is up to him to come to me and to cast himself on God's mercy."

"But he's having a stroke!"

"Be that as it may, there can be no forgiveness without repentance," Mom snapped.

"Then we need to get him arrested or locked up or something before he ruins everything."

"I don't think it is that simple, dear. The Swiss authorities are difficult to deal with."

"But he's gone *nuts!* You *have* to do something!"

"Oh, the filthy, *filthy* man!" Mom burst out furiously. Then, after a few loud deep shuddering breaths, she added, "Sadly, it is no longer illegal to desire to commit adultery in Switzerland. Poor John Calvin would be so shocked. I'm not even sure that fornication is against the law here any longer. And Ralph's desire to smoke and drink would not be seen as a sign of insanity. The Swiss are very lax."

"But maybe we can put something in his food to put him to sleep and get him home that way."

"That's not practical, dear. I admire your ingenuity, but the best thing for you to do is simply beg him to come home and seek my forgiveness."

The phone was beeping. I had run out of coins.

"I don't think it'll work," I said hurriedly, "but I'll try! Do something about the bank account!"

"I will be praying all night for heavenly leading. You have done the right thing by calling me. Think of yourself as a righteous Jew in the camp of the Midianites. If the Lord be for you, who can be against you! And—"

The last coin dropped. With a whirr and a click the phone went dead.

Chapter 26

I SAT IN THE PHONE BOOTH for a few minutes, pondering, and absentmindedly using the ballpoint pen that hung from a chain above the black metal rack of phone books to punch holes in the squishy yellow soundproof tiles that lined the walls. I did not feel bad about doing this. The tiles were already scrawled with numbers, train departure times, and doodles.

The Germans finished their drinks during my phone call. Their dirty glasses were still on the big round glass coffee table. Like all the other guests they had gone upstairs to change for dinner, or to wait their turn for the bathroom. Peering disconsolately through the glass panel in the booth's heavy door, I watched one of the Italian assistant maids vacuuming the lobby area.

Talking to Mom had been no use at all! One thing I knew for certain: I had to come up with something better than simply asking Dad to take us home. I sighed deeply and went to find Eva. Things were not going well.

"Eva?" I said as I walked back up to the bar.

"Oui?" said Eva.

"Did I tell you our chalet is less than two miles from the seven peaks of Les Dents du Midi?"

"Oui, c'est très joli."

"My bedroom is at the front of the chalet, so I have a great view."

"Oui?"

"Les Dents du Midi never changes her shape, but she does change her mood almost every hour."

Eva gave me a blank look. She was washing the Germans' glasses in sudsy steaming water. I swallowed hard a couple of times. I wished I had the courage to just come right out with it and quit stalling.

To myself I was saying, "Say it! SAY IT!" To Eva I was breathlessly babbling, "At night I wake up in moonlight and lie staring at the mountains and the moon and stars and the snow on Dents du Midi and listen to the chalet creek as the temperature outside falls and the beams adjust to the warm air that's inside and the cold wind on the outside. I love our chalet, the mountains, and the pine forest stretching up behind our house up to the peaks! You'll love it too! I love the woods and fields; so will you! I love the peasants' kitchens where I get to eat cabbage soup! I love the goat in Mr. Ruchet's barn! I love the sound of the cowbells in the spring as the herds make their way up to the high Alps!" I glanced around to make sure we were still alone. We were. I lowered my voice and leaned toward Eva and whispered, "You're saved, right?"

Eva nodded. She began to quote a Bible verse. I held up my hand for silence. Here goes, I thought, *HERE GOES!*

"Not now, Eva. The thing to remember is that *Jésus* is Lord!"

"*Oui.*"

"*Jésus* said give to him what he asks of you."

"Yes, eet ees een zee Bible. I have read thees thing. Eef he ask for your coat you must geev heem your cloak also."

"Yes! Good! Because *I'm* the guy he meant! *I'm* the one asking!"

"What ees eet you are weeshing, Calvin? What ees 'cloak'?"

"Listen and remember that the Bible has lots of unusual heroes, including ones like Rahab."

"*Oui? Qui est?*"

"The Lord often works in mysterious ways. Think of Jael and the tent peg. She drove it through that guy's head. This, too, was the work of the Lord, because he makes his ways manifest any way he wants to. So don't be shocked when I tell you my idea. It's a little bit more Old

Testament than New Testament but the book of Revelation is in the New Testament and *it's* weird too," I said breathlessly.

"*Oui,* I am read thees. Calvin, what ees ze mystery, Babylon zee great, zee mother of harlots and zee abomination of zee earth?"

"Mom says it's communism and Russia . . . but never mind that for now!" I took a deep breath and drew myself up to my full height on the barstool and tried to look prophetlike and wise. "*Eva?*" I thundered.

"*Oui?*" said Eva. She looked startled.

"*Eva, thus sayeth the Lord!* Go into the room of Ralph Becker and lie with him as Rahab the harlot lay with the Canaanites, Hittites, and Levites—no, not the Levites, they were the priestly tribe—but . . . but the rest. This is the Lord speaking to you, Eva, through the mouth of Calvin Dort Becker, just as I spoke through Balaam's ass and the prophets of old!"

"*Ah, oui?*" said Eva, her brow furrowed into a puzzled frown.

"As I commanded my servant Abraham to sacrifice his own son as a kind of test, and that was unusual too, and as the sons of God lay with the daughters of Noah or somebody, and then they looked upon his nakedness and all manner of things like Ruth and Naomi when she went to that other man, and then there's all the women lying with their sister's husbands to raise up their seed when somebody dies and all . . . just like that, Eva, I *command* you to go into the tent of my servant Ralph, and by tent I want you to understand I mean his hotel room, and do unto him that thing you did unto his son, Calvin, through whom I am now speaking to you, O Woman!"

I gasped for breath. Eva's eyes were wide open and she was staring. Her mouth was puckered into its tightest rosebud.

"Tell Ralph Becker that you would like to keep doing this thing unto him but will not unless he goes home to L'arche because you want to come to know the Lord better and want Bible studies. And this may not make sense to you, but I think it'll work, O My

Daughter! And you shall tell Ralph Becker that if he goeth home you shall be unto him his concubine as Solomon had a thousand wives, and King David had that young virgin put in his bed to warm him when he was old, and you'll do this in return for Monday morning Bible studies. So you shall bring him unto his dwelling and his people, and his people shall be your people! *Thus sayeth the Lord of Hosts! Amen!*"

Chapter 27

DAD WALKED INTO the dining room. There was still ink on his fingers but otherwise he seemed fine. He was dressed for dinner and looking cheerful. Dad's hair was combed and he had shaved. Other people were strolling in too. I was already seated at our table waiting for dinner and trying not to look in Eva's direction. She was at the bar. Janet was nowhere in sight.

Eva had called my idea "deesgusting." She had not liked my idea at all. She quoted that Bible verse about a dog returning to his own vomit. For once the verse was relevant, not that that made me feel any better. I was in despair.

Dad sat down at our table. My heart was pounding. My Last Ditch Eva Plan had failed, just as calling Mom had failed. There was only one thing left to do: The Final Last, Last Ditch Plan. I could feel my resolve trickling away. I steeled myself with the thought that I was saving my father's life and my parents' work, let alone the Thermometer of Blessing and our family's future. I took a deep shuddering breath.

"D-dad?" I said in a shaky voice.

"Uh-huh?" Dad said absently and without bothering to look at me.

I bit my tongue a couple of times to try and get my stammering under control. Now or never, I thought, *now or never!*

"I have s-something to tell you."

"Well, make it snappy. I'm meeting the English General for before-dinner drinks. Ah, there he is!" Dad said, and waved.

"It won't take long."

Dad turned to me and smiled. He looked happy.

"What is it?" he asked in a kindly voice.

I took another deep breath. Dad was acting so nice and reasonable that I could hardly stand to carry on. *This is for his own good,* I thought, *It's up to me to save my family! Besides, just because he is acting nice does not mean he is well.*

Dad waved to the General, who by this time was settling down on one of the bar stools.

"I want to thank you for . . . for . . . uh . . . "

"Yes?"

"For showing me there is no God!" I burst out, much louder than I intended.

Dad stopped waving to the General midwave and frowned. For the first time since he had walked in, Dad gave me his undivided attention.

"Calvin, I don't know whether there is a God or not. I never said there isn't. I'm just thinking certain things over."

"Well, I want to thank you for o-opening my eyes to . . . to . . ."

I hesitated. Now that Dad was staring at me, my Final Last, Last Ditch Plan seemed hopeless. I was wilting under Dad's gaze. What did he mean by "just thinking certain things over"? He had said he was going to get women! He said he was going to leave Mom! He was going to empty the Thermometer of Blessing! He was—for goodness' sake!—about to have a "before-dinner drink"! Dad was clearly having a stroke! There was no turning back!

"I wanted to thank you, to . . . uh, thank you for . . . f-for—"

"Calvin, I'm going over to get my drink. We can discuss theology later."

Dad smiled. He took two steps away from the table.

"I want to thank you for all the great things you can do without Jesus in your heart ruining it all!" I called after Dad.

Dad turned and stared at me. The General shouted out, "I say, old chap! Time for a bit of the life-giving, eh? What, what?"

Dad was not paying any attention to the General. He was staring at me and looking worried.

"Calvin, what are you talking about?"

Dad took two steps back to the table. He stood looking down at me.

"Oh, I d-don't know . . . just things," I muttered while staring at the tablecloth.

"I hope you're not doing anything stupid. Are you, Calvin?"

"No, just all the great things I get to do now that I've got my body back from the Holy Spirit and know it's not a temple and all, since you said the Bible's like the *New York Times* and all."

There was a long silence. I shot Dad a quick sideways glance. He was flushed. I felt a glimmer of hope. Dad passed a hand over his forehead, then rubbed it down over his face so hard that his nose flattened out then popped up as his hand passed over it. His eyes closed. Then he opened them wide and stared at me for a moment before he spoke.

"Calvin, what have you been doing?" Dad asked in a low worried voice.

I looked away from Dad's face. He looked sad. I concentrated on my over-size soup spoon. I gulped a few times. I felt bad about making Dad look so sad, when moments before he had seemed happy and carefree for the first time that I could remember. Out of the corner of my eye I saw Dad slowly sit down on the edge of his chair.

"Nothing much, just enjoying all the worldly pleasures and all that. Isn't the, uh, flesh great?" I said.

I stared at the heavy silverware and fiddled with the thick, stiffly starched tablecloth.

"Calvin, what did you just say?" Dad asked softly.

I took a deep breath. Then, with my cheeks feeling as if they were on fire, I turned and faced Dad squarely.

"I have been fornicating with Eva. It's terrific!" I gasped out.

I was glad that my voice held steady, though it did go up an octave or two from where it should have been. I forced my eyes to stay glued to Dad's. His face was turning purple. There were blotches of white on his cheeks. Dad stared at me with his mouth open.

"I say, padre!" called out the General. "Come along and have a spot! Cheers!"

The General waved his whisky glass. Dad's eyes did not even flicker toward him. I battled to keep my gaze steadily on Dad's face. There was a ringing in my ears. My heart felt as if an ice-cold steel hand was squeezing it.

"She's become my stark-naked c-concubine," I said. Then, for good measure, I gasped out, "Maybe I can get her pregnant and we can all travel together with the baby, you know, begging in stations after you've spent all our money. We'll get more money with a baby, won't we, Dad, like the Gypsies in Milan station, right?"

The white blotches on Dad's cheeks soaked up the purple and turned the same vivid dusky hue as the rest of his face. The vein in his neck was pulsing.

"Calvin! What have you done?" gasped Dad.

"You said that all the Christian stuff, you know, all the rules and all, are stupid," I blurted. "So then I thought, well, since there's no God, and I won't be struck by lightning just like Dad says and all, it'll be all right to do my animal desires to Eva. So when she suggested it, she was very helpful and took off all her clothes . . . and lay upon me!"

Dad slowly turned to stare at the bar. Of course I knew that even though, in a way, I was finally telling the truth, I was really lying, since Eva took off her clothes in my room way *before* Mom left and Dad doubted God. But my lie was for his good. How else could I get Dad home to the doctor unless I found some way to snap him out of his stroke-induced backsliding?

"She has wonderful big breasts, Dad. You ought to see them," I muttered. "She made me play with them. At first I was nervous, then later I—"

Dad lurched across the dance floor with his legs stiff as boards, as if he had forgotten how to bend his knees. I sat rooted to my seat. Some of the other guests, including the German family, were already at their tables. They were all staring. Janet walked in.

"Eva, what have you done to my boy?!" Dad roared.

Eva stopped pouring the manager's drink in midpour. The General's arm froze in mid cheery wave. Then Dad seemed to hesitate. He passed his hand over his face again.

"Excuse?" asked Eva in a high, terrified squeak.

Dad collided with the bar. Eva backed away. The bottles rattled as she pressed herself against the glass shelves in front of the mirror. Dad was leaning over the bar, thrusting his upper body and face at Eva. I could see his face in the mirror.

Dad's eyes were wide as he yelled: *"Eva, I want an answer! Have you been molesting my child?"*

"Good God, man!" roared the General. "What the blazes do you mean by this nonsense? Good God!"

"You mind your own business, you stupid Limey fart!" yelled Dad. "He's only fourteen!"

"The rotten Yank's gone off his onion at last!" the General called out to everyone in the room.

"Oh Daaaaddy!" wailed Janet.

"Absolutely mad as a hatter," said the General as he glanced around at everyone. "Look, he's positively frothing!"

"EVA, ANSWER ME! WHAT HAVE YOU DONE TO MY BOY?!"

Eva's face crumpled into a quivering pink blob. Her mouth was making all sorts of weird little shapes as it twitched and grimaced. She started to sob and talk fast all at once.

"Herr Becker, I am sorry and repenting to *Jésus!* Before I know *Jésus* as my Savior I 'ave been *très méchante fille.* Now I 'ave *le* new life of

Jésus! I change! Yes, I 'ave made thees weeth Calvin een zee morning when I bring hees *chocolat chaud complet.* I 'ave 'ad zee sexual!"

"Damn it, woman, what are you saying?" barked the General.

"Oh C-C-C-*Caaaalvin!*" sobbed Janet.

"Strumpit!" said the General, then he laughed and barked out, "You were never so friendly to me, damn you! I'll jolly well order hot chocolate m'self tomorrow! Damn the tea!"

"Mein Gott in Himmel!" said all the Germans.

Dad crashed to the dance floor with a knee-splitting thwack that made me wince. The drummer dropped his drum-tightening wrench. The German family wailed things in German. The General seemed to be swallowing his false teeth and was backing away from Dad till he stumbled over the edge of the dais and fell heavily to the floor along with one of the music stands.

"O Lord, forgive me!" Dad called out, and he looked up beseechingly to the dining room's dark rough-hewn ceiling beams, as if he saw the Lord Jesus Christ sitting astride one. "Lord, I have sowed the wind and reaped the whirlwind! Let his blood be upon my head! Count not his sins against him! Strike *my* name from the *Book of Life!* It is *I* that has led him astray! Strike *me,* Lord! Spare Calvin!"

Chapter 28

THERE WAS NO REFUGE in the peasants' kitchens or in the frosty gloom of the winter forest. The Lord and his works were not to be escaped. For three days and nights I was confined to our chalet along with Janet and Rachael. We were ordered by Mom not to venture out of our rooms except to use the bathroom. Mom had sent our young people next door to the Keegans' chalet before Janet, Dad, and I even got home. Our family was alone. Mom, looking happy and scrubbed, the way she looked when she was preparing to teach a Bible study, said, "We are in a time of family crisis, children. Your job is to stay in your rooms and pray and fast as we dedicate ourselves to wrestling before the Throne until He has made His way clear."

I did not pray. I stared listlessly at the familiar knot-and-wood-grain face-shapes in the age-darkened pine boards paneling my tiny bedroom. Throughout those awful three days and nights I was gripped by the same sickening frozen sensation I was seized by when—the summer before—Dad and I hiked up the peak of the Dents Blanches de Champéry and I was nearly killed.

On that cloudless, perfect July afternoon I had looked over the edge of the cliff and almost fallen. As I teetered on the edge I felt as if an icicle got shoved up my rectum all the way to my heart. That was how I felt while I sat in my room waiting.

The Dents Blanches de Champéry was behind and far above our chalet. She stood at the head of the Val d'Illiez, the deep narrow valley our village was nestled in. Dad and I had hiked up the steep southern slope. The northern face, a sheer merciless cliff, loomed over our village. After a sweaty five-hour climb to the summit—the pine and larch trees got shorter and scrawnier as we trudged higher, till they were no more than stunted little bushes—we stepped at last onto the open mountainside above the tree line and then began to hike up the steep windswept slope. It was strewn with house-size gray boulders. Some of the huge rocks had small patches of dirty gray snow left over from the winter nestled around their bases. I tossed slushy snowballs at Dad, and he made a few and threw them back.

When we arrived at the top I stepped gingerly to the edge of the cliff to gaze at the view. Looking south I could see into France. Range after range of mountains led up to the snow-clad peak of Mont Blanc shimmering in the far distance. To the north "our" Alps—in other words, the mountains that were part of the view from my bedroom window, from the twin peaks of the Dents de Morcles to the square-topped Grand Muveran—stood familiar as the faces of my family. With the snow melted off them I could see every crack, crag, and vein on their rugged pale-gray granite faces. In the middle distance, looking like a toy town, was our village. Far below our village, where the Val d'Illiez opened into the flat plain of the Rhône Valley, a smudge of dirty reddish brown hung above Monthey and the iron-works and chemical factories.

Dad and I had hiked up to the top of the Dents Blanches two years before. That time I was too afraid even to get close to the edge. (Looking over high places always resulted in a sick squirmy feeling in my chest and stomach.) Dad had said, "Never mind, Calvin. We'll come back some other time. There are plenty of things that scare me, too." He had given me a hug after he said it.

I was determined not to chicken out again. There was an iron rail running along the edge of the yawning abyss, to, as Dad explained, stop "nutty English tourists" from breaking their necks.

As I reached for the rusty, inch-thick iron rail the warm wind roared up the cliff face, ruffling my hair. The rail was fastened to a couple of heavy iron posts cemented into the bedrock.

I slowly pushed my face forward into the sweet-smelling warm breeze and relaxed enough to enjoy the view of the Rhône Valley miles below—distant, hazy, and opening out wide in a patchwork of yellow and green fields, orchards, roads, and small towns before it ended at the sparkling edge of Lake Geneva. I sniffed in deeply, then, cautiously and with heart pounding, peered straight down.

Six inches from where my feet were planted on the spongy carpet of grass, a thick cluster of bell-shaped, vivid purple-blue gentians stirred in the wind. An inch from the flowers was the edge and the dreadful nothingness. My stomach felt as if it were tumbling into the void.

I jerked my eyes away from the yawning chasm. Then I resolved to look down again. I had heard from Farmer Ruchet that eagles nested on the cliff, and I wanted to try and find them. I gripped the rail tightly and slowly looked a second time. I could not see the cliff wall, only the vast expanse of hazy air between me and the dark pine forest more than a thousand feet below. Clutching the rail in my clammy hands I inched my head and shoulders farther and farther out. The bolt fastening the rail to the post broke, leaving nothing between my rigid trembling body and the abyss. Paralyzing cold fire shot up my spine and through my stomach.

Dad must have lunged in silence. The next thing I knew he was hurling me to the ground. We landed so close to the brink that my arm was hanging down the cliff face and I felt the vertical wall of sun-warmed rock under my fingertips.

When Dad helped me to my feet all he said was, "Close call there, buddy." He put an arm around me and gave me a tight hug and added, "We'll have to tell somebody about that rail!" Dad laughed and squeezed my hand. "But we better not tell Mom about this or we'll never hear the end of it."

I never loved him more than at that moment.

We had taken the first train home the morning after the Hotel Riffelberg dining room cataclysm. Before we left, Dad had called Mom. I do not know what they said, only that afterward he was pale and silent. Janet said nothing either. I stared out the frosted window of the cog railway during the slow, presunrise ride down to Zermatt. I saw nothing, though I know what we must have passed, since I had seen it many times.

I was full of sickening doubts. I had succeeded in getting Dad to go home through a trick, a half-truth. I had done it for his good. Now he looked so pale and sad I was wondering if I had done something horrible. We had said almost nothing to each other ever since Dad was helped, stumbling, from the dining room by the manager. Janet and I had followed until Dad's door was closed. We waited a moment. We could hear nothing.

Then Janet and I sat in her room. She did not speak to me or even look at me, but we still huddled together until finally, many hours later, Dad knocked and said quietly through the door, "Tomorrow we go home. Pack tonight. The manager will wake you for the train." After that I went back to my room. I did not sleep. That was the last time Dad spoke until we got home.

By the time we arrived at our chalet, at about five in the afternoon, it was getting dark. Mom met us at the door. All she said was, "Go to your rooms, children," then she marched up the steep rickety stairs. Dad followed Mom with his head down. Mom did not even glance at Dad. Janet and I did not look at each other. We waited for a moment for our parents to get up the stairs, then followed them. Rachael was nowhere in sight.

There was no shouting or arguing. There were no doors slamming. The chalet was absolutely silent, except for the timbers creaking as the stars began to shine out of the velvet darkness above the pale snow-covered peaks.

Chapter 29

FOR THREE DAYS and nights I felt as if I were living in a tomb. There were no Bible studies, no prayer meetings. The young people were gone. I slept and woke at weird times, as if day and night no longer mattered. I hardly dared to leave my room, afraid of what might be happening between Mom and Dad, and at the same time sat for hours straining every nerve trying to hear some scrap of conversation that would give me some sort of clue as to what was going on.

Mom brought me a daily portion of some sort of soup. She must have made up one big pot the first day, because the soup was the same for all three days. Each noon—I knew it was noon because I could hear the bell in the village church tower ring out the hours, then chime merrily to let everyone in the village know it was lunchtime—Mom arrived with my bowl of soup. All she said was that I should keep praying. I do not remember eating the soup, though later when she collected the bowl it was always empty, so I must have. All I remember was asking Mom if Dad had seen the doctor yet. Mom did not answer me.

On the fourth day at about noon, Mom knocked. She was dressed up wearing a nice dark green knee-length skirt that hugged her slender figure, a crisp white blouse, and a soft turquoise cardigan. She looked clean, pretty, and cheerful. Dad, she said, had something to say. As I made my way to Mom and Dad's room the icy looking-over-the-cliff-while-the-handrail-gave-way feeling grew so intense, I had to reach out to the wall of the narrow hall to steady myself.

My parents' small bedroom was darkened. The only light was coming through the tulip-shaped cutouts in the wood shutters covering the two windows and the door that opened onto the top-floor balcony that ran the length of our chalet under wide eaves. In the dim winter light, the pine walls and ceiling looked gray rather than their normal dark honey color. Even the yellow linoleum appeared colorless. The heavy mahogany bed against the wall to my right and the yellow upholstered divan against the opposite wall loomed colorless and dark. Dad's favorite picture—a New England seascape he had brought over from America as a memento of my parents' honeymoon in Kennebunkport—was barely visible above the bed. The air was stale.

Rachael and Janet were standing by Mom's old chest of drawers next to the door I had just stepped through. They were shivering. The girls were wearing their flannel flowered pajamas and the matching bathrobes they got for Christmas. I was in my pajamas too and had been since the first night home.

Dad looked (and smelled) as if he had not changed or bathed since we got home. He was standing at the foot of his bed waiting for us. He was still in his travel clothes: baggy black ski pants, black-and-white checked flannel shirt, and a gray V neck sweater. His clothes were rumpled and slept-in looking. I could smell the odor—something like a whiff of burning feathers—that Dad emitted after long hikes on hot summer days. It was the same smell I had gasped in that day when we had crashed to the ground above the cliff. Dad's eyes were red and his cheeks streaked with the narrow paths his tears had cut in the grime. When he spoke, his voice sounded so flattened out and tired that I recognized it as his only because I was staring at his pale face and saw his lips moving.

"Children," croaked Dad, while not looking directly at any of us, "I have sinned, and through my sin Calvin was driven to sin."

"But God is merciful!" exclaimed Mom cheerfully.

When Mom spoke, she made me jump. She sounded so loud compared to Dad. Her tone was bright.

"Yes," said Dad quietly and sadly. "The Lord forgives those who cast themselves on His mercy."

"But still, there are serious consequences!" said Mom brightly.

"As Elsa says, there are consequences."

Dad sighed. I noticed that he did not look at Mom when he spoke, or at us, but at the wall. Mom, on the other hand, never took her eyes off him.

"As with King David," Mom said, and smiled.

"God forgave him, but the child conceived in sin died," Dad said, then sighed heavily and added, "That was the consequence . . . that never changes."

"Because the Lord doesn't break His own rules!" Mom chimed in.

Mom waited but Dad said nothing.

"We live in a cause-and-effect universe," Mom continued. "Say Ralph was to walk through that glass door onto the balcony without opening it first; I mean if the shutters were open, what would the effect be?"

"I'd be all cut," Dad said. "I turned from the Lord as Jonah did when he refused God's call on his life and would not go to Nineveh to be a missionary."

"He was cast from the ship into a raging storm!" Mom exclaimed exultantly. "*That* was the effect of *his* choice!"

"Yes," whispered Dad, "There are consequences. Now, because of the fact that I have committed the sin of Jonah . . ."

"By turning away from the Lord," Mom added, "and other sins too. You drank, Ralph, and you swore!"

Dad nodded sadly, then said, "I almost destroyed the Lord's work here at L'arche."

"When I came home alone I hardly knew what to tell the Keegans or the young people!" exclaimed Mom.

"Your mother's a brave woman," Dad mumbled. "She held things together . . . all . . . all during my time of rebellion."

"Just like Esther in the Bible," Mom chimed in.

"Yes," said Dad. "When all else failed, Esther stood alone and saved the Israelites. Your mother stood alone while I drank and swore and denied my Lord."

Then Dad started to cry. His choking sobs seemed to be pulled out of him in big bursts that made Janet, Rachel, and me jump each time he barked one out. His heavy shoulders heaved up and down. There was some groaning mixed in with the sobs. Mom was crying, too, but her crying was kind of happy-sad, the same as when someone got saved and she announced it at Bible study. She dabbed the corners of her eyes a couple of times with the lace handkerchief she was clutching.

Janet turned redder and redder but did not cry. Rachael got even paler than she was when we walked in. She started to sob and squeal so shrilly, I could barely hear her. She sounded something like the dog whistle a visiting missionary from India once demonstrated for me.

I tried not to look at anyone and wondered how all this would end. I felt as if the rail had just come away in my hand and I was staring down the cliff again. My knees were feeling watery.

"My sin of doubt and denial almost destroyed us," said Dad, as he choked back another sob. "And though I was the human agent of Calvin's sin with Eva, still, like David's child, the Lord must give and take away, for the child David conceived in sin died, though King David was spared," Dad said. Then he turned his bleary eyes on me. "Calvin?" Dad whispered.

"Y-yes, Dad?" I stammered, and hurriedly looked away.

"We have sinned," Dad whispered.

"Janet did too," Mom chimed in. "*She* chose to stay with you! She danced! This too caused Calvin to stumble!"

Janet moaned softly. But she did not say anything.

"Yes, and we'll deal with her later," murmured Dad. "But now it's Calvin's turn. Calvin?"

"Yes, Dad?"

"Do you repent?"

"Yes, I repent very much," I whispered in a shaky, barely audible voice.

"Girls!" commanded Mom. "Come here and stand with me while your father, like Abraham with Isaac, presents a sacrifice to the Lord for he that He loves He will chastise. To spare the rod is to spoil the child!"

My heart sank though I was not surprised. I knew that somewhere along the line, after all that had happened and after all the talking and prayer was done, things would end up this way, with me getting a monumental strapping, a historic strapping longer and harder than any I had ever received. But knowing this might happen did not stop my heart from thumping wildly when Mom mentioned the rod.

Dad slowly took off his braided leather belt, the one with the silver "John 3:16" buckle.

"Calvin?"

"Yes, Dad?"

"You deserve death eternal," Dad intoned in a voice so tired, so flat and miserable, that I peered intently at him to see if he was all right. Dad sounded as if he was dying.

"Yes, Dad," I said, while wondering what kind of strapping he had in mind and why Mom and the girls were still there, since Dad always punished me in private.

I stumbled and almost fell. I shut my eyes and struggled to regain my balance, to put some strength back into my buckling knees. When I opened my eyes, Dad was staring at me. The light from the tulip-shaped cutouts illumined only one side of his face. On the other side, all I could see was the glitter of tears in the eye peering at me.

Dad stepped over to where I was standing. He turned away from Mom and the girls and gave me a sad smile only I could see. Then

Dad took me by the shoulders, pulled me to his chest, and whispered, so low I am sure Mom and my sisters did not hear him, "Keep your chin up, boy." Then he pushed me back, and in a loud voice he said, "God is merciful and it is better to be judged by God than man!"

The room smelled more strongly than ever of burned feathers. In the distance the village church tower clock struck noon, then began to chime.

"Do you cast yourself upon his finished work on the cross?" Dad asked quietly.

I nodded, while wondering how long I could bear the buildup to my strapping before I rushed from the room, down the hall, then down the stairs and out the front door. A vision came into my mind of myself running barefoot down the steep snow-covered pasture below our chalet, clearing the single-strand electric cattle fences with great leaps and bounds that took me hundreds of feet farther down the mountain, as if I were flying. . . .

The silence was broken by Rachael's sniffing. The vision faded. Dad looked at me for a long moment. I held my breath.

Dad took a step toward me, then stood up straight and squared his wide shoulders. I cringed and waited for the order to bend over so the strapping could begin. Then Dad started to speak in a dry tense voice.

"God is merciful," said Dad. "He sent his Son that by his stripes we might be healed. You were led astray by my wickedness, and just as the sin of the wicked kings of Israel brought calamity upon Judah, even so for my sins the family has suffered. For the sins of the fathers have been visited upon the children. And it is written that it is better for one who causes a little one to stumble to have never been born." Dad paused and took a deep breath. "It is *I*, Calvin, who drove you into the arms of that woman!" Then Dad shouted hoarsely at the top of his lungs: *"That you may know the Lord lives and that his mercy endures forever, that you may understand that Christ took our punishment, I will take yours, Calvin!"*

With trembling hands Dad yanked off his sweater, shirt, and undershirt in one big fat roll. The girls gasped. I glanced at Rachael. Her face was drenched in tears. I looked at Janet. She was staring fixedly at one of the little tulip cutouts and trembling violently. I looked at Mom to see what she would do about this. Her face was shining like Stephen's when he beheld Jesus at the right hand of God, just before the Jews stoned Stephen and made him into the first Christian martyr.

Dad took off his pants. I shifted uneasily.

"Dad?" I whispered. "Dad, what are you doing?"

"Quiet, Calvin!" Mom hissed.

Dad pulled off his socks and, after a moment of hesitation, his boxer shorts. He stood naked at the end of his bed and made no attempt to cover his nakedness.

I was sure that Mom would, at last, do something or at least call the doctor.

"Forgive me Lord, for it is I who sinned!" Dad cried out, and then he slowly sank to his knees at the foot of his bed.

"Calvin!" Dad bellowed, and looked up at me from where he was kneeling.

I tried to answer but could not get my mouth to work.

"I will take your punishment for you," Dad said quietly. "I love you boy."

Then it started. Dad raised his arm. The belt was gripped in his hand, the buckle dangling loose and swinging in front of his thigh. He began to whip himself. Not measured strokes the way he usually strapped me—two or three tidy hits across my bottom, just enough to raise a small red welt, but all over, crazy and wild. As best as I could see through the glimmer of tears, the belt was whipping around the way I once saw an air hose whip around on a truck when the hose came unstuck.

"Please don't, Dad!" I sobbed. "Please, Daddy! *Please!*"

"Calvin! *You just be quiet!*" hissed Mom angrily. "It's a picture of Christ and his Church! This is a wonderful and beautiful thing for you to see, however hard it may be to bear! Isn't it beautiful?"

"What?" Rachael sobbed. "What's beautiful? Stop it, Daddy! Please, Daddy sto—"

Mom put her hand over Rachael's mouth so she could not keep begging Dad to stop.

Dad whipped himself all over his pale muscular body. There were small cuts on his legs wherever the buckle happened to hit.

"Please, Dad!" I cried out. *"I did it before you fell away! Punish me!"*

"Quiet!" snapped Mom. "Don't you *dare* start telling more lies!"

Dad never cried out in pain. Other than the whistle of the belt, the slap of the leather on his skin, and his heavy breathing, the furious beating was given and taken in silence.

Mom and the girls were huddled in a knot in the corner of the room clutching each other. The girls were sobbing. I collapsed back onto the divan.

At last Dad dropped the belt. He was gasping for breath as he struggled unsteadily to his feet.

"Very good, children, now you may go to your rooms," said Mom in a calm steady voice.

I tried to stand up. I could not.

"Help one another," said Mom.

Janet stepped over and tried to help me to stand. Her shaking hands were so slippery with ice-cold sweat she could not get a grip on mine.

The last thing I saw as I stumbled out of Mom and Dad's bedroom was Mom stepping over to the dresser. She was reaching for a small stainless-steel mixing bowl, the one from her Mixmaster she got as a gift from the missions board. It was filled with water.

As Mom picked up a washcloth lying next to the bowl she must have tapped it with her fingernail. I heard a soft "ping." That was when I turned to look. The dusty brown bottle of Mercurochrome disinfectant from the bathroom cupboard was sitting next to the bowl, and so was a little blue-and-yellow metal box labeled VINDEX. (It contained squares of gauze saturated with a gooey yellow antiseptic cream. "Sulfur-based," Janet once said.)

I do not know why my sisters and I went to our rooms alone. No one told us to. I suppose we could have gone to Rachael's or Janet's room, but we split up in the hall. We each went our own way, eyes staring down at the cracked yellow linoleum, without saying a word or exchanging any looks. I turned right, Janet and Rachael turned left.

The hall was frigid. I could see my breath. As I passed the tall tiled wood-burning stove, it was cold to the touch. I idly wondered if anyone was bothering to keep the coal furnace in the basement lit, and if they were not, when the pipes would freeze. I took a deep breath of the cold smoky scent that always lingered in the hall. The smell oozed from the darkened walls and low blackened ceiling. The paneling reeked from years of smoke seeping out of the stovepipe that, after two bends, ran ten feet or so up the hall till it made one final turn and disappeared into the stained cement chimney.

I heard two soft clicks as my sisters' doors shut one after the other, just before I closed mine. As I stepped into my room it hit me: there could only be one explanation for the Vindex, the bowl, and the Mercurochrome. *Mom knew!*

Chapter 30

AS THE LIGHT FADED from the sky I did not bother to turn on my bedside lamp. The snow-covered mountains turned a cold mauve color, then glimmered white and ghostly as darkness fell. Mom brought no soup that night. I did not dare to leave my room to go looking for food, though I did wonder if we were going to fast for the rest of our lives, or if the next stage of Mom's plan included starving all of us.

I felt hungry but stayed put. I took a drink of lukewarm water from my sink's big old-fashioned zinc-and-enamel hot tap (the cold tap seized up years before and was never fixed), then peed into the sink. I wanted to avoid the hall and maybe meeting Mom, my sisters, or Dad.

Other than the chalet's creaking I heard no sounds, no voices, not even footsteps. I began to tremble. I tried anything I could to stop picturing Mom's smiling face as she reached out for that washcloth. She had looked so pleased! Mom had known what Dad was going to do! *She had planned everything!*

The house was getting colder. I climbed under my puff. I remembered how sad Dad's voice sounded when he whispered to me to keep my chin up, the way he tried to comfort me, secretly, so Mom would not hear. Had he agreed to take my punishment in some sort of bargain with Mom to spare me? I pulled the lumpy puff up over my head and breathed in the musty smell of the old feathers and let the cover soak up my tears.

After I stopped crying, I popped my head out from under the warm smothering puff into the cold night air. I stared at the craggy white peaks of the Dents du Midi, which, in the moonlight looked impossibly high and absolutely deadly and forbidding as they towered into the black starlit sky. Dad had whispered to me, "Keep your chin up, boy." Was the part of him that took me on hikes, the part that sometimes swore, still there? Would Dad hold his knife and fork the way Mom wanted him to from now on?

Sometime during the middle of the night I lay on my side and touched my Little Thing while I thought about Jennifer diving off the big boulders that the cyprus trees clung to on the point between the Paraggi bay and Portofino's harbor. I pictured her long, ash-blond hair turning silver in the water as it fanned out behind her slender figure while she dove deeper and deeper into the blood-warm turquoise water. I had peered spellbound through my goggles at her receding figure. After she pushed off from the rippled silver sand on the sea floor, and shot back through twenty feet of clear water toward the surface, her bathing suit's straps slipped off her strong shoulders. I pictured her small new breasts, so pale beneath her sharp tan-line.

I had been shocked when, from one summer vacation to the next, her breasts sprouted, filling in her flat bathing suit top with soft little upstanding cones, turning my old vacation-friend from a child into an almost-woman, someone who—for a few days at the start of that holiday—I was too shy to roughhouse with. I had glimpsed Jennifer's breasts for one tantalizing instant—pale, perfect, as if carved from ivory . . .

I squeezed my eyes tight shut and, for one brief moment, conjured up Jennifer's beautifully kind laughing face, saw her as clearly as if she had been lying next to me in the dark. I pictured her hazel-green doe-eyes; wide friendly mouth; and her sharp little chin with water streaming over it; her high freckled cheekbones; and the water clinging to her long lashes glittering in the dazzling Mediterranean noonday sun, running down around her lips, dripping down her straight nose, off its soft rounded tip. . . .

She had popped to the surface, adjusted the straps of her suit, and said in her clear sensible English accent, very matter-of-factly, "Hope you got a jolly good look, boyso!" I wanted to kiss her laughing mouth so badly that my chest ached—it still ached—for her. I suddenly felt so homesick I could hardly breathe. . . .

Chapter 31

I WOKE TO THE SOUND of cheerful singing. The voices of the young people were loudly wailing my mother's favorite prayer meeting hymn, "Trust and Obey," in various thick European accents.

> Trust and Obey,
> Trust and Obey,
> For there is no other way to be happy in Jesus,
> But to trust and obey . . .

Janet always played at Mom's prayer meetings, and not so well. Her style—lots of false notes and way too much use of the pedal, which made the piano sound echoey—was very recognizable. Mrs. Keegan only played for Sunday church services. That way, she said, Janet could learn how to accompany her future missionary husband as he led whatever congregation the Lord called them to someday. Mrs. Keegan was giving Janet lessons.

Janet hit enough wrong keys so that even from way upstairs in my room I could tell she was doing a particularly bad job that morning. From the sounds of their singing, the young people were having a hard time following.

For about ten seconds it felt like any other morning. I lay, enjoying the feel of the hot sun blasting through my window, wondering why Mom had not woken me up to come downstairs to the prayer meeting. Then I wondered why, if it was Monday morning, we had not had church the day before and, for that matter, why I had forgotten to shut my shutters. Then I tried to remember why I was so incredibly hungry. That was when the beating and the mess my family was in now came flooding back.

The sunshine pouring through my window seemed to grow cold. I began to shiver just as I heard a light knock.

"Mom wants you to come down," Rachael said softly through the closed door.

"Are they down there?" I asked.

"Who?"

"Mom and Dad."

"No, just Mom and the young people."

"Where is he?"

"In their room, I think."

"What did Mom say to all of them?"

"That he's alone praying and seeking God's will for his life and that's why he's not down there."

"Is that all?"

"Yes."

"Have you seen him today?"

"No. Now hurry up, Calvin."

I heard Rachael's footsteps pitter-patter away down the hall and then the creak of the stairs.

I slowly walked halfway down the stairs to the second floor, when I remembered that I was in my pajamas and went back to my room, got dressed, washed my face, and combed my hair. There was hot water. Someone must have lit the furnace.

There were two living room doors opening into the downstairs first floor hall. One door was up at the front by the fireplace, and one at the back next to the piano. My parents had the wall between two rooms knocked out to make one big meeting room where prayer meetings and church services were held. That is why there were two doors.

When I stepped into the living room, I crept in at the door farthest down the hall and pressed myself against the wall next to the old black upright piano. Janet did not look at me, though I am sure she knew I was standing six feet from where she sat hunched over the keys. I looked for Rachael. All I could see was the back of her head by the fireplace.

Because our chalet was built on a steep mountainside the back of the bottom floor was cut into the hill and had no windows. At the front, the ground floor was level with the garden. There were five windows and one glass door on that side, all with little square glass panes, opening out to the front yard and facing the magnificent view of the Dents du Midi.

The living room was about fifteen feet wide and thirty feet long. It had a low ceiling, with beams running diagonally about two feet apart. The narrow pine boards between were set in a cross-hatch pattern running one way between one set of beams and the other way between the next, so if you looked straight up it seemed as if the ceiling was paneled with hundreds of W's. The dark brown paneling on the walls was wider than anywhere else in the house and had a deep scalloped molding that gave the living room a fancier look than our other rooms. The fireplace was made of rough-hewn gray fieldstone.

The living room was filled to capacity with twenty-five or so young people. Some were sitting on the dozen or so chairs (mostly armchairs upholstered in a burgundy flower print), and the rest sat cross-legged on the olive green throw rugs on the pine floorboards. The young people on the floor sat huddled at the front facing Mom. She was standing between them and the fireplace. The fire was burning brightly. The air was hot and stuffy.

Mom was going strong. As usual she was dressed up to be as "attractive an ambassador for the Lord as possible." She had on her best black wool suit, the one with a little jacket and matching skirt edged with red satin ribbon. I could smell her perfume from where I was standing way over next to the piano against the back wall. Her face was flushed from the heat of the fire or from excitement or both. Her cheeks were rosy and her big eyes sparkled.

Mom always looked her best when she gave a Bible study or led a prayer meeting. She seemed to shimmer. Mom often said that most missionaries made the "tragic mistake of forgetting the fact that young people do not wish to be witnessed to by unattractive ambassadors for Christ."

When Mom led Bible studies, she paced, carrying her Bible in one hand. She would wave it around when she was making a point. The young people sat with their Bibles open on their laps, crunched together on the floor to give Mom room.

Mom was certainly doing her best that morning! Her words poured forth out of her mouth in a cheery flood. The Good News gushed out of her in a tide of giggles, laughs, tears, and illustrations, all pouring forth from the loveliest smiling mouth and white teeth any Temple of the Holy Spirit ever proclaimed Christ with.

"The Lord has shown me a precious truth I just have to share with you dear, dear young people," Mom said. "But, before I do," she giggled, "I just have to share something the Lord told me this morning as I lay awake wrestling in prayer before the Throne. He said, 'Elsa.' 'Yes, Lord,' I said. 'Elsa, you've been up all night for seven nights wrestling before my Throne in prayer.' 'Yes, Lord,' I said. 'Elsa,' the Lord said, 'I will do a mighty work in your life as I did a sign to My people in the wilderness.' 'Speak, Lord,' I said. He answered, 'You are tired, Elsa, worn out by the cares of this life and with having wept and wrestled before Me for seven days and nights to see My will for your life and the Work I have given to you!' 'Yes, Lord,' I said. Then He said, 'In human terms it would be impossible for you to lead the Monday morning Bible study today.' 'Oh yes, Lord,' I said. 'But,

Elsa,' said the Lord God of Hosts, 'My strength shall be made perfect in your weakness!' 'Speak, Lord!' I answered, 'for your servant is listening.' 'Elsa,' said the Lord, 'Fear not, for I AM with Thee!' 'Oh, just give me a sign, Lord!' I cried out. And he *did!*"

Mom spun around and laughed. And the young people all bent forward eagerly. Mom waited as the silence built up and up, till everybody was just about vibrating with anticipation. She smiled and smiled and let us all wait.

"Well!" said Mom, at last, with a laugh. "The Lord told me! He said, 'Elsa, my chosen handmaiden and my favored daughter, my vessel of living waters, my very own mouthpiece in the courts of men, Elsa, my dear, darling little Elsa.' 'Yes, Lord,' I said. 'I am your very own little Elsa who gave You her heart when I was just three years old at four-twenty in the afternoon at my dear mother's knee, where she gently led me to the foot of Your Cross to introduce me to You as my Personal Savior and helped me invite You into my heart to change my life and to become my best friend!' 'Elsa,' said the Lord God of Hosts, 'Elsa, my darling child, My sign to you is that *in spite of seven days and nights of fasting and prayer in secret before me,* in spite of your *faithfulness* in weeping before Me and carrying the burden of the *whole world* in prayer before Me, alone, I AM who *I AM* and I shall give you this sign! My sign, dearest Elsa, is that *in spite* of your ceaseless selflessness'"— Mom giggled and spun around twice and waved her Bible around—" 'in spite of weeping before Me, in spite of your weariness from doing My will, I, the Lord God of Hosts, shall lift you up and you will give *the greatest Monday morning Bible study ever! That will be My sign!* ' "

Mom spun around three times, then said, "And God said to me, 'You will give the greatest Bible study you have ever given unto seventy times seven!'" Mom spun around again. " 'And you will be more beautiful than ever in spite of how tired you are!'" Mom giggled and smiled and paused and bent forward and all the young people leaned toward her. " 'For,' said the Lord my God, 'My strength shall be made perfect in you, Elsa, and you shall shine forth with My love and will speak Truth! I will hold up your hands as Aaron and Hur supported Moses' hands when he lifted them up in victory over the Amalekites!' "

Then Mom held her Bible up over her head, closed her eyes, and swaying gently back and forth, began to quote: " 'And so it was, when Moses held up his hand, Israel prevailed; and when he let down his hand, Amalek prevailed. But Moses' hands became heavy, so they took a stone and put it under him, and he sat on it. And Aaron and Hur supported his hands, one on one side, and the other on the other side, and his hands were steady until the going down of the sun. So Joshua defeated Amalek and his people with the edge of the sword.' "

Mom opened her eyes and smiled and, still holding her Bible aloft, said, "And for those of you who are young in the Lord and do not yet know your Bibles well enough, that passage is from the book of Exodus, chapter 17, verses 11 to 13, and is where we learn that as long as Moses held up his hands as a sign unto the Lord, the armies of Israel prevailed over the Amalekites!"

Mom took a breath and smiled while the young people rustled the thin paper of their Bible's pages and looked up the passage. When they all had found the verses, she said, "So the Lord spake to me, 'Get up, Elsa, and dress in your finest raiment and anoint thyself with perfume and precious oils, as Esther was anointed in the court of the King, and I will give you the words to speak as I did to my servant Esther!' "

Mom spun around and around five or six more times and laughed. She seemed about to cry for a moment. And all the young people clapped. Mom smiled and smiled. I pressed myself against the back wall and wished the wood grain would open and absorb me. Mom's carrying on always made me feel as if I had bugs crawling inside my spine.

"So," said Mom, and she held up her arms as if she were Jesus calming the storm over the waters, "And so," she cried out, *"Here I am, giving the Bible study just as the Lord said I would and it is a sign to all of us to strengthen our faith!"*

Then she burst into tears and sobbed, and the young people gathered around to comfort her and tell her how much her great Word from the Lord had just meant to them, and how honored they were just to sit at her feet.

After a few minutes Mom regained her composure, wiped her eyes, and smoothed down her skirt. Her audience seemed to be holding its breath.

"My dear, *dear* young people," Mom said, and smiled her sweetest smile.

Everyone smiled back and nodded and sat back down. Mom looked straight at me. I stopped breathing.

"Calvin has something to share, don't you, Calvin?"

I felt as if I were turning to stone. Mom could never resist using everything that happened to our family—no matter how private—to share with the young people. Everything that I ever did, every argument Mom and Dad had, every question Mom's children asked, all of it—got folded into the story of our lives, told to the young people, again and again, updated and explained, added to as proof of God's love and how he had used our family to "bring forth a demonstration of His existence to an unbelieving world."

Our story, the "L'arche Story," seemed to be just about as important as the Scriptures. Mom never tired of sharing what the "Lord was doing in our lives" and updating the latest "marvelous new chapter that the Lord is unfolding." *That* was why I was pressing myself against the back wall and wishing that the boards would absorb me, turn me into just one more weird face made of knots and wood grain, peering out!

"You—you d-don't . . . " I stammered.

Mom smiled and nodded.

"There is nothing to be ashamed of, Calvin! All have sinned and come short of the glory of God!" she said, and smiled sweetly.

"Mom . . . " I whispered pleadingly.

"Calvin, our trials and tribulations serve as a demonstration of God's love for all mankind. They are sent to us for a purpose!" said Mom, and then she smiled her most implacable smile.

All the young people turned and stared at me. Some nodded encouragingly. Others just gaped. The fire crackled. The ornately flower-painted green Neuchâtel clock was ticking loudly from where it sat on its specially carved pedestal that was fastened to the wall above the piano. I heard my own labored breathing. The icy feeling was spreading through my chest.

"Mom?" I whispered. "Do I have to?"

"Calvin, do you need a little help?" asked Mom with a light cheery laugh. "Fine," she said, "I don't mind helping out." Mom beamed at the young people. "You know, you young people come here for spiritual guidance and to deepen your walk with the Lord. And sometimes you think just because the Lord has raised our family up to act as spiritual midwives at your second birth that we Beckers are special. Well, we only *seem* special, but actually we're sinners just like you! And the Lord has had to reach into each and every one of our lives to draw us to Him just like he did with each and every one of you precious young people."

The young people had all turned back to face Mom now, though some of them glanced at me from time to time. I shifted my weight from one leg to the other. I had been standing so still while trying not to get noticed that my leg had gone to sleep. I had a terrible case of pins and needles in one foot. I glanced in Janet's direction. She would not look at me or at Mom and sat hunched over the piano, looking down at the yellowed keys. Rachael was sitting up very straight and absolutely still with her pigtails sticking out stiffly from her head. She had not turned to look at me when Mom tried to get me to share.

"Now, I was wondering why this certain thing happened while we were on vacation," said Mom. She smiled and paused. "And now I want to share this marvelous new thread that has been woven into the tapestry of our lives! You see, salvation can't be inherited! Just because someone is born into a Godly missionary family doesn't mean they've accepted Jesus as their own Personal Savior, does it? Calvin doesn't magically inherit salvation from me, even though, from the earliest age, I've loved the Lord Jesus Christ as my Personal Savior and walked close with Him, never taking my eyes off His shining face! But, you see, each and every person has to accept the Lord Jesus Christ *individually!* We don't believe baptism is magic! Baptism and communion and all the other so-called sacraments are just symbols of a greater truth. *Only a personal commitment to the Lord Jesus Christ, when you invite him into your heart, saves you!*"

Mom stopped talking and smiled. Then she turned her hot gaze on me. Everyone else in the room, except for Rachael and Janet, turned to stare at me too.

"Now, Calvin had never yet made such a commitment, had you, Calvin?" Mom asked cheerfully.

All eyes were riveted on me. I stood stock-still, trying not to breathe or twitch or meet the wide curious staring eyes. I tried to count the W's made by the cross-hatch paneling in the ceiling. I tried to look sideways, out to the mountains.

"So," said Mom with a giggle, "Calvin needed to make his very own commitment. And guess what? The Lord did a work in Calvin's life!" Mom smiled and smoothed down her skirt and studied her reflection in the window next to her, then she turned back to the young people. "The Lord chose our vacation in Zermatt as the place to reach out and touch Calvin!"

Mom waited. Everyone stared at me. At last I nodded yes. If I had not responded, they would have stared at me and waited all morning, for all I knew.

"Thank you, Lord!" said Mom. "See, the Lord can choose *anyone* and *any place* to reach out and touch us. He chose Zermatt for Calvin. Now there was a certain young woman at, well, actually up at Riffelberg, which is the modestly priced little hotel we stay at, and Calvin lusted after her in his heart, as King David lusted after Bathsheba in the matter of Uriah the Hittite. And you might ask, 'How on earth could that be the Lord allowing *that* to happen?' Well, the Lord has *bigger plans* for us than we can ever imagine! And the Lord knew all along, from before the beginning of time, that the only way to get dear little Eva, that's her name—and I'm sure she won't mind my sharing it or my telling you that she's the young woman Calvin lusted after, since it helped both her and him into the Kingdom—well, even in the middle of deep and grievous temptation, Calvin was still my son, just as the Covenant still applied to King David in the midst of his sin! And, as *my son,* Calvin has been held up, day and night, by my prayers every minute of his life! And the Lord had a great plan for his life and answered my prayers! So the Lord allowed Calvin to stumble just a teeny bit, so that the Lord could use that sad event to not only touch Eva's heart but to touch Calvin's, too! 'How?' you ask. Well, *because* Calvin was raised up by me, even in the midst of the deep waters of temptation in the Physical Area, he *longed* for Eva's salvation! Didn't you, Calvin?"

I stood, frozen. Mom waited. Everyone stared. Mom looked at me harder and harder till at last, with a great effort, I slowly nodded yes. All I could see was Mom's smiling face. It was as if I was looking down a long dark pipe. The rest of the room was a blur.

"*See?!*" exclaimed Mom. "And so, instead of acting on the impulse of the moment and giving in to his temptation, Calvin *shared the Gospel with Eva* and she got saved!"

All the young people sighed. Some clapped. Janet slumped farther over the piano keys, as if she were trying to scrunch herself into an invisible ball. Rachael's head was rigid and still facing the fireplace. She had not moved a muscle the whole time.

I felt grateful to my sisters. By not turning around, I knew they were refusing to participate in Mom's show and my humiliation. It was my sisters' way of saying they were on my side.

"Yes, is not God's timing so marvelous?" asked Mom. She paused and took a deep breath. *"It is the next chapter in the unfolding of the L'arche Story!"*

All the young people clapped. Janet and Rachael were still sitting frozen, still refusing to look at me. I saw Mom shoot them an annoyed glance.

"Well, then *another* remarkable thing happened! Ralph heard about how Eva got saved. And he was so glad for her salvation, but he was grieved that what brought her to the Lord was Calvin's inappropriate curiosity about certain Physical Things—things that would only be appropriate to even *think* about *after* marriage to a person God has chosen for each and every one of you from before the beginning of time—for Ralph wanted Calvin to be presented to his bride spotless, pure as a little lamb, like an unopened Christmas present, one where the ribbons have not even been tugged! Ralph wanted Calvin saved for that *one girl* God had chosen to be Calvin's sweet bride from before creation! *So Ralph decided that Calvin should be punished for his temptation, even though God used it to bring Eva to Himself!* So then the Lord showed me what Ralph was to do! It was to be something unusual, yet marvelously beautiful, that would demonstrate God's love to Calvin for all eternity and then, in turn, help me help you precious young people to understand *exactly* what it is Christ did on the cross for us all!"

I heard Janet's miserable sigh. By now, her knees were tucked up under her chin. Her head was almost touching the black keys. Janet's knuckles were white as she clutched the edge of the keyboard. The ringing in my ears was drowning out Mom's voice and the crackle of the logs seemed unusually loud. Rachael was rigid.

"What Ralph did was to take Calvin's punishment on himself, just as Jesus took our eternal punishment!" Mom proclaimed in a triumphant voice.

The young people gasped and leaned forward. Mom's face was

shining bright as a new moon on a clear winter night. Mom's silver necklace and bracelets tinkled as she spun around and around and smiled and smiled.

"Now, until *that very moment,* Calvin had never really understood the Word of God, had you, Calvin?" said Mom, and she held up her Bible so that everyone could see exactly what I had not understood.

I waited. Mom looked at me. I waited some more. She looked at me hard. I knew that the only way out of that room was to do what she wanted. I slowly nodded.

"So a wonderful work was done in Calvin's life when he saw Ralph chastise himself—just symbolically, you understand. Then Calvin understood the Gospel and invited Jesus into his heart, and it all happened *just yesterday while you were staying at the Keegans, after the Lord led me to send you all away for a few days!*"

The young people gasped and clapped. Some cried. Others jumped to their feet. Then they hugged me and welcomed me into the Kingdom. Janet and Rachael were the only ones in the room to not move.

Chapter 32

WE WERE IN MY BEDROOM. Mom had come to pray with me and say good night. She was still wearing her black wool suit from the morning. She must have added fresh perfume. It smelled sweet and strong.

I had been in my room all day since the Bible study, avoiding my family and the young people. Janet and Rachael left me alone. I did not see or hear Dad. In the afternoon I snuck down to the kitchen—after listening at the top of the stairs to make sure the coast was clear—and took half a loaf of crusty village bakery white bread, which I ate in my room over the sink so I could wash the crumbs away.

"But that *is* what happened, darling!" said Mom.

"It isn't," I answered.

"That's exactly what happened!" she snapped.

"No, it's not, Mom! Why make stuff up?" I snapped back.

"I do not 'make stuff up,' " said Mom, glaring at me furiously.

I glared right back at her, kept my eyes steadily on hers until she finally looked away.

"Why did you talk about me anyway? You know I hate it when you say stuff about me."

I felt so angry I was trembling and no longer cared what she did or said. Mom looked at me and the expression on her face went from glaring to surprise when I just kept staring at her and did not look away. Her face flushed.

"Calvin, everything we have is the Lord's! It *all* belongs to Him! We can't hold anything back!"

"I wish you'd just tell your own stories, Mom, and not put me in them. It wasn't true."

Mom gave me an annoyed sideways glance. I stared straight at her and she looked away. Then she turned back to me. There was a splash of red on each cheek. Her hot breath smelled like cheese rind. Mom fixed me with her angriest expression. I stared right back. Her eyes dropped.

"Calvin, do you know what the unforgivable sin is?" she asked in a furious whisper, while she stared down at her hands.

"No."

Mom looked back up at me.

"Blasphemy against the Holy Spirit!" she whispered. "God has done a great and marvelous work in your life!"

When I laughed, the splashes of red on Mom's cheeks spread over her whole face till it was red as a tomato. I was laughing at Mom before I knew I was. I heard my own voice laughing. It made a strange scary sound in that little room, more like choking than anything else.

"To deny what I'm saying is to deny the Holy Spirit! Be very careful, Calvin!" yelled Mom. *"You came to know the Lord yesterday while Ralph took your punishment!"*

Mom grabbed me by my shoulders and began to shake me. I grasped her little wrists and held her arms away from me so she could not touch me. She tried to pull away but I held on and suddenly realized how weak Mom was and how strong my hands were. I felt her tense up and try to yank away from me.

"I could see it on your face!" shrieked Mom, as she struggled to pull loose from my grip. "I could see what was happening in your heart even though you didn't say anything! NOW LET GO!"

"Not unless you stop shaking me. And I wasn't even thinking about God!" I yelled. "I was thinking that Dad had gone nuts!"

I let go of Mom's wrists and she did not try to shake me anymore.

She sat next to me rubbing her wrists as if I had hurt her. I knew I had not. I held her firmly but gently.

"That's because you only later understood what it all meant," said Mom in a small sorrowful voice.

"What I understood," I said, "is that you were in on it. I *understood* that you had the water and Vindex ready and that you *wanted* Dad to hurt himself, and was glad he did! What I *understand* is that I never should have gotten Dad home! You didn't even call the doctor! It was all lies! What I *understand* is that compared to you, Dad has the best manners in the world!"

Mom's face suddenly turned pale. I kept my eyes on her. She was the one who would not look up at me now, not even to give me a sideways glance.

"I needed to help you see that it was part of the tapestry," said Mom at last in a breathless rush. She waited for me to answer. I said nothing. "It's the next chapter in the L'arche Story," Mom added, still without looking me in the face. "It would have been nice if you spoke up a little more forcefully this morning and told the young people what the Lord had done in your life. 'For if we deny Him before men He will deny us before the Father.' Don't deny God, Calvin!"

"I didn't accept Jesus while Dad whipped himself. You shouldn't lie," I answered.

When Mom spoke again her voice went up an octave. Her face was working and twitching and she clenched and unclenched her jaw.

"Your father *never* 'whipped' himself! He gave himself a few symbolic strokes to demonstrate a theological principle. That's all. Don't exaggerate."

"A 'few symbolic strokes'?! He was cut all over!"

"Calvin, I said don't exaggerate!"

"I'm not exaggerating, and don't lie, Mother!"

"Not another word or I'll have to get Ralph and tell him all his efforts to bring you back to the Lord have been wasted! Calvin, how can you talk like this? How dare you call me a liar? Who knows more of the Lord's will, you or I?"

I closed my eyes. As if in answer to her question, Jesus descended into my room in a bright white robe and stood next to my mom. He reached out and touched her on the top of her head. A spark went from his finger into Mom's head and light flashed out of her feet and she pitched forward and fell with her head under my sink and the soles of her feet smoking. And the Lord turned to me and laid a finger over his lips, winked, smiled, and said, "Shhh!" And in the twinkling of an eye he was gone.

I hoped that if I kept my eyes closed long enough it might really happen, if not on my planet then at least on one of the dust worlds floating in my room or in some other universe where their Jesus actually answered the prayers of boys with born-again fundamentalist mothers.

My eyes were still closed when I heard my door open, a few steps, then the sound of the door shutting softly. When I opened my eyes, Mom was gone.

Chapter 33

THE NEXT MORNING RACHAEL KNOCKED.

"Mom says we have to get back to normal and do our jobs," whispered Rachael as she poked her head around my bedroom door. "She says the time of testing is at an end."

"She does?" I asked, and looked up sleepily.

"You're to help with the trash same as always," said Rachael as she closed the door softly behind her.

She knelt down next to my bed, leaned close, and hugged me. The narrow shaft of sunlight coming through the tulip cutout in my shutter lit Rachael's face. She was pale. There were tears on her eyelashes.

"I'm so, so sorry about what happened to you," Rachael whispered. "Sometimes I . . . just . . ." Rachael's words trailed off into silence.

"Hate her?" I asked.

Rachael pulled away and stared aghast.

"Oh, no! Not that! It's just that sometimes, well, Mom seems to go too far."

" *'Too far'?!* Is *that* what you call her taking everything we do and twisting it around into lies? She knew! She made Dad do it!"

"Oh, Calvin . . . " There was a shake in Rachael's voice.

"Forget it," I muttered.

We worked in silence as we collected wastepaper baskets and carried them down to the basement.

We all had certain chores. One of Rachael's and mine was to empty the wastepaper baskets and take the paper trash to the furnace room in the basement. We fed the furnace slowly. If you put too much trash in at any one time, smoke would billow out the vents in the furnace's sides and the papers would not burn properly and would leave too much ash.

"I don't think we'll ever be normal," I muttered as I emptied a wastepaper basket.

Rachael did not answer me. She walked out and took the empty baskets back upstairs with her. I started to feed the furnace. I loved to open the heavy cast-iron door and gaze at the hot bed of coals glowing inside, emitting little tongues of flickering blue flame. I liked the glow from the furnace so much that I would turn off the light so that the only illumination in the room was the blue-orange flush from the furnace mouth. When I fed in the paper trash, I liked the way each sheet hovered over the rippling bed of blue fire for an instant, floated on the hot air, then suddenly burst into flame.

I reached into the box for some trash while keeping my eyes on the flames. As I tossed a paper into the open furnace I realized it was one of the sanitary-napkin-disposal bags from Riffelberg that Dad had written on. I snatched it back, dropped it on the ash-dusted concrete floor, and stamped on it to put out the flame licking up the bag's edge just as Rachael walked back in.

"What are you doing?" Rachael asked, as she turned on the light.

"Look at this!" I said. "It's Dad's writing from the hotel."

"What writing?" asked Rachael.

"He locked himself in his room for the whole time and wrote all this. Where did you get it?"

"Mom brought me their wastepaper basket. She told me to make sure all this stuff was burned with it."

"Does Dad know we're burning his writing?" I asked.

"I don't know. He wasn't there when she told me."

"He read some to Janet and me. It was all about doubting God and how the *New York Times* and the Bible are the same."

"Oh, how awful!" exclaimed Rachael. "No wonder Mom wants it burned!"

"But if Dad doesn't know, I mean it's his and all, we shouldn't . . . well, what do you think we should do?"

"Mom said, 'Burn every vile scrap.'"

"I think we should ask Dad first," I said, and picked up a handful of Dad's papers. "Can you read his handwriting?"

"Kind of," said Rachael. She squinted. "Boy, look at this, he must have written on every piece of paper in the hotel."

Rachael picked up a big sheet of wrapping paper used to line a drawer. It was written over in Dad's tight jagged handwriting. Rachael stepped under the single dim lightbulb that hung from a short wire in the center of the furnace room and held the paper close to her face. She began to read out loud.

" 'A Holiday from God by Ralph Becker.' " Rachael looked up and frowned. "What is *that* supposed to mean?"

"I don't know," I said.

"Was he writing some kind of crazy book? That sounds like a title. I don't think we should read this. It sounds *very* blasphemous!"

I wanted to hear what Dad had written. I knew that unless Rachael read it out loud I might never get the chance. Reading was tough for me and I could not read Dad's handwriting.

"We should, uh, know his state of mind in case, in case we need to help him or something—spiritually, I mean and all," I mumbled.

Rachael looked doubtful.

"Please?"

"Okay, but if it's too demonic I'm not going to. And you have to promise me that if I do read it you'll burn it all up like we're supposed to."

"Okay."

Rachael picked up a scrap of hotel stationery. She started to read, pausing once in a while to figure out Dad's messy scribbles.

" 'Love slows time down. The repeated motions of love, the rituals, can give life a shape that gives the passage of time a familiar face, like meeting an old friend. Love resides in the familiar.' " Rachael looked up. A perplexed furrow wrinkled her freckled brow. "What *is* Dad talking about?"

"Just read."

"Okay. 'Those who lie to themselves and who think that there is such a thing as starting over have forgotten the saddest fact of all: Wherever you go, there you are! We cannot escape ourselves or our past. Love only grows where we are willing to take the rough with the smooth.' "

Rachael handed me the sheet. She raised her eyebrows.

"Okay, that's all there is on that one. Burn it!"

"I will in a minute."

"No. Do it now."

"All the scraps are out of order. Say you read something that continues on another page and we've burned it. Then what? How could we figure out what he meant?"

"Okay, but as soon as I'm done it all goes."

Rachael fished another scrap out of the box. It was the blotting paper off the desk pad and had soaked up Dad's ink. The words were big and blotchy. Rachael squinted and read haltingly.

" 'Work always brings us back, face-to-face, with reality, the reality of necessity and also the reality of the need for the recognition we seek from others that gives our lives shape and meaning.' " Rachael looked up. "He sounds *so* nutty. What on earth happened to him?"

"I don't know. Just read it, okay?"

Rachael sighed heavily. As she read she turned the paper this way and that. Dad had written up the edges as well as down the center of the sheet.

" 'We are eating, drinking, sleeping, and looking for our place in the order of things, by which we mean the human order. We are pretty much stuck where we are. The pretense that somehow we can rise above the system of reality is absurd. We cannot climb out of the universe and see it whole. We are in it. We take everything we are told on faith. Every belief is, therefore, religious in nature. There is no final objective evidence for any belief. "I think, therefore I am" is just another statement of wishful thinking.'"

Rachael picked up another sheet. She moved the paper under the lightbulb so she could see it better.

" 'Since the very nature of reality as we understand it is nothing more than the words we use to describe what we experience, we can really know nothing more than the fact that we like to describe things. To that extent, all faith rests on the faith that we can communicate meaning to ourselves and to others. Everything is, therefore, religious, as we understand religion, because every thought depends on an act of faith in affirming our own sanity and the sanity of others who will understand us.

" 'There is no such thing as the scientific method in an objective sense. There is only the scientific method within the framework of the accepted notion of the human game of communication that we have all agreed to, assuming there is a "we" anyway. I am so alone as I write this.' "

Rachael handed me the sheet with a frown. She picked up another.

" 'Once we surrender to this lesser rule, and begin to live within the framework of the second and lesser rule, we can say we "know" things as long as we do not really claim to KNOW them. We can speak of Shakespeare's being a "better writer" than, say, P. G. Wodehouse. We can speak of standards and say that the *New York Times* is the "paper of record" and not have that statement appear farcical. It is, of course, only the "paper of record" in the sense that we accept our ability to communicate some meaning, even though overall meaning, if there is any, is unknowable.' "

"He read this part to Janet and me out loud," I said.

"He did?"

"Yes."

"He was really backsliding, huh?" Rachael picked up another sheet of hotel stationery. " 'Why do we try and make sense out of suffering, want to learn from it? We find hope in beauty and, above all, in our response to it. If there is no meaning, if there is no soul peering from our eyes, just eyes reporting to a brain that will rot away along with all its memories, then our desire for there to be more is a madness that has shaped our lives in some very terrible ways. If we have souls that will carry the memories of our experiences with them to some other life, not dependent on our rotting bodies, then beauty will not be wasted.' "

Rachael shook her head sadly. She picked up a postcard of Zermatt and read off the back.

" 'Faith is our response to loss, to the fact that, in time, we grow up and see through the self-perpetuating myths that seek to control us. We see through this. And yet we still pray! Love is called forth from us in spite of everything! We cannot imagine a life where sacrifice and love do not exist hand in hand and become the foundation for everything we hold dear.' "

Rachael dropped the postcard back into the trash box and picked up another sheet of drawer-lining wrapping paper. While she read from the back, I looked at the pictures of little blue gentians printed on the front. I thought about the flowers growing next to the cliff face Dad had pulled me away from.

" 'Is our longing for God more than an elaborate cover for our fear of death? Why does the silence of God need to be covered up by a torrent of human words? Is theology more than an excuse for God's bad behavior? That we seek meaning is another way to say we fear death. We call our desire for meaning the voice of God. Maybe the desire for meaning is itself an indication that there is a God, indeed, the voice of God in us. Does a child call out for her mother in the night if she has never known her? Perhaps our longing for meaning is the echo of God. I hope so.' "

Rachael tossed the paper aside with a sigh.

"That's enough. Never mind the rest, I'm going to get the wastepaper basket out of the men's four-bed dormitory. Now you have to burn it all, Calvin! We don't want any more trouble with Mom and all. I'll be back in a sec."

"I will," I said hurriedly, and picked up a handful of Dad's papers.

"There's no way the Lord will bless the Work with awful stuff like this under our roof," said Rachael over her shoulder as she walked out.

I laid the papers back in the box. Then I slowly opened the door and peered out into the darkened hallway. No one was around. I ducked back into the furnace room. I picked all my fathers' papers out of the box, and off the floor where Rachael had dropped a few of the sheets after she read them. I carefully laid the papers on the edge of the old stone laundry tub that was built into the wall opposite the furnace.

I threw the rest of the trash into the furnace so Rachael would see plenty of ash if she checked. Then I cautiously stepped into the hall, clutching Dad's papers under my sweater.

I hoped I could make it up to the attic without getting caught. I wanted to hide Dad's writing under the board next to the chimney where I kept my five copies of *Mad*. Maybe someday I would learn to read well enough to figure out my dad. Maybe someday he might want his writing back. And even though I could not understand much, I thought Dad's writing sounded kind of beautiful.